LOVE TO BELONG

Caroline Bell Foster

Scan for free reads

Copyright © 2023 Caroline Bell Foster

All rights reserved

The characters and events portrayed in this book are fictitious. Any similarity to real persons, living or dead, is coincidental and not intended by the author.

No part of this book may be reproduced, or stored in a retrieval system, or transmitted in any form or by any means, electronic, mechanical, photocopying, recording, or otherwise, without express written permission of the publisher.

ISBN-13: 978-0-9930673-6-5

Cover design by: Sunshine

My last words in my diary as a teenager were about you. You continue to be my Sunshine. x

***

The Nottingham Story Weavers

What can I say? I could not write Love To Belong without you all. From the bottom of my heart, I thank you for keeping the encouragement going and cheering me on.

Mars, Carol, Vasiliki and Talia, I love you all. xx

***

I would also like to thank the influencers I call my besties: Marika, Fumi, Racquel, Patricia, Lydia and many others, whose content let me into their daily lives.

Thank you for inspiring my character Chilli. She has a little bit of all of you. x

CONTENTS

Title Page
Copyright
Dedication
Chapter One · · · · · 1
Chapter Two · · · · · 9
Chapter Three · · · · · 20
Chapter Four · · · · · 25
Chapter Five · · · · · 30
Chapter Six · · · · · 36
Chapter Seven · · · · · 44
Chapter Eight · · · · · 55
Chapter Nine · · · · · 61
Chapter Ten · · · · · 69
Chapter Eleven · · · · · 75
Chapter Twelve · · · · · 86
Chapter Thirteen · · · · · 94
Chapter Fourteen · · · · · 104
Chapter Fifteen · · · · · 112
Chapter Sixteen · · · · · 118
Chapter Seventeen · · · · · 126
Chapter Eighteen · · · · · 134

Chapter Nineteen	142
Chapter Twenty	150
Chapter Twenty-One	157
Chapter Twenty-Two	163
Chapter Twenty-Three	174
Chapter Twenty-Four	181
Chapter Twenty-Five	189
Chapter Twenty-Six	195
Chapter Twenty-Seven	203
Chapter Twenty-Eight	210
Chapter Twenty-Nine	217
Chapter Thirty	224
Chapter Thirty-One	230
Chapter Thirty-Two	238
Chapter Thirty-Three	248
Epilogue	257
About The Author	263
Books By This Author	265

CHAPTER ONE

She was beginning to dislike it, but plunged ahead.

"Okay guys, I'm super excited. I'm at St. Pancras train station and finally on my way to Paris. Got my portable chargers, my favourite bag with all the pockets. Remember, it's about convenience when you're travelling," she advised, with a swiftness she was famed for. "And look at this beauty," Chilli aimed her camera to showcase the furry pink, totally impractical suitcase at her feet. "How cute." Angling the camera back to her face, she fluttered her freshly in-filled eyelash extensions and giggled. "See you on the other side."

With a sigh of relief, Chilli swivelled the camera screen into its housing, signed off and carefully placed the expensive camera into her bag, before grabbing the outrageous suitcase, entering the train, and making herself comfortable in First Class.

Ten minutes later, she was joined by her friends and fellow influencers, Candace Mason, and Vinny Sang.

They'd been friends via cyberspace for years, but had only met physically two years ago at a media conference in Berlin.

Fortunately, although beauty vloggers, Candace took the healthier, hemp, aloe vera, au natural approach, and Vinny's content was wild and theatrical.

"So, what's the deal?" Vinny asked, re-arranging his bucket hat on his head. His clothes were loud and vibrant, his hair shaved on one side from the left temple, right around the back of his head to the opposite ear and he sported a chin-length fringe tipped in platinum blonde. Last week it had been deep purple.

"We have the fashion shows and the after-party at the hotel." Candace explained, checking her emails.

They talked about fashion, influencers, designers, who they wanted to interview and definitely what they'd hoped to be gifted.

For the three of them, content creation was big business. They each had followers in the millions. Two years in a row, Chilli was voted Social Influencer of the Year.

Yep, life was good, and she revelled in it.

"Love the hair, Chilli Pepper," Vinny teased, using his nickname for her and reaching across the table to tug the strands sweeping over her shoulders.

Chilli leaned back out of his reach and shook her head. "You know the rules, Vinny," she scolded seriously. "Don't touch the lace front." She wagged her finger at him in warning. She was wearing a prototype for a collection they had approached her to endorse from an American wig manufacturer. It was a shoulder-length brown bob with a deep parting on the left. Apparently, if she sprayed a little water on it, the bone straight strands would turn into a tousled wavy beach babe look. She was going to try that later when she changed for the party, although she had a long wavy lace front wig as backup in case it didn't work.

Chilli had been creating content for years and covered everything from fashion trends and makeup to talking about her daily life and pop culture.

She collaborated with large, well-known brands. Wearing their clothes and using the products that had been sent to her. And also shopping in their brick-and-mortar shops. Almost everything Chilli did was documented via video, and she shared her views publicly and was paid handsomely for it.

Anything Chilli endorsed, sold out and her last makeup tutorial had received over three million views in a few days. She was liked and in high demand.

She was aware she couldn't rely on content creation as a stable income. The money was good but influencing fickle. Trends came and went. Popularity could disappear like a puff of smoke. It was becoming saturated, and Chilli was missing the enthusiasm she had had when she had started out. With the help of her staff, she was looking at other ways to monetise her brand.

Born in England, Chilli, whose real name was Chillitara Laurent, was bi-lingual and as comfortable in France, where her beloved grandmother lived, as she was in Britain and frequently travelled between the two countries.

"How's life with the boyfriend going?" Candace asked, interrupting the pleasant thoughts of her grandmother, whom Chilli intended to visit before she left France in a few days.

Chilli sighed, thinking of Paul. He'd lasted all of three weeks and was only a boyfriend on paper. She couldn't get past his large sweaty hands, much less have him kiss her. Besides, it soon became apparent he'd wanted to use her for her contacts for his T-shirt business.

"It's not," Chilli answered without remorse, barely concealing a shudder.

Vinny laughed. "You go through men like I go through–"

"Men," Chilli finished for him with a teasing wink.

"Oh, *touché*," he waved his hand about.

"Who knows, maybe we'll both find somebody rich to snog at the after-party tonight," Vinny declared.

Chilli laughed. "That's right, we're only snogging rich men from now on," she proclaimed.

They high-fived each other as they laughed. None of them had much luck with relationships. Candace flittered from man to man. Vinny was continuously looking for a lover who could support his extravagant lifestyle and Chilli wasn't looking to be in a relationship at all, but played along, contributing to their outlandish list of what Mr. Rich Man should be like.

***

Arno Tournier cringed and swiped his finger across the surface of his tablet a little too aggressively. The passengers in front of him laughed and talked loudly about their love lives. Generation Z, he thought, knowing he'd just about escaped that label being thirty-four himself.

Arno couldn't concentrate on the blog he was reading and

with a huff, put his tablet down and glared at them. The Generation Zs were gossiping with no consideration for the other passengers.

He was tired. He'd been in England for a nine o'clock appointment, and because of the lateness of one of his suppliers, the meeting hadn't started until after eleven, ruining his entire day.

Arno slumped in his seat to rest his head against the headrest and closed his eyes. He wanted to return to the vineyard. He was a vigneron at heart, but with his grandfather's steady decline in health, there was no one else to manage what he liked to call the sterile side of things.

Arno hated it. Hated life in Paris and couldn't wait to head home. But his beloved grapes had to wait because of a conference in the morning.

A loud burst of laughter captured his attention, and there was nothing for him to do but look and listen to the conversation going on not three feet from him. Unfortunately, he'd forgotten his headphones so couldn't tune the world, *them*, out.

The girl directly opposite was beautiful in a lanky blonde sharpness kind of way. She was probably a model or something, seeing the long willowness of her arms. Her shoulders protruded rather sharply from the cut-outs of her black top, and her breasts were small. She did nothing for him. Paris was full of women who looked like her.

He shifted his gaze to the girl sitting beside her. She was smaller, wearing a hot pink felt hat placed at a jaunty angle on her head. Her features were soft, and her face was round. A dimple played by the side of her mouth. Her complexion was dark gold, and the hair poking out from under the hat was slightly darker. She was wearing a long-sleeved black, V-necked, T-shirt thing, and the hands that she waved expressively about were tipped in hot pink too.

He mentally rolled his eyes. High maintenance was stamped all over her. And as for the vicious way she dismissed her boyfriend, Arno knew the poor bastard had had a lucky escape.

He closed his eyes and didn't open them again until jolted by someone landing on his lap.

"I'm so sorry," Chilli apologised in a rush, trying to get up. But between the table at her back and the hard-muscular chest at her front, not to mention the arms now holding her, she couldn't move. "I tripped on something." She explained, trying to wriggle free.

Arno looked at her. Up close, her skin was flawless, her eyes the darkest brown he had ever seen. They could even be black. Her eyelashes were very long and thick and her lips full and tempting. He had to force the inappropriate urge to lean forward and run his tongue along her succulent bottom lip from his thoughts.

"I'm sure that you did," Arno drawled, gritting his teeth when his body reacted to the soft cushion of her bottom. She was well within her rights to slap his face and call him a pervert, knowing she couldn't help but feel the hard ridge of his lengthening arousal beneath her. He'd gone too long without a woman and couldn't remember the last time he'd enjoyed the smoothness of a woman's thighs locked around his waist.

Chilli gasped at his harsh tone and heaved herself up. Or she tried to. She'd noticed him earlier as she'd waited for her friends. He was hard to miss with his deep olive skin tone, and dark wavy hair she'd had the mad compulsion to touch and remembered curling her fingers into a fist to control the tingling.

From a distance, she hadn't been able to make out his eye colour, although they hadn't looked run-of-the-mill brown. Now, with only inches between them, Chilli was fascinated to see they were deep forest green. Funny how the colour reminded her of the dream she'd had this morning.

It was weird, and she knew there was some psychobabble explanation about it, but she dreamt in one colour. She thought it was some kind of premonition or something, so whatever colour it was, she'd always wear it close to her skin that day. The dark green of his eyes matched the colour of her satin bra and panty set perfectly.

His shirt was unremarkable, plain crispy white. She glanced down to see what colour his trousers were. Please don't be black, she prayed silently to herself and looked down to stare at the patch of cloth between her legs. His trousers were dark. Black, or maybe navy, she mused curiously, but with a stripe running through it and she peered to discover what colour the line actually was.

"Do you mind?" Arno barked. The girl was practically looking at his crotch. Did she have no shame?

"What?" Chilli looked at him wide-eyed.

Arno all but growled. "Get up!"

"Oh, I'm sorry," Chilli declared, with an embarrassing gasp, "you see I have this thing about colours," she explained quickly. "I wanted to see what colour your trousers were, if they were like your eyes or boring like the rest of the suits on the train." She tipped her head towards the businessmen in the carriage, clear by their white shirts, generic ties, and black trousers.

Chilli, feeling the heat still scorching her cheeks and thankful her skin was dark enough to disguise her embarrassment, wriggled about, trying to lever herself up without touching his chest or wrapping her arms around his neck.

"I'm really sorry," she repeated with difficulty. It was as though he'd sucked in all the air surrounding them and her heart was struggling to beat. He continued to stare into her eyes as though she were a crazy person, before dropping his gaze to track all over her body. "Can you at least help?" she ordered eventually. Everywhere his eyes touched sent tiny flames of awareness through her. If she could, she would fold her arms over her breasts to cover her peeking nipples.

Chilli wasn't fat, but half-African genes ruled over her figure. She had curves. Curves that when growing up had been embarrassing, especially beside her petite French grandmother. Now she embraced them, but unfortunately, they were still the first thing men noticed.

Arno opened his legs, and she slid between them. He didn't

dare look at her, having already lost the battle with his body and just wanted to move her on as quickly as possible to save them both further embarrassment. He'd seen the heat in her eyes, the brazen sexual awareness as her nostrils flared. Her scent had changed, reminding him of the shift in the air when a summer storm was coming. He was close enough to see a flush of red gently touch her cheeks to sweep down her neck. He wanted to map the enticing colour with the tip of his tongue, knowing she was as aware of him as he was of her. The ever so slight rocking of her hips told him so. But this was neither the time nor the place. He did not pick up loud young women on trains.

Turning to his left, Arno twisted away, placed one hand on the back of the seat, the other on the table, and hauled himself up.

Chilli quickly scrambled out and stood to face him.

"Thank you, and again, I'm really sorry," she said, hoping she didn't sound as breathless as she felt. She didn't know what this was, but wow.

"Think nothing of it, *Mademoiselle*," his tone was formal, icy, and unpleasant.

Chilli gasped and stepped back in indignation. He made it sound as though she had intentionally fallen on him, and she wouldn't be surprised if he checked his pockets for his wallet. Forget the wow, she thought, pursing her lips. She wanted to smack that arrogant sneer off his face, and she wasn't a violent person.

Instead, Chilli tipped her chin up and spoke to him as he towered over her. He was tall, with broad shoulders she didn't want to think about. He could be an athlete, she guessed, trying not to notice the distracting broadness of his chest. "I really did trip," she defended tightly.

They both looked down, staring at the pale blue carpet with a narrow red line running through it. There was nothing to trip on.

"Run along," Arno said, sitting down to pick up his tablet in a blatant display of dismissal.

With a chilling look, completely wasted as it landed on the top of his head, Chilli straightened her spine and went to the bathroom.

On her return, instead of sitting in her old spot, she sat beside Vinny. Her back to the rude Frenchman.

CHAPTER TWO

It was almost one in the morning.

After a late meal in the hotel restaurant, Arno made himself comfortable in the foyer. It was a beautiful space, decked out in creams, golds with deep red trimmings, that reminded him of the full-bodied Cabernet he produced.

His mouth twisted, and he shook his head at himself. He was such a wine freak and was precisely what one past lover had called him.

Five, no, six generations of prized winemakers coursed through his veins.

One past relative had planted vegetables with the vines and they had lost much of the vineyard to disease, and it had taken another generation to recover.

A sexy server walked over to him in a tight black skirt and white shirt that strained across her breasts. She flirted outrageously with him, and the thought of asking for her number almost tumbled from his lips. Paris was perfect for a one-night-stand.

Once he went home, it was long days in the vineyards and even longer nights in the office, doing the sterile admin things that bored the life out of him.

His last girlfriend had left him months ago, or was it a year now? He mused, trying to recall what she looked like. He clenched his fists. The server, although pretty, wasn't doing anything for him. He'd gone about his business with the girl on the train skirting the periphery of his mind all day, distracting him. The subtle scent of her perfume had clung to him. He'd felt the whisper of her breath across his skin when he should have been listening to one of his distributors. And he definitely remembered how her luscious bottom had felt pressing against him. Added together, and the memory of her had kept him in a state of semi-arousal all day. He wanted her. He should have got *her* number.

Arno declined the server's invitation with a polite smile and ordered a glass of red wine. Hell, if he was in Paris when he wanted to be home, he may as well check out the competition, he thought, relaxing into the plush armchair.

The server walked away with a swing to her hips, and a look over her shoulder to let him know her offer was still open.

Arno pulled out his phone and checked his messages instead. There were plenty of emails, and he steeled himself, hating all the paperwork, and thought about hiring a firm to manage it all. Although felt like he was betraying his ancestors.

Tournier Wines was one hundred percent family-owned. He and his grandad were the only ones left. Past generations had killed off his workforce by not reproducing enough, Arno mocked, saluting them with his glass.

The elevator doors opened with a soft ping, but it was the raucous laughter skittering across the polished porcelain tiles that made him look up with annoyance, and his breath caught. It was the girl from this morning with her loud friends. Did they never shut up? He thought with irritation, watching them and then *her* as she tipped her head back in laughter.

Her dress was sexy as hell, electric blue and soft looking. It looked complicated to put on. Much less take off. Rope-like things crisscrossed her otherwise bare stomach, connecting the top half of the dress to the skirt.

The rest of her body was covered from the hip down. Tight sleeves billowed at her wrists, covering her fingers. It was dramatic and seductive, and he found himself wanting to lick those patches of skin on display at her waist.

Her hair was longer than this morning, and he frowned, knowing he'd thought it to be shoulder length on the train. Maybe it wasn't her. Perhaps it was someone who looked like her? he thought, watching her closely. But no, her laugh was the same, her lips ripe and as kissable as he remembered, and, oh yeah, her bottom was definitely the same, peachy and pert, he noticed with a smirk appreciating her curves as she turned to link her arms with her friends when they made their way to the bar to his right.

He had been tired, but Arno suddenly felt excited, like when his grapes were ready to harvest.

The server brought his glass on a dainty brass tray, hovered for a moment, then, realising he really wasn't interested, walked off without a wiggle to her bottom. Women. Arno laughed to himself, how fickle is thee, he misquoted.

With the glass held loosely in his hands, he looked at the colour, swirled it around, sniffed and then tasted, letting the wine slide along his tongue and fill his mouth. The flavour was good. His was better. Without thinking, he walked towards the bar with his glass, his tiredness gone.

***

Chilli saw him enter the dimness of the room and her heart skidded to a halt.

She was still on a high because style icon Annika had said her name in greeting and that high now shot to mega heights.

After pausing in the doorway, the man from the train sauntered over to one of the semi-circular seats and sat down, sliding to the centre. He was directly opposite to where Chilli was standing at the bar with her friends. She moved, turning her back to the room, knowing she could watch him openly via his reflection in the mirror behind the glass case.

The soft lighting from the five-fingered brass chandeliers scattered here and there lent a romantic feeling to the intimate room. It was a new modern hotel, yet the bar had a quaint 30s feel about it. A white piano with an enormous vase of red roses on top dominated an elevated stage, but Chilli didn't see any of that. She was locked on him.

He was beautiful. Definitely French by the aristocratic angles of his cheekbones and jawline. His hair, brushed back from his face, was thick and glossy, but it could do with shaping, she noted.

Funny how this morning she took him to be a boring businessman, probably an accountant. Watching him now, his long fingers slowly smoothed up and then down the stem of his wine glass, she would say he was an artist or something else, passionately creative.

He could do with a makeover, though. His clothes were as boring now in dark trousers and a plain shirt as they were this morning. Yet there was an exciting restlessness about him. Chilli could feel it. The sleeves of his shirt were rolled up in defiance of rigid formality. He didn't want to be here.

Their eyes connected via the mirror and Chilli could not look away. Neither acknowledged the other, and Chilli was grateful when the shots arrived, and she had an excuse to escape his intense gaze to pick up her glass.

Only she couldn't help herself and watched him surreptitiously under her lashes, very much aware of him staring when she clinked her glass with her friends, toasting the success of the day. She spilt some and licked it from her fingers.

Almost defiantly, Chilli did another shot, even though her first drink still scorched a trail of fire down her throat. She raised her chin, noticing a single dark eyebrow lift ever so slightly as he watched on.

Chilli loved Vinny and Candace, but after twelve hours of togetherness, they were rattling her nerves. Thankfully, they were returning to England in the morning. However, she was staying on.

Tomorrow she was going to an all-day AXP Centennial Conference, a foreign exchange programme she had taken part in a few years ago. She was a guest speaker. Afterwards, she was going to spend time with her grandmother.

"Okay," Chilli suddenly turned to Vinny and Candace, "I'm going to do a quick update, and then I'll be back," she promised, digging into her designer bag shaped like a gold cherry tomato and pulling out her beloved camera.

Chilli was looking for a quiet corner to film when she spied him. Boosted by the alcohol, she straightened her spine and walked over.

She really needed to call him something else *'the man from the train'* made him sound like a serial killer, she acknowledged, giggling to herself before stopping in front of his table.

"*Bonjour*," she greeted in French, "remember me?" she finished in English.

Chilli hovered by the table and licked her suddenly parched bottom lip. Now that his dark green gaze was trained on her, she'd lost her nerve. The tiny amount of alcohol she had consumed had rapidly evaporated under his sizzling stare. He was intense, his regard giving nothing away, although the fingers skimming his wine glass had stopped.

"I remember you," Arno replied.

Chilli scooted in beside him. "Can I borrow your table for a moment?" she asked.

He canted his head to one side, then looked around the room before pinning her with his gaze, his forehead pleating into a puzzled frown.

"What for?"

Chilli beamed. "I'll show you," she invited. Opening her handbag, she carefully pulled out her beloved camera she called Frankie.

Knowing exactly how her camera worked, she adjusted the settings to facilitate the dim lighting in the room. She fluffed her hair and angled the camera just where she liked it–slightly above her–before turning somewhat. Then, clearing her throat, she smiled into the lens.

"Hi guys," Chilli said, then talked excitedly about her evening and everything that had happened throughout her day.

Arno listened as she talked into her camera. She was talking about herself and reeling off names and details of her meal as though she were writing a diary.

She talked and talked and said something about rating her foundation ten out of ten.

Then repeated everything in French.

Arno found her speech fascinating as he listened keenly and deduced she didn't live in France. Her pronunciation, though perfect, was accent-less.

"And finally," Chilli turned towards the man from the train, "I'm going to find out his name," she angled her camera at him for a split second, "And then ask him to buy me a drink." She winked. "When in France...?" Chilli left the rest unsaid.

"Thanks," she said, placing her camera carefully on the table.

"What was that?" Arno asked.

"I'm a content creator," she explained, but at his baffled look went on. "Vlogger."

"Blogger?" he'd heard of the stuff people wrote on the internet were called blogs and read many articles on the winemaking industry, but he didn't delve much further than that.

"No," Chilli explained. "Vlogger. I don't write about things so much anymore. I film myself talking instead. It's more exciting."

"Isn't that how you say?" he cocked one silky brow at her. "Pretentious *oui*?"

"What's pretentious about giving people an honest diary of my life?"

"The fact you are giving people a diary of your life?" he shot back.

He didn't quite sneer, but it was there, hovering in the corner of his well-shaped mouth. Chilli really hoped he would not disappoint her and be an arse, she thought. Good looking, but still an arse.

"Everyone loves my content," she defended, losing the excitement of the day to his moody disapproval. "I have my own YouTube channel." She announced, tipping up her chin.

His dark eyebrows dipped, and he reached over to pick up his glass. He swallowed down his wine disrespectfully–wine was supposed to be honoured across the palate–before turning to look at her.

"Is that what you will do?" he inquired. "Put it on YouTube for people to watch?"

"Yes."

"With me on it?"

Oops. Chilli should have seen where this conversation was leading.

"Not necessarily," she hedged. But by the tilt of a single eyebrow, knew he knew she was lying.

Time to go. He was an arse, she thought, fighting her disappointment and scooting across the seat, but he grabbed her camera and put it on the other side of him, out of her reach.

"Hey!" Chilli gasped in horror, nobody touched Frankie, "give that back!"

"As I see it," Arno charged, fighting to keep from smiling. "You took my image without my consent. I own that image." He declared. "I now own your camera."

"I'll erase it."

"You will."

"Give it back. I will do it right now."

"What is your name?"

"Chillitara Laurent."

"You are French?"

"West African father. French mother. Live in England." She revealed automatically, as she mentally calculated how fast she could dash across the table and get her camera back. It was worth over two thousand pounds.

"You speak French?" He asked, stating the obvious.

She looked at him then, hearing the curiosity in his deep voice. This morning she hadn't noticed the gravelly sound of his speech, being distracted as she was by his moss-coloured eyes, but now she did. She liked it. "Why?"

"Curious."

"What's *your* name?" she thought to ask.

"Arno Tournier."

"Nice to meet you, Arno," Chilli repeated his name in her head. It suited him. Masculine and sure. "Can I have my camera back now, please?"

"No," he shook his head slowly and tipped his mouth down

before saying, "I will erase it myself."

Chilli gasped in horror. "Are you crazy!" She sputtered, thinking of all the videos she had made today. She would make a fortune when they were uploaded. Not to mention all the new followers. Followers meant revenue. "You know nothing about Frankie."

He looked at her in confusion, his wide forehead pleating into a tight frown. "Frankie? Who is this, Frankie?"

"My camera," Chilli could feel the sting of tears behind her eyes. Frankie meant everything to her. Her grandmother had bought it for her twenty-first birthday.

Arno leaned forward. She was closer than she had been a moment ago, her arm brushing his as she sneakily inched nearer to launch for her camera. Arno hadn't had this much fun in years. He moved the camera further away, out of her reach, even if she did lunge for it.

"How old are you?" Arno asked.

Chilli pursed her lips and rolled her eyes. "Old enough to tell you I'm not interested," she answered harshly, her tears forgotten as she planned how to retrieve her camera.

Arno laughed; he couldn't help himself. She didn't seem to have any of that British stiff upper lip thing they were famous for, and had more of the French passion he appreciated.

Winemaking in South Africa and Ethiopia aside, he knew little else about Africa. However, he was looking forward to exploring that side of her culture, preferably tonight.

"Then why are you breathing so," his eyes dipped to her chest, "erratically?" Arno usually wasn't like this; he never teased or showed his interest in a woman so blatantly. He didn't need to. But she was an exception. She wanted him. Had wanted him from the moment she had landed on his lap this morning.

"Because I'm upset!" Chilli shouted with annoyance, wanting to thump him or the table. The table won.

Arno laughed at her outburst. She was so fiery. Was she like this in bed? "It is only a camera."

"But it's mine, and I want it back," she charged. "Right now!"

Without thought, Chilli lunged across him and touched her camera, but instead of capturing it, she ended up pushing it beyond her reach, and she was lying across his lap in an even more intimate position than this morning.

"Tut-tut *Mam'selle*," Arno quickly rearranged her on his lap, sitting her up and placing one of his arms on the table at her back. He placed his other arm below her breasts to grasp the edge of the table, ultimately caging her in when he leant forward. Anyone looking from afar would think they were taking advantage of the shadows and kissing. "Now look what you have done," Arno accused softly.

"Let me go," Chilli breathed. Erratic didn't explain what she was feeling. His masculine scent bathed her all over, vanilla, spicy bergamot and the subtle smell that was all him. She remembered it from this morning. His thighs were rock solid beneath her bottom, and his warm breath fanned her ear. She was one massive pulse of awareness for him. She had never been so turned on.

"Why?" he whispered, close to her ear.

If Chilli were to move her head just a bit, those lovely lips of his would caress her ear when he spoke. She so wanted to turn her head.

"Because you're a stranger," she answered softly, feeling his finger insinuate itself between the soft latticework of her velvet dress, to find her skin and make small circles on her side. She stopped breathing.

"We met this morning." He shifted and spanned both hands around her waist.

"What are you doing?" Chilli whispered. This was improper on so many levels. But she couldn't move. Her usual confidence had dissolved with the alcohol, she reasoned, because if she'd had her wits about her, she would have slapped his handsome face already. Why did he inspire such violent thoughts? She went from wanting to run her fingertips under his shirt to wanting to throttle him!

"Rearranging you," Arno lifted her slightly and, with one

hand going to the small of her back, brought her forward. Liking that she didn't resist.

"We are French," he declared, with great importance, "we greet each other properly, *oui*?"

Before she could answer, he kissed one side of her cheek, and then the other.

His lips were warm and soft against her skin. She didn't know when it happened, but her hands were on his broad shoulders as their movements synchronised and they flowed together like water running over pebbles in a brook.

"Hello Chillitara Laurent," he whispered, ever so close to her lips. Like this morning, he knew she could feel his arousal, and like this morning, he felt the subtle rocking of her hips.

"*Bonjour Monsieur*,"

"How old are you?"

"How old do you want me to be?"

Arno smirked, his eyes smouldering as they trailed over her delectable curves. He flexed his hands, wanting to stroke the inner softness of her sex until she bathed his fingers.

"Twenty-six." He answered honestly.

"Lucky for you." Her smile was small but confident when she walked her fingers from his shoulders, up to his neck, to spear her fingertips into the long hair at his nape. She leaned in close to whisper. "I'm twenty-six," she paused, allowing the tip of her tongue to skim the sensitive spot below his ear. "And a half."

They looked into each other's eyes. A secret moment shared.

"Will you come to my room?" Arno asked, his lips almost, but not quite, touching hers.

Chilli's body ignited all over.

She knew what he was asking. What he wanted. She wanted it too, she convinced herself.

Dark green, she remembered. This morning she'd woken to the harmonious glow of her dream on her mind. She'd felt excited. Safe.

She licked her lips and watched as his eyes dipped to track the movement. There was a heavy pulsing of promise beneath her bottom. He wanted her, was blatantly reacting to her, and didn't mind her knowing it.

The stars aligned.

She squeezed his shoulders as though needing to hold on as her next words sent her into an emotional free fall.

"Yes."

CHAPTER THREE

Chilli held on tight to Arno's hand, allowing herself to be guided across the packed room.

She was so self-conscious she felt as though everyone knew she was about to have sex with a man she had just met.

Naturally, her friends saw them and Vinny, the walking announcement he was, gave her a thumbs up and teasingly thrust his hips provocatively several times.

"Wait," Chilli paused, pulling Arno to a stop when they were about to pass her friends.

Arno braced himself. If she were about to back out, he would respect her wishes, but his body wouldn't be happy. He had never been this turned on in his life.

Chilli looked up at him, feeling the heat rolling off him. "What's your room number?" she asked, catching her breath.

"Seven zero five," he answered and watched when she turned and repeated his room number to her friends, telling them to ring her there in ten minutes, and ordering them to take a picture of them both.

Capturing her hand again, Arno brought her fingers to his lips and kissed them slowly. He didn't know why, but what she had just done, putting her safety first, sent his levels of respect for her that much higher. She was smart as well as beautiful, and entwining their fingers, guided her towards the bank of elevators.

It's now, or never, Chilli thought as they waited. It was the longest wait of her life. She didn't dare look at him, but studiously faced the brass-coloured doors that muffled their silhouette.

The elevator arrived. They were alone. The doors slid closed and silently swished them up to the seventh floor.

With his fingers entwined with hers, Arno brushed his thumb over Chilli's knuckles like a soothing caress. She hadn't known she'd needed his reassurance until the numbered buttons on the panel lit up like a runway, quickly announcing their destination. Oh my God, what was she doing? Her stomach turned over.

"I've neve–"

"Shh," he said, interrupting her nervous confession, "I know," he answered. Somehow, he already knew she didn't do this type of thing. Her whole body was shaking, she was biting the corner of her bottom lip, and she looked ready to bolt. She was clinging to him as though she needed his strength to hold her together.

He paused outside his room door.

"Do you still want to go in?" he asked gently. He was six-one, and she was a whole foot shorter. From his vantage point, he could see her nipples pushing against the soft fabric of her dress. She wanted him. But her eyes were anxious.

Chilli took several internal deep breaths because she was so far out of her comfort zone, she was floundering like a fish on the sand. She had only dated once she got to university. She'd never had a one-night stand. Even then, it wasn't until her second year, and he had lasted a year and a half. She could count the number of lovers she had had on one finger.

Arno stepped closer and pushed aside the lock of hair that had dared to move over her right breast. When he had seen her earlier, her hair had been swept away from her face to cascade down her back. He pushed her hair over her shoulder.

Arno captured her hand and raised it to his lips when she continued to maul her bottom lip when the seconds ticked by. He kissed her knuckles once, then twice, and with a small reassuring smile, turned to walk her back to the elevators and deposit her with her friends.

It took a moment for Chilli to realise what he was doing.

"Wait!" she stumbled to a stop. "I mean no."

Arno waited patiently. His body was raging, and he was

already preparing his brain for a night of long, cold showers.

"I want this," she stated, swinging his hand between them. "I do."

"Are you sure?" Arno asked, not daring to get his hopes up. "It's okay."

Chilli pulled her shoulders back and tilted up her chin as she smiled and nodded at the same time.

Arno noticed the tiny dimple had appeared beside her mouth again.

Chilli took a single step which brought her into his space, and on tiptoe, reached up to pull him down to her. Their first kiss was more of a smoothing of lips. Back and forth and back again. It was gentle and sweet. Innocent and fresh. Safe. He was leaving it up to her to take charge of the pace.

They only pulled apart when the brass doors of the elevator slid open to reveal an elderly couple in black-tie. The man looked ruffled and smiled at the lady at his side, who was smoothing her hair.

"I'm sorry. We've changed our minds," Chilli apologised and waved. "Have a good night." She called out in French and heard a tinkle of laughter before they replied, 'you too.'

Without looking at Arno, Chilli pulled him down the softly lit corridor to his room and waited for him to open the door.

On the threshold, he dipped his head and kissed her. Properly.

Chilli's knees gave in as his tongue danced with hers. He was a good kisser. No, he was a great kisser. Her body already primed to be with his, shot to mega sensation. She felt him everywhere, her entire body tingling with awareness, yet he was only touching her mouth.

She groaned, plastering herself along his long hard body, stretching to wrap her arms around his neck, to haul him down, making it easier for her to kiss him back.

He brought them into the room, kicked the door shut, and leaned against it. Arno was finally touching her. All of her. Her body was soft, where he liked softness to be. Urgently, he swept his hands up and down her narrow back, over her generous hips, mapping her curves, to haul her even closer. He growled with deep appreciation when he finally palmed her beautiful bottom, moulding and massaging the heavy globes as his groans singed the air. He was losing his damn mind and didn't care.

"Ringing," he gasped against her mouth, hearing the obnoxious sound infiltrate his brain like a foghorn over misty water.

"Huh?"

"The phone," Arno realised it was the room telephone and needed to be answered. "Your friends, Chillitara."

Arno reluctantly released her leg where he'd held it against him.

Her breathing was shallow and rapid, matching his as she fumbled through the daze, finally realising what he was saying.

"Oh my gosh," Chilli squealed, diving to answer the phone. "Yes," she rushed, picking it up. "I'm here." She listened, rolling her eyes. "No, he isn't a psycho, and yes, I'll see you at breakfast." She all but slammed the phone down, placed her bag on the desk, and stepped out of her heels before turning to Arno.

The interruption heightened their hunger for each other.

Arno strode towards her.

***

Chilli was deliberately late for breakfast, and valiantly ignored the knowing grins from her two friends when she approached their table.

"Have a good night?" Vinny asked, spooning thick yoghurt over his bowl of grapes and peaches.

She could see Candace's influence and smirked down at him. Usually, he was a full English breakfast type of man.

"Yes, very," Chilli admitted briskly, knowing if she didn't give him something, he'd keep going on about it. "Is that all you're eating?" she deflected, pulling out a chair to join them.

Vinny glanced sheepishly at her. "Yeah."

Chilli ordered herself a pot of tea and toast, then thought

better of it, ordering a full English instead. She was ravenous. Lovemaking made for a good workout. She smiled to herself.

Her skin was tender in places where Arno had rubbed against her with the rasp of his low beard. Her face, across her breasts and oh my, her inner thighs.

She'd had the best night of her life. Doing things she had never done before. She was well and truly loved up, with a stock of orgasms to last her years. Her privates were throbbing, and her body still strummed with awareness.

Her one-night stand will be forever in her memory as the best twenty-four hours of her life. Arno was an amazing, caring lover, and this morning after making slow, gentle love to her again, walked her to her room and kissed her goodbye. It had been perfect.

Chilli tucked into her breakfast as the three of them talked and planned new ways to make money online.

After an hour, with a wave and a promise to catch up next week, she said her goodbyes to her friends to get ready for the AXP conference across town.

CHAPTER FOUR

The AXP conference was a lot of fun. She'd been an exchange student in Sweden for three months. Her grandmother had compromised on Europe when Chilli had threatened to take a gap year and go travelling in Australia instead.

Little did her grandmother know, the exchange program had been her first choice. Her grandmother had been overprotective, and it was only as an adult that Chilli knew the reason behind it.

Chilli still volunteered for AXP, knowing the experience lasted a lifetime and was life-changing, and she visited her Swedish host family often.

The conference was being held at the French Regency hotel and after informative talks and a buffet brunch, Chilli waited for her turn to speak.

She'd been asked to talk about her experience with the youngsters and their parents. It was a group of eighty people, and she was comfortable with it.

She talked, they listened, they asked questions, and it became a great conversation that from the applause they had appreciated.

She had just finished live streaming about her morning, the conference and the branded stationery she was using when she spotted her fellow exchange student Jose, who had been in Sweden with her.

With a scream, she leapt up and ran into his arms, where he spun her around and around, kissing her neck and holding her tight.

"I missed you, Chilli!" he exclaimed, hugging her again.

They had been inseparable in Sweden, and when he'd had trouble with his host family, her host family had allowed him to stay for the last month of their program so that he didn't have to return to his home country of Brazil.

Arms entwined, they moved to the seating area to catch up. Seeing Jose in the flesh was rare. He was only in France for a six-hour stopover en route to Tunisia, where he was a football coach, and she snuggled into his side as he showed her pictures of his new girlfriend.

Jose excused himself to take a call and Chilli looked around. The lobby was crowded because another conference was about to start. Wine bottling the sign beside the door announced.

With Jose gone, Chilli and made a quick live stream about seeing her old friend. She was used to people watching her, but this time she felt different. This time, the air felt hostile.

Finishing quickly, she lowered her camera. All she saw were other AXPers chatting. A group of dark suited businessmen were walking towards another conference room. Their backs were to her so she couldn't see what colour their shirts were, then chuckling at her nonsensical thoughts. With a shrug, Chilli took several selfies to upload later and waited for Jose.

***

"Hi, outstanding event, isn't it?" A lady said. She had a plate and a bottle of water in her hand. "Is this seat taken?" she inquired with a smile, looking at the empty seat beside Chilli.

"No," Chilli said, making space for the lady to sit down. She had seen Jose off an hour ago and was eating her lunch. As was jokingly the case with AXP, you stated your name, country and year. Military style. "Hi, I'm Chilli Laurent, AXP Sweden," she named the year. "You?"

"AXP America. Too many years ago to remember," the lady chuckled. "I'm Kerry Oswald-Jones."

They shook hands and started talking about their experiences, with Kerry telling her with pride that she was now engaged to the boyfriend she'd had back in Golden Acres, Georgia, when she had been an exchange student.

"You've been together all this time?" Chilli asked with envy.

"Sadly no, we were involved in a car accident, and I left early," Kerry explained with a grimace. "We didn't get our goodbyes."

"I'm sorry. How sad."

"He came looking for me ten years later, though." Kerry looked down at the diamond ring winking on her engagement finger.

"Newly engaged?"

Kerry laughed again, wriggling her fingers. "Can you tell?" her brown eyes sparkled, and Chilli immediately liked the older woman. She put her to be in her late twenties and was very sophisticated.

Being an observer of the finer things in life, Chilli knew Kerry came from money. She was British, with that elegant upper-class way of talking. Her hair had a slight kink where it had fallen victim to the Parisienne humidity, and her skin tone was warm and vibrant. She was stunning.

"What's your role in AXP now?" Chilli asked, knowing a good deal of ex-AXPers volunteered in some capacity.

"I'm trying to get AXP to resume the Georgia chapter because it ended in my year, which is a shame."

They talked about the programme and how politics and religion were changing which countries the organisation now deemed as safe.

They went to the dessert table together and buddied up for the rest of the conference, becoming firm friends and promising to catch up in England.

"Let's take a selfie," Kerry suggested, taking out her phone, and the ladies put their heads together and took several photographs. "I'll send you them." she said, flicking through the images.

"Is it okay to post one or two on my social media?" Chilli asked.

Kerry grinned as though she had a secret. "It's fine," she whispered, slipping her phone into her bag.

Chilli had noted the authoritative aura of her new friend. Kerry seemed older and more worldly than anyone she knew at the same age.

"What did you say you do?" Chilli inquired curiously.

"I'm in politics."

"Ah."

Kerry stopped, "ah?"

"Hmm-mmm, there's just something about you," Chilli pondered, then lightly added. "I'm a content creator."

Kerry winked. "I know. I'm a massive fan and follow you on everything, hence the selfies." She revealed, grinning.

"You do?"

"That clip with you unboxing the packages sent to you from that online male apparel store and you trying on the boxers over your jeans had me in stitches!"

"Thanks," Chilli answered, beaming. Why they had sent her men's boxer shorts she didn't know, so she made a video anyway, clowning around and suggesting different uses for them. She had got over six hundred thousand views for her efforts.

"It's great seeing another woman of colour making it. Well done," Kerry praised. "You should be proud."

"Thank you."

They talked some more, lingering over coffee, missing one session to talk, before eventually going into another area to listen to the Vice President's speech.

"That was fantastic," Kerry praised an hour later.

"Another coffee?" Chilli suggested.

Kerry looked at her phone. "No, sorry, I'd better start looking for my husband-to-be." She glanced around and smiled softly when she spotted him.

Chilli followed her gaze, noting the man with a baseball cap pulled low over his eyes and dark sunglasses. He had that American, broad shoulders, thick neck, square jaw thing going on. He was very handsome, but paled against the image of Arno. An image that remained from the moment he'd left her at her door with a smile and a gentle kiss, smoothing a finger down her cheek as he'd looked into her eyes. They'd said goodbye, but Chilli really wished they hadn't.

"Would you like to meet him?"

Chilli nodded, trying to banish the image of her one-night stand from her thoughts to focus on her new friend. "That would be nice."

When they approached Chilli watched as Kerry's fiancé straightened away from the column he was leaning against, to pull his hat even further over his eyes, as though he was hiding from someone, Chilli noticed curiously.

"Hey babes," Kerry sidled up to her fiancé, then turned towards Chilli. "This is Chilli," she introduced. "Chilli is the influencer I watch online."

He nodded and held out his hand. "Nice to meet you, Chilli. So, you're the one to blame for my wife buying all that stuff?" he accused with an amused grin.

Chilli put her hands up. "Sorry," she turned her puzzled eyes to Kerry. "I thought you said you were engaged?"

"It's a long story," Kerry leaned in close to whisper. "But we got married in Golden Acres before I left the program."

Chilli gasped, knowing the rules inside out. Kerry would have been a teenager. "Seriously?"

"Seriously," she looked adoringly up at her husband. "We're getting married the right way when we can figure out when and where."

"That is so romantic," Chilli expressed, pleased for the other couple. "Well, it was lovely to meet you both."

Kerry's husband pulled off his sunglasses and tipped up his hat. Chilli was hit by startling blue eyes. It wasn't the colour that made her frown, but how familiar he looked to her.

Chilli clasped his hand, said the usual pleasantries and then, after hugs and promises to keep in touch, walked away, thinking how beautiful it must be to be in love.

What a fairy tale, she thought, wondering if she were ever to have a fairy-tale ending like that. No chance her subconscious ridiculed her. She'd had a one-night stand, and nothing ever came out of those, it told her savagely.

CHAPTER FIVE

Arno knew himself well enough to admit that he missed her. With every thought, his body clenched with a need to be inside her.

Chillitara Laurent.

The woman with flawless skin and dark eyes. He'd thought them to be black, but they weren't. They were the deepest velvety brown that, when she was overcome with emotion, flashed pure antique gold. He'd worked hard to see those moments that night so long ago.

In those few hours since she had been in his bed, he'd learnt to watch her. Watch, when her closed eyes would snap open just as she was about to fall apart in his arms. It was a beautiful thing to witness.

The memory of those regrettably brief hours stayed with him. They got him through the long nights when he should have fallen into an exhausted stupor but lay thinking of those smooth legs of hers wrapped high around his waist, or over his shoulders, or better yet, when her luscious bottom bounced against him, urging him on. He had to bring himself relief, then take another bone-numbing shower before he even attempted to fall asleep.

Arno entered his office and flung himself in the chair that had been his father's and his father's father. Hell, there had been so many Tourniers using this office, who knew who had sat in this leather armchair that creaked with the slightest movement.

Arno closed his eyes and allowed the memory of Chillitara to settle him.

Her dress had been complicated, and he remembered spending long erotic moments smoothing his hands over her soft dips and curves, looking for an opening. He'd been desperate to get it off her.

She'd stepped back, and for a dreadful moment, he'd thought she'd changed her mind. Her lips had been swollen with his kisses, and she'd looked at him from under her lashes before sexily pushing out one hip to slide down the zip, which was hidden there.

With a tug, the skirt separated from the top and fell to the floor, and she'd stepped free of the fabric.

He remembered trying to swallow, seeing the tiny scrap of triangular silk between her legs hiding her sex from him.

The top went over her head, and he'd died. Died and went straight to heaven.

Her body was luscious with curves that tempted him to kiss, suck, lick and savour. Her nipples, dark and dainty, had teased him, and his mouth had literally watered.

Her breasts weren't overly large, yet balanced the dip of her waist and the curve of her hips to perfection.

Arno had dropped to his knees. He'd never in all of his thirty-four years seen a body like hers. She was made for him.

He remembered tugging her closer and smoothing his hands up and down the backs of her shapely legs. Her fingers had been in his hair, pulling his head back, and she'd bent at the waist to kiss him long and hard.

Moving her hands to the sides of his face, her fingers had pressed the back of his neck, urging him closer, her thumbs sweeping over his ears. He had never known his ears were erogenous zones.

He remembered the scent of her, the subtleness of her legs as he'd raised one over his shoulder to bathe his senses in everything that was her. She was so excitingly swollen and aroused, he'd lost his mind. When he finally nudged his mouth against her sex, she'd whimpered and all but collapsed against him. He'd held her hips tight, keeping her steady as he sucked and teased until her hands tangled into his hair, directing him where she had wanted him.

She'd screamed when he'd pushed his tongue inside her,

drinking her very essence until her body trembled and her knees finally gave way.

He'd crawled up her body, pulling her nipples into his mouth, sucking hard, then moving to kiss her deeply before lifting her boneless body to the bed, laying her down and starting all over again.

He'd never had a lover like her. She'd been entirely selfless, giving as good as she got.

He had turned her every way he could imagine. She'd pushed him to his back and had her way with him, picking up the pace and then slowing them tantalisingly down. She'd teased. She'd demanded. She'd faced him, her dark gaze unwavering as she'd ridden him, and he had lost his mind.

It had been erotic. It had been memorable. It had been raw. It had been tender.

As the morning light had filtered softly into the room, with mutual smiles and tender caresses, Arno had laid back to watch and memorise everything about her, as she had dressed in his white shirt, rolling up the sleeves and using his tie to cinch her small waist.

She'd picked up the two pieces of her dress, lay them gently over one arm and held her shoes in her other hand.

He'd pulled on his grey jogging bottoms and a black T-shirt.

It had all been very slow. Both of them keenly watching the other.

He recalled looking at her bare feet, her toes painted a pretty blue colour. She couldn't walk barefoot around the hotel, he remembered thinking.

Arno had given her a pair of his white athletic socks to wear. With an evocative smile tossed over her shoulder, she had pulled them up to her knees. Slowly.

Unwilling to let her go, Arno had happily accepted her invitation, caught her around the waist, tumbled her onto the messy bed, and made love to her again.

The morning sun had warmed the room when they'd eventually taken the stairs to her floor. Kissing along the way, and at her door, he'd told her goodbye.

He shouldn't have.

What they had, what they'd done, didn't come around often.

But first, he had work to do. Arno shook himself, took a deep breath, grabbed the heavy ridge of his arousal, and thought of cold water, brick walls, anything to ease the pleasurable agony thoughts of her always evoked, before letting his breath out in a harsh whoosh.

After a moment, he was controlled enough to think clearly and with a sigh, switched on his laptop to get down to the tedious task of accounting. It was never-ending. He had a vineyard to run. A wine to produce. A damn fine wine, and with the market getting increasingly crowded, he needed to spend money to bring the vineyard up to the level where production costs could be reduced, and he could compete with the supermarket screw-top wines.

Two hours later, the figures blurred and at some point, his housekeeper Agnes had brought him a chicken casserole with crusty bread for dinner. It lay on the tray half-eaten. He wasn't hungry. Wasn't hungry for food, picturing Chillitara as she had lain beneath him. He could not get her out of his mind and knew either he found someone else to erase the memory of her–and that didn't sit well with him–or he went after her.

It was too early to go to bed, knowing he would only toss and turn with dreams of that long-ago night on replay. Two months since that night in Paris, and he relived it every damn chance he got. Two months!

He shut down the spreadsheet he'd been working on, and with his open laptop balanced in one hand, poured himself a small glass of Hennessy Cognac and walked into the living room.

He wasn't one for TV, but turned it on anyway, flicking mindlessly through the channels before settling on a cheap American film, knowing he wouldn't have to concentrate too much. Shootings, spectacular car chases, and the hero getting the girl was about all he could manage in the mood he was in.

He settled in, and typically it didn't hold him. He reached for his laptop, and with his fingers hovering over the keys, opened YouTube.

She had a channel he remembered her saying, so typed in her name with one finger. A list of Chilli's dropped down on the menu, partway through what he perceived to be the spelling and he selected the first one as there weren't any Chillitara's. And there she was. Image after image of her filling up his screen.

He glanced at the titles while scrolling. She talked about everything under the sun. From makeup tutorials to unboxing–he didn't know what that was–wigs and hairstyles, to spending too much money on clothing and hauls. He was open to finding out what hauls were.

Arno changed the sixty-inch TV on the wall over to Smart Mode and settled on her latest video.

Chillitara, whom he now realised called herself, Chilli filled the screen. She was smiling, and Arno leaned back to sip at his Cognac and watch as she talked about looking for office space and the perils of that. She was animated. Her face was flawless. Her hair was long and a vibrant red colour that reminded him of a rich burgundy wine.

She changed her hair often; he noticed. She was flirty and playful and totally at ease talking about herself. Her mouth was lush and laughing with the camera. He remembered those lips wrapped around him, first shyly and then with growing confidence as she literally brought him to his knees, holding him captive.

When the video ended, he watched more. They weren't overly long, twenty minutes or so, although the makeup tutorials were longer. He skipped those.

At the end of each one, her name, social media platforms and a request to like, follow and subscribe came on the screen in glittery gold script. After several videos, and knowing he had to rise early, Arno turned off the TV.

He felt energised and excited, finally having a direction.

He went upstairs, pulled off his clothes–as he always slept naked–and slipped under the covers. With his phone in his hand, he did what he should have done weeks ago and googled Chilli's name to read everything about her.

CHAPTER SIX

She looked like a teenager, Arno thought in horror, seeing her sitting on the metal steps with her legs sprawled open and be-ringed hands dangling between them, taking photographs. Her clothes looked like what his neighbour's daughters would wear, he thought in shock.

She was wearing dark baggy ripped jeans, gold glittery trainers with high white heels that looked like bricks and a black torn T-shirt with *'Hate Me'* written in blood-red.

Her hair was shoulder length and mostly pink, and she looked nothing like how he remembered her. She didn't look like this in her videos! Where had her sophistication gone? Her glamour? Was she too young for him? How *old* was she again? He thought swiftly and then remembered twenty-six. Age was more than a number in his book, he acknowledged, watching her make the peace sign with two fingers and move into another pose. And just who was the guy busily adjusting her top where it had fallen off her shoulders, her boyfriend?

Arno made an effort to unclench his hands where they held the steering wheel of his rental car as the questions flew thick and fast inside his head, and he asked himself, yet again, what the hell was he doing here? He was Arno Tournier. He didn't chase women.

Arno didn't like England, but he'd timed this visit with a string of meetings he had. So why not to see if Chillitara wanted to go out or something?

Predictably, Arno's body clenched at the heated images the 'something' conveyed. Even now, looking as ridiculous as she did and flirting with the photographer, he should have been turned off; he wasn't.

His phone rang via the in-car system. It was one of his

leading distributors who asked if he could bump up their meeting. Arno looked at Chillitara. She was draping herself over the rusty railing on the steps, taking direction from the photographer. With his mouth tipping down, Arno decided to talk to her later and with a last glance, started his car and pulled away.

***

Chilli, with a member of staff, was outside doing a photo shoot. The rusty warehouse exterior of her building made for a dramatically urban setting.

Although she was an influencer and available to the public, she was super strict when it came to her personal safety, especially in her day-to-day life. It had to be.

Chilli posed with a light spring jacket and baggy jeans. It was not something she would normally wear, but this was business.

A black car swept past them to park on the far side of the parking lot. Chilli waited for the shadowy figure of the driver to alight, but they remained in the vehicle and, not wanting to waste the natural light, Chilli slipped easily into another pose.

***

Two hours later, Chilli had finished the meeting with the hair company, and her lace front wig line was now one step closer to fruition. She was excited as well as exhausted.

Her staff had left.

Walking to the corner of her office where her video equipment was set up, Chilli prepared to do her last task for the day. A video vlog.

She turned on the spotlights.

She had changed her hair and felt more like herself, wearing a green tartan pencil skirt and a simple black polo-neck jumper, with capped sleeves. A pair of bright yellow stilettos finished her polished look.

Touching up her makeup, Chilli pressed extra translucent

powder over her tee zone, re-did her nude lipstick and settled in the bubble-gum pink bucket seat.

Chilli talked about the brand she'd been modelling and how hard and demanding the sector was. She complimented those who paraded up and down the runway, spoke about the skinny vs plus-sized debate and promised to re-visit the world of modelling at a later date.

When she finished, Chilli sat back and reached for the glass of water beside her and toed off her shoes. She was tired after a long day and was ready to go home, order something in for dinner, mushroom risotto possibly, and have a nice long bath using the luxury bath products they had sent her to try.

She was startled by a noise. However, with the spotlights on, she couldn't see past the bright circumference in her immediate vicinity. The rest of the room was dark.

"Hello? Anyone there?" she asked out loud, spooking herself and then laughing at the gory cinematic images that fleeted through her head. She replaced her glass and bent to scoop up her shoes.

Footsteps coming in her direction made her freeze, and a terrified scream lodged in her throat.

Chilli watched, half bent and frozen, when the shadow of a man came forward. The end of her life flashed before her. She could not physically move. Fight or flight. What about freezing? She forced herself to look past her killer's slightly scuffed boots, up his indigo-coloured jeans, over his white jumper, to his face. Chilli stopped and heard a thud close by. She glanced down. She had dropped her shoes.

Looking up, Chilli couldn't believe who she was seeing. It didn't make sense. Arno Tournier lived in France. He should not be in England. Much less on an industrial business estate on the outskirts of London.

"*Bonjour Mam'selle*," Arno stepped closer but remained by the large white table in the middle of the room.

Chilli straightened. He looked casual and foreign. His hair was not as long as she remembered. It curled around his ears and was brushed away from his face. He was holding a small bouquet of red roses tied with a red satin bow.

"Arno,"

"*Oui*,"

"What are you doing here?"

"I came for my socks," he answered with all seriousness, but his lovely mouth slid into a smile on one side.

"Socks?" she repeated faintly, still in utter disbelief that he was here.

"You left with my socks. I want them back."

Chilli crossed her arms over her chest when the penny finally dropped, so to speak, and she smiled, remembering the white athletic socks he'd given her to wear the morning he'd walked her back to her hotel room.

"They're at home."

"*Bien*, good," he repeated. "We will collect them now."

She laughed. He looked so serious and so blooming sexy. "I don't think so, *Monsieur*."

Arno stepped towards her, holding out the flowers. "For you." He said simply.

She accepted the roses, being careful not to react to his touch when he lay the perfect stems in her arms. "Thank you," Chilli dipped her head and breathed in the delicate fragrance, but also caught his scent of vanilla and something lighter, lime maybe. "They're beautiful."

Chilli turned off all but one light. She moved around the table where she wasn't lit by the spotlight.

"As are you, *Mam'selle*?"

"You have developed a smooth tongue since we last met, or maybe you always had it?"

He smirked over at her, leaning his hip against the long table, watching with amusement as she put as much distance between them. He didn't answer.

"I like this place. But it is not safe late at night," Arno said instead.

"How did you get in?" she thought to ask, remembering one

of the other tenants tapping on her door and telling her goodbye several hours ago.

"Too easy," he shook his head in dismay. "Someone was leaving, and I caught the door."

"Oh,"

Arno, having enough of the yawning space she was trying to put between them, walked with determination around the table towards her. It was dark enough for what he wanted. He was hungry for her, and in one move, hooked his arm around her waist and plastered her body against his. At her gasp, he leaned forward and kissed her.

She tasted even better than he remembered, her lips softer, her mouth sweeter.

At her whimper, he plucked the crushed roses from her fingers and pulled her into his arms.

They kissed like they were thirsty. Starved for months, and it was true. It had been two months since their one-night stand, and at this rate, with Arno's hands roaming over her body, and the way her hands were in his hair urging him on, their one-night stand was about to become two in the next few minutes.

"Arno," she breathed against his lips. She didn't know why she said his name; it just felt right.

He groaned and, palming her luscious bottom, hauled her even closer, making her feel the blatant demand he had of wanting to be inside her body this very second.

Her moans bounced around the room as she flung her head back, giving him access to the column of her neck. He swept his tongue down and then up behind her ear, nibbling at the patch of tender skin he knew would make her whisper his name.

Arno squeezed her breasts, sampled, and carried their weight in his palms, but needing more. Impatiently, he hauled her top out of her skirt and sucked on her neck as his fingers found her nipples straining against the confines of her bra. Arno hadn't come here for this. Well, not yet anyway. But holding her, touching the smoothness of her skin, knew he was losing what little control he had. And when she moaned his name deep in her throat and leaned back against the table, pulling him with her, he completely lost it.

He picked her up and sat her on the flat surface, pulling up her top, urgently bathing her breasts with his kisses. Her breasts were overflowing, and he scooped them out of the delicate cups, holding them, pushing them together as he licked one straining nipple and then the other before pulling it deep into his mouth. He'd dreamt of doing this again, of feeling the hard nub across his tongue and the roof of his mouth. Jesus! He couldn't get enough of her taste.

It was Chillitara who found the buckle and undid his belt. She reached into his boxers and released him. She opened her legs wider, guiding him, hot and heavy, into her. But with everything he had, Arno pulled away, quickly sheathing himself before slamming into her again.

Arno rapidly rocked into her. The time to savour was later. The way she was holding him, one arm around his neck, the other clinging to the hardness of his hip, urging him on and her ankles locked at his back, sent him into a free fall and he gladly drowned in everything that was her.

It was rushed but perfect. They came together. They clung when they both exploded around each other.

He was still inside her as they wrestled to the surface. She could feel him pulsating, feel herself throbbing around him, and the tears escaped to run like tiny rivulets into her hairline.

"*Mon chou?*" Arno whispered, feeling the change in her breathing and a slight hiccup.

He moved back slightly and frowned, seeing the tears. "I'm sorry," he said, wiping the tears away with his thumbs, cupping her face. "I hurt you?"

Chilli sniffed, then smiled. "No," she admitted softly, feeling all sorts of embarrassment and thankful for the dark corner they were in.

"Then why the tears *Mam'selle*?" he pulled away, slipping out of her.

Chilli felt the loss. "I didn't realise I missed you so much," she revealed quietly.

His smile was gentle, and using his fingers tipped up her chin to look into her eyes.

"I missed you too."

Her heart turned over and went to burst out of her chest. "Really?"

"*Oui*, yes," he pulled her up and off the table, "that was not how I planned tonight to be."

"Oh? How should it have gone?" she asked, righting her clothes, well trying to, but his large hands were one step ahead of hers. He was the one to smooth down her skirt. He was the one to push her jumper back into her skirt, and he was the one who kissed her every chance he got.

"You kissed me hello," he began his list. "You thanked me for the roses, and we went out for dinner."

She leaned into him and looped her arms up and over his broad shoulders to interlock her fingers at his nape. "We got two out of three, right."

"Come," he removed her arms and nibbled at her lips before pulling her towards the door.

"Wait!" she giggled and looked down at her feet, wriggling her toes.

Arno chuckled and released her hand to search for her shoes.

"You have a penchant for bare feet, Chilli," he mused affectionately, kneeling to place them on her feet.

"You called me Chilli," she said instead, stepping into one shoe.

"You did not tell me what you called yourself," he accused with a shrug, holding out the other shoe for her to step into, and smoothing his fingers over the firm curve of her calf muscle when she did. Her legs were perfect. "So, I went looking."

"That was very stalker-ish."

He stood up, capturing and holding her playful gaze. "You left an impression," he confided with a telling smirk. "Too many nights filled with dreams of your kisses and falling apart in my arms, *Mam'selle*."

"I'm sorry," she said, although she was smiling. Who wouldn't smile at such a compliment? "Come on, let's lock this place up."

"We need to talk about your security," Arno said, looking around. All the other offices were dark, leaving her vulnerable in the massive building.

Chilli looked around, nodding. "I got distracted," she admitted warily. "And I don't normally stay so late."

Arno nodded. "Tell me what to do," Arno ordered.

Following her instructions, he put her camera equipment away and smirked with amusement, watching her wipe down the table.

With one hand holding her camera case, together they walked hand in hand out to his car.

Seeing the black car, Chilli asked, "You were here earlier?"

"*Oui*, I was coming for you," he explained. "But then business demanded my time, and I had to leave. I saw you over there." He nodded towards the steps.

Chilli laughed. "I was modelling for Dutty Urban. They're a wacky Grime streetwear brand."

"Ah, so you dress for them, not for you?"

"Exactly," she stopped beside his vehicle. "My car is over there," she pointed to her vehicle further away. "Shall we meet later?"

He shook his head and waited.

"You drive behind me and come to my flat?"

"*Oui mademoiselle*," he smirked. "You are very smart."

She laughed, feeling light-hearted and as happy as she'd ever been. Arno had tracked her down. He'd wanted to find her.

CHAPTER SEVEN

Arno spent two days with her. Two days in which they went to work during the day, but came together every evening, spending hours upon hours pleasuring each other.

They talked, and when it was time for him to leave, she walked him to his car and cried her eyes out.

Arno called once he'd arrived at St. Pancras station, and he called when he was on the Eurostar. She called to make sure he was comfortable, and they talked whenever they had a strong enough mobile signal, as he travelled through France until he arrived home hours later.

However, they didn't talk about what they were or if they'd ever see each other again. France wasn't far. In fact, it was faster to get to France than some areas of England, but they had made no plans for their future.

Over the weeks that followed, Chilli threw herself into work, observing the number of views and followers increase as she marketed brands for other people.

She also spent a lot of time brainstorming with her staff as she wanted to do something with more substance and, for continued success, knew she would have to diversify.

Her team suggested podcasting, being as she was a talker, they'd teased. The problem they had was how to integrate her brand, or even branch off completely without losing her income streams.

The Women of Colour Excellence Conference, Kerry Oswald-Jones, had involved her in, exposed her to new followers and an edge towards a brand with more maturity and depth.

She and Arno talked almost every night. He said little about his life, saying it was nothing exciting compared to hers and that he worked in a vineyard and that he lived in the Southwest region of France.

One day, she'd video-called him, and he'd answered while outside within a row of waist-high grapevines. He'd looked hot, sweaty and tired. A red bandanna had been tied around his forehead, holding back his long hair. She had demanded he show her what he was wearing, and oh my. Dusty-looking jeans, scuffed boots, and a charcoal grey T-shirt that moulded his chest and strained across his biceps.

Later that night, with a smirk and a twinkle, he had demanded she show him what she was wearing and looking down with one eyebrow slanting into a tease, watched as his eyes darkened when she showed him her pink slip of a nightie in satin and lace.

She'd enjoyed watching him freeze and then swallow, and for the first time, they'd indulged in video sex.

That night had been extraordinary. Both of them vulnerable as they'd watched each other pleasuring themselves. When it was over, they'd smiled and talked into the night. But they hadn't made plans for any tomorrows.

***

Hearing her Diana Ross ringtone, which she had assigned to her lover, Chilli happily grabbed her phone.

"Hey Arno," she said, angling her phone so that she could continue to apply her makeup and talk.

"Hey,"

His voice never failed to make a delicious throb travel down her body, and she melted when she looked at him. He'd showered as his hair was damp and brushed away from his strong face, she noticed.

"Going out?" Arno asked, noting the lush red lipstick and the long glittery earrings. She was wearing her white robe, and he could tell she was naked beneath the satin because he could easily see the dark discs of her areolas. Chillitara was so damn sexy he could barely keep his hands off her. She was as eager to make love with him as he was with her. Unfortunately, they hadn't physically been together in weeks, and he was feeling the strain. Video sex didn't take the edge off these days.

"Hmm-mmm," Chilli answered. If she weren't so busy applying her eyeliner, she would have noticed the beginnings of his deep frown.

"Where?" Arno didn't even try to hide his annoyance.

She looked at him then, not because his voice had cooled but because she liked to know what he was wearing and to match accordingly. It was a 'thing' she'd ever since she'd dreamt in forest green, and he had come into her life that morning on the train. It had been a sign, and she took it seriously.

"What colour shirt is that?" she asked lightly instead, oblivious to his changing mood. She couldn't tell if his shirt was pale pink or something else. Arno's wardrobe was not adventurous, and she couldn't wait to take him out shopping. Actually, she couldn't wait to introduce him to her followers either.

Arno didn't indulge her and look down at himself like he usually did. "You said you were going out?" he prompted, crossing his arms over his chest and leaning back in his chair.

"Yes, but I can't decide which dress to wear." She picked up the phone and pointed it at the two dresses hanging from the wooden curtain rail in her room. "The short white or the multi?" she asked. The white clung, and the multi-coloured flowed about her legs but had long thigh-high slits on either side. It was sexier than the white and naturally in shades of green which had fast become her favourite colour.

"Neither." Came the terse reply.

Startled, Chilli returned the phone to her face. "Excuse me?"

"I said neither," Arno repeated, his voice dripping with ice chips. "It's already," he checked the time on his phone, "nine," he charged, looking at her with lowered brows. "Why are you going out?"

"It's a launch party for Hopetone and Pinks," she explained, only because she wanted to. "And they delivered the golden envelope through the post yesterday." She turned to pick it up from her dresser to show him. "Do you know how privileged I feel getting this golden envelope? Think Charlie and the Chocolate Factory excited." She had been giddy with excitement ever since she'd signed for it. She turned the phone back to the dresses. "Which one?"

"I don't want you going out by yourself." He growled.

Arno felt a fire burning in his stomach. Chillitara was too good-looking to be going out without him. Then he recalled that scene in Paris. Chillitara was an outrageous flirt, young with questionable morals. She'd given herself with little effort from him, he remembered as anger surged through him, and there was nothing to stop her from doing the same again with another man!

Chilli laughed at his ridiculousness. "I've been going out by myself for years." She placed the phone on her dresser and angled it to the wall where a black and white retro frame of Diana Ross and the Supremes held pride of place, and walked over to the dresses, snatching down the white.

She'd felt sexy and fabulous in it when she'd tried it on. "What are you really saying here, Arno, because from where I'm standing you can't order me about." Out of view, she dressed quickly, only turning the phone when she was fully clothed and arranging her boobs within the built-in cups.

The dress stuck to her curves. Her breasts looked fuller as the fabric stretched enticingly across them, to dip low, showing off her cleavage. There were small foldy things of cloth in the middle, showcasing her tiny waist. The fire blazed in Arno's stomach, and his jaw locked.

"You are not going out dressed like that!" Arno blasted before he could stop himself. She looked sensational. Predictably, his body tightened with a need to sink into hers. That dress screamed sex. I want sex.

Chilli shot him a dark look. "Are you blooming insane?"

"You look like a *prostituée*!"

Chilli gasped with hurt. "How dare you!" She couldn't believe he'd called her that.

Arno raised slowly out of his chair at his desk to lean over his laptop. "I dare because you fucked me the first night we met!" he charged, his temper scorching through his veins. "I dare because you flirt with every man you meet! Every photograph you take. Every video!" He yelled. "I *saw* you in that hotel not three hours since leaving my bed with the scent of our sex still clinging to your skin!" he flung at her savagely. "So, yes! I damn well dare!"

Shaking with rage and hurt, Chilli grabbed her shoes, absolute showstoppers he liked her to wear when they played in bed, and more recently when they had video sex, and all she wore were the gold strappy shoes with the platform sole and red lipstick.

"Well not to disappoint you," Chilli began coldly, holding up the shoes to the screen, "I'll be wearing these tonight to see who I can," she couldn't use his word, "so I can–" she tried again and then just said it, repeating his filthy word back to him.

Arno's eyes flashed, and he leaned closer to his laptop as though he wanted to reach through the screen and throttle her. "If you dar–"

Chilli hung up on him, overcome with rage. How dared he? Just who did he think he was?

Tears slipped down her cheeks, and she stripped off the dress and left it on the floor before stomping to her bathroom to wash her face. She looked at herself in the mirror, seeing the ravages he had done with just a few words. Her eyes looked wide and tortured. Her bottom lip trembling and her hair a tumbling mess from where she'd dragged the dress over her head.

She was no prostitute! And what did he mean about seeing her? When? Her hands were shaking so much that she turned on the cold water tap and ran water over the insides of her wrists, trying to compose herself.

Diana Ross's singing didn't muffle her sobs. He was ringing her back, and Chilli snorted and turned away.

Then, because she was hungry, stomped over to her kitchen

and went to the fridge. Stupid man, she thought, grabbing open the fridge door to peer inside as she sniffed and wiped away her tears. Stupid. Stupid. Stupid man!

There was nothing else besides a loaf of bread and a block of cheese. Chilli broke off a piece of bread and buttered it liberally. She peered inside the fridge, wishing the ingredients for a mushroom omelette would magically materialise.

The phone kept on singing *Chain Reaction* and then stopped. She turned towards the bed where she had left it. Then the rude and obnoxious ringing of her landline began insulting the air. She ignored it too, until fearing the persistent ringing would annoy her neighbours, strode over and pulled the connection from the wall. Take that Arno Tournier, Chilli thought maliciously, looking at the end of the cable in one hand, the bread in the other and finally, the golden envelope over on the dresser.

It was nine thirty-six, the red digital clock on the microwave said. Stuffing the last of the bread into her mouth, Chilli came to a decision just as her mobile phone started singing again. She turned it off.

***

It should have been a rubbish night. Chilli had even been sobbing when she'd re-done her makeup, but it wasn't, she'd had a brilliant time.

The building that hosted the event used to be a bank. Mahogany counters were now used as bars. The grand ceilings adorned with elaborate chandeliers danced gentle light over the exclusive crowds. It was a great space and the pink champagne flowed from tall unicorn ice sculptures. Hopetone & Pinks knew how to launch their luxury bath products in style.

Candace and Vinny were there as well as several other content creators Chilli knew.

She was glad she'd worn the multi-coloured dress as celebrities were in attendance and many sought her out. She was glowing with accomplishment. You knew you had made it when stars asked for selfies.

She exchanged numbers and almost accepted an invitation to dinner from an actor who appeared on an evening soap. But no, her heart may have got a trampling on tonight by the one person she had given it to, but–*What*?

Chilli gasped at that revelation when she sat between Vinny and his boyfriend, Dr Gabriel, in the back seat of the taxi on their way home. She loved Arno. Two days of real togetherness and she was in love.

She felt the tears again, hovering just below the surface. Arno, the tall Frenchman who adored her body. Was that all, though? They'd spent a lot of time in bed those two days he'd been in England and talked most days since. But this streak of jealousy tonight spoke volumes, and ordinarily, Chilli would have blocked every access he had to her and probably moved to a new house. But one argument didn't end a relationship inevitably, surely? Were they even in a relationship? They'd just slid into nightly chats and phone sex.

Did you throw in the towel or talk it out? She wanted to give him another chance, but to call her what he did was unforgivable, and she wasn't sure she could forgive the ugly word he'd used. And what did he mean by seeing her the morning after at the hotel? Was he at the AXP conference? And if so, why? Had he been stalking her? She shivered, not liking the direction her thoughts were taking her. There was always a risk you would attract psychos when you were in her kind of business, she knew.

It had started to rain. Not the down need an umbrella kind of deluge, just the odd speck on the windscreen she could count, she mused absently thinking back.

She'd met Arno on the train. She'd seen him again later in the hotel bar. Had he followed her to the hotel? Stalked her?

Chilli went over the conversations she'd had with her friends on the train, realising they'd talked about the boutique hotel they'd be staying in, and what they would do that night. It wouldn't be hard to wait for her, *stalk* her, she thought with unease.

For that matter, what did she know about him? She knew he lived in the southern area of France. He worked in a vineyard and picked grapes. She'd seen evidence of that many times, in fact, but what else did she know? Was he married, only coming to see her when he told his wife he needed to go to England on business? The thought made bile rise and stick in her throat. He talked to her via video link all the time, but even so.

If she saw him again, she would ask the right questions and behave like a grown-up. Not because she was inexperienced when it came to men, did it mean that she was stupid, she scolded herself. She needed to take control. Control Chillitara! She mentally ordered herself. Control.

The taxi pulled up outside the Victorian house that had been sliced into four equally sized flats. She was on the top floor, flat B.

"Lunch next week?" Vinny asked, peering across the seat. He didn't bother to get out, but his tall, shaved-headed boyfriend with tattoos on his neck held out his hand and gallantly helped her out. He even adjusted the neckline of her dress. Dr Gabriel Coxwith, a doctor specialising in Paediatrics was Vinny's much older, on-again-off-again lover.

"Thank you and no," she bent to say to Vinny. "Week after?"

"Got it," Vinny confirmed. "See you then."

She kissed Gabriel on the cheek before waving them off, yet was unsurprised when the taxi remained idling, until she unlocked the front door, waved and stepped inside before it drove off.

***

It was the ringing of her phone several hours later that pulled Chilli out of a deep sleep, where she had been dreaming of a gentle stream and trailing her feet through it. The entire dream had been bathed in a soft, rosy glow. Not pink, but a delicate, sultry red.

"Hello?" she answered sleepily, knowing the only person who

would ring her at four in the morning would be Arno. She'd turned her phone back on just before she'd fallen asleep, not liking the silence. Like teenagers, they usually talked until one of them fell asleep.

"*Je suis désolé*," he immediately apologised as she answered.

"I'm sorry too," Chilli said in English, snuggling into her pillows. She was bilingual, but when she was tired and emotional, she could only speak in English.

"Did you have a good night?"

Chilli wasn't sure what he was asking. She didn't want to start a fight. Did he mean, had she actually gone out? Or was his question exactly that and enquiring about her night out? Why she was overthinking it, she didn't know she scolded herself, turning over to look at the antique ceiling cornice that framed the entire room like trimmings on a birthday cake.

"Depends," she hedged.

She heard him sigh, followed by a deep rumble in the background.

The Southwest of France was having torrential rains, she knew, because Arno had told her not two days ago. The grapes needed the rain, he said, as it was unusually dry.

"I am a jealous fool," he admitted. "I miss you and then to see you dressing up, looking so beautiful, and I wasn't there to bask in your beauty made me jealous, *mon amour*."

A flash of bright light shot across her bedroom, and she turned to her window to watch the lightning. She hadn't bothered to close her curtains when she got in, as she had no problem sleeping through the bright morning rays. In fact, she liked to wake naturally. She had a partial blind affixed to the bottom half of the sash window for privacy, but the top half was bare. Rain pelted the windowpane, and the lightning was putting on a magical show.

"I didn't like it, Arno."

"I know."

"It's what I do," Chilli explained. "I have to network to keep my numbers up, keep my sponsors happy and my followers interested. I've invested a lot of time, money and energy into what I do. And besides, I like it."

"I know that too."

They were both silent.

Chilli watched the sky, wondering if there was a thunderstorm in France.

"Arno?" she began carefully, as a tear slipped down her face. "I don't think we're going to–"

"No!" he interrupted quickly. "I won't let you break us up because of my foolishness," he stormed in a panic, holding the phone tight to his ear. "This is on me. My problem, *oui*?" he admitted. "I will do better, I promise you."

"But Arno..." she sighed, as more tears fell.

"I'm sorry *mon amour*."

Chilli wavered. He had never called her his love before. Was she? Was she really his love? Why was she feeling so insecure and needy all of a sudden? Chilli asked herself. She wasn't like this.

She wiped her eyes and sniffed un-ladylike.

"Please don't cry, Chillitara."

Chilli could hear the pain in his voice.

"I can't help it," she hiccupped. "You're so far away, and I miss you, and I want you here with me," she poured out honestly. "I'm sorry I'm so pathetic, but I miss you." Chilli wailed, not even bothering to hide her crying.

She looked at the phone after hearing him chuckle. She was crying, pouring out her heart, and he was laughing?

"I'm here."

"Huh?" she sniffed, sitting up to look about the room, believing she had misheard him. "What?"

"I was going to wait until you woke up, but I am too close. Look outside."

"Outside?"

She heard him laugh again.

"Wake up *mon amour*."

Chilli flung back her covers and rushed to the window, pulled up the blind and peered outside. It was pouring, and there he stood, getting soaked. Arno was easily noticeable from the glow of his phone glued to his ear, standing beside a rental car. He waved up at her.

"You're here," Chilli touched the window as though caressing him, then pulled herself together. "You silly man, come inside," she ordered. "You're getting wet."

She watched him shrug his shoulders in that rueful French way of his and felt her heart melt. He was here.

"I'm coming."

Chilli dashed around her flat, pulled on her robe. Then stumbled to a stop, spying her reflection in the mirror. She screeched and dragged the black do-rag from her head to search her drawers for a silk scarf she could cover her flat curls with. Finding one in a red tribal print, she wrapped it over her head, tying it in a stylish bow above her forehead, before running barefooted down the stairs.

The first impression she got when she flung open the door was that he was soaked. Rainwater was dripping from his hair, clumping his lovely eyelashes together and dripping down his face. He was still. The rain lashed down behind him, drowning out any sound he may have made. He was holding a small bouquet of roses down by his side. Rose-coloured roses.

They stood looking at each other. Arno eventually broke their trance to trail his verdant gaze over her, and then he sighed, his shoulders dropping before he stepped over the threshold.

"*Mon amour*," was all he said, and Chilli jumped into his arms, wrapped her legs around his waist and cried into his neck.

Arno locked the front door with her clinging to him, climbed the stairs and once inside, secured them into her flat, before kissing her.

It was gentle and sweet.

"I missed you too." He said between kisses.

CHAPTER EIGHT

Surprisingly, they didn't make love. Arno took a quick shower and slid into bed beside her and snuggled her into his side.

Together, they fell asleep with her head on his shoulder.

Chilli woke to his hand stroking the length of her body.

"Have you now become my alarm clock?" she asked sleepily, grappling to the surface.

Arno's hand became sure and intent, slipping between her thighs and wiggling his fingers, encouraging her to open her legs.

With his chest pressing against her back, Arno pushed against her, making her feel the evidence of how aroused she made him feel. He was always like this around her. His first thoughts were about her. From the moment she'd intentionally fallen onto his lap on the train and every moment that followed.

"Open for me *mon amour*," he whispered into her hair and kissed her nape as she opened her legs to place one over his.

With one hand now stroking both nipples, first one and then the other, Arno slid in deep and made slow morning love to her, taking her ever higher, and then slowing it down until she was practically begging him to finish.

When he did, grasping her hips and raising her to meet his thrusts, she moaned deep and trembled as she fell apart in his arms with her leg still over one of his hair-roughened thighs.

It was the perfect way to wake up.

"Hmm, that was nice."

"I'm here to please *mon amour*," Arno said groggily. He'd left straight from the vineyard, luckily caught a direct flight from Bergerac and drove the rest of the way. He'd eaten two chocolate bars, grabbed from the vending machine while the rental people prepared his car, and now that he had satisfied one appetite, he was ready to satisfy the other.

Tapping her bottom, he said. "Breakfast."

"I have nothing in the fridge," Chilli replied, remembering how dismal the shelves looked last night.

Slipping from under the covers, her nightgown slid down her body and settled high on her thighs. Hearing Arno's sharp intake of breath, Chilli turned to look down at him. His eyes were hot and heavy as he tracked his gaze over her, making her nipples peak and self-conscious heat flood into her cheeks.

Her breasts had always been lush. Arno could see them delightfully overflowing in the confines of the satin. They just looked and felt extra bountiful this morning, he thought with appreciation.

"Not to worry *mon chou*, we can go out," Arno stretched and watched when she walked to her bathroom. Her bottom bounced like it had a mind of its own. With a hungry smile to himself, he followed her into the shower.

Two hours later, they were sitting, having a sizeable English breakfast at a gastro pub chain.

"Are we going to talk about yesterday?" Chilli asked. While lying in his arms last night, she'd promised herself she was going to ask the questions she should have asked weeks ago.

Barely hiding his impatience, Arno sighed warily. "*Oui*, yes, if you insist."

"Oh, I insist all right," she replied, placing her coffee down to spear the last button mushroom onto her plate. "Do you have a significant other in France?"

Arno laughed.

"*Now* you think to ask me that?" But his laughter died when he noticed her seriousness. "No, I do not have a significant other in France, Chillitara," he stated tightly. "And if you knew me better, you would not insult me with such a remark."

"I didn't mean to offend you," she cajoled, looking at his plate. He hadn't eaten his mushrooms yet. "I don't know you though, do I?"

He snorted, and she narrowed her eyes at him. "What do you do? Aside from picking grapes. What do you do when the picking season is over?" She knew nothing about grape picking. Did he pick the bunches that she bought at the supermarket, for instance? Did grapes grow all year round?

"Research grapes." Arno answered. "Next question."

"Do you have a family?" she shot back, ignoring his militant look. "Brothers and sisters?"

"I am an only child." He crossed his arms over his chest and leaned back. "Next question."

His terseness was to put her off, but tough. She wanted answers. "Parents?"

"Both dead," he snapped with a huff. "I don't remember them."

"Oh, I'm sorry."

He didn't acknowledge her words of sympathy, but went on, "grandfather living."

Chilli licked her lips, changing direction. "What am I to you?"

He lost the mutinous look and stared unblinkingly at her.

Chilli held his gaze; she knew it was vital that she did. They had never had a more candid conversation.

The seconds ticked by.

"Would you like me to help you?" she inquired, switching his plate with hers without asking to finish his mushrooms before they got cold.

He shifted as though he were sitting on a pile of pebbles. "You are important to me," Arno confessed tightly.

Chilli smiled. "Thank you. You are important to me, too."

"*Bon*, let's go," Arno placed his napkin on the table, signalling the end of the conversation.

"I've not finished," Chilli ignored his sigh of impatience. "And you are being quite rude," she chided. "Tell me what last night was about."

"I've already apologised for that."

Chilli shook her head at him, "Arno, your jealousy was unreasonable, and admittedly, scary," she pinned him with her stare, "I was leaving you today." she confided, waiting to see how he was going to react to her words, but he surprised her.

"And look," his lovely mouth curved into his cheeks, and he reached across the table to capture her hands, entwining their fingers together. "Today we are closer than ever." Arno leaned forward and kissed her knuckles. "You are important to me, and I was jealous," he revealed. "It is normal to be jealous when I see *my* woman, my beautiful woman, in a sexy dress, her legs on display, going out without me. I didn't like it. I *don't* like it."

Chilli pulled her hands away at his possessiveness. Some women liked that kind of talk, but she wasn't one of them.

"Is this going to be a problem?" Chilli challenged. She knew he was aware that they had no future if it was. "Because this is business to me, Arno. Not only that, but I also enjoy doing what I do, and you live in France."

By the sudden coolness of his stare, she knew he'd read between the lines. She would go out regardless of what he said.

"It is my problem, *oui*," Arno said eventually, when Chilli continued to look at him with silent questions in her dark eyes.

"Last night, you said you saw me?" Chilli asked, remembering his disturbing words. "When?"

He named the hotel and at her confused look continued. "I too was at a conference, albeit not as large as your student exchange thing," he explained, then reluctantly admitted. "I saw you being very familiar with a man in the lobby."

Chilli raised her brows, before shaking her head in disappointment, realising he was referring to her friend. "Jose?" she asked more to herself, remembering sitting with her friend in the lobby. "Jose is like a brother to me. We were exchange students in Sweden together," she explained, not because she had to, but because it led to her next question. "So," Chilli drew in her breath slowly, "I really should ask why *you* didn't come over and talk to me?" she questioned. "We'd spent the night together." Only to continue in dismay, her eyes flaring at his veiled look. "Ah," she shook her head in understanding, her mouth tipping down on one side, realising where he had regulated the most magical night of her life. "It was a one-night stand that meant nothing to you."

"*Oui*," he said, however, quickly amended, "*non!*" Arno held her gaze steady with his before shrugging his shoulders. He'd already admitted more about himself than he ever would to any woman. Why couldn't she just leave it at that? He was here, wasn't he? "I knew you were different, special," he tacked on. "Even then. I just—" he slammed his mouth shut, frustrated at the hoops she was making him jump through.

If he hadn't tracked her down, Chilli would have laughed at that blatant lie, and she watched him, wanting to read more into his words, but he dipped his head, and raked his hair away from his face, before flashing his hands about as though shooing away a fly. His face was blank when he looked up.

Obviously, *he* didn't want to talk about his feelings. Chilli breathed in deeply before saying what she had silently spent the morning rehearsing. "When you go back to France, I'm coming with you." She challenged, lifting her chin to watch him closely.

"What?" Sitting forward, all insulting nonchalance disappearing at her words, Arno asked, "To live?"

He couldn't look more horrified than if she had dropped her dress and danced naked on the table.

"Your reaction is enough," Chilli said, wiping her mouth before throwing the crumpled napkin onto the table. Her disappointment was obvious by the look she didn't bother to hide. *He* obviously wanted her on his terms, but she was nobody's part-time lover or a fool. "I'm leaving now," Chilli stood, picking up her bag and jacket, before turning back to him. "And I don't ever want to see you again."

Arno sat there stunned, wondering what the hell had just happened, and didn't snap out of it until he saw her stalk past the window, her long hair swinging in time to her angry stride. She couldn't walk away fast enough!

Swearing under his breath, and thankful the bill was already paid, Arno dashed outside to catch Chilli by the elbow, swinging her around to him. Her eyes were drenched with tears. The anger and panic Arno had been feeling quickly disappeared when two fat teardrops fell onto her cheeks.

"You can come home with me," he stated, placing his hands on her shoulders and bending slightly at the knee to look into her eyes.

"Promise?" Chilli sniffed.

Arno wiped away her tears with his thumbs and kissed her temple gently. "I will make the arrangements," he promised, before moving back to capture and lift her chin with his fingers. "But I warn you now, *mon amour.* Don't *ever* threaten to leave me again, because you are mine!"

With that, Arno pulled her into his arms and held her close, before kissing her deeply right there in the car park, where rain-soaked leaves littered the tarmac from the thunderstorm the night before.

Only Chilli couldn't go with him the next day or the one after. A broken water pipe where her office was located interrupted their plans, and Arno reluctantly returned to France alone.

CHAPTER NINE

Chilli looked up at the flight timetable and watched in disbelief when her flight turned from green to red with a big X and the word 'cancelled' on either side of the flight number.

Scrambling with the things she had scattered over the two seats beside her; she picked up her bag and balanced her tablet and phone in one hand as she approached the desk.

"Excuse me, my flight has just been cancelled," Chilli said, waving behind her.

She had flown the same itinerary on one other occasion, when Arno couldn't make it to her, taking the evening flight on Friday night.

"I'm sorry," the unhelpful, overly made-up uniformed woman said.

She didn't look the least bit sorry, Chilli noticed.

"Is there another flight I can get?" Chilli suggested when one wasn't forthcoming.

The lady looked at her screen, tapped away, shook her head once, tapped again and then looked at the board over Chilli's head.

"If you run, you can fly into Beauvais and then connect to Bergerac. It'll be tight," she checked the time on her watch. "But I'll let them know you're coming."

"Thank you." Chilli praised and waited for the new boarding passes to be printed and directed to a different gate which, naturally, was the furthest away.

They were waiting for her, and she sat in the nearest seat. With her fingers shaking and her breath rushing, she sent a quick text letting Arno know the flight had been cancelled.

She was about to send off her new flight times when the flight attendant asked her to please change her phone over to flight mode.

With heated cheeks, Chilli changed the settings, pocketed her phone and smiled her apology at the attendant.

She arrived at Beauvais Airport but didn't make the connection, so diverted to Paris instead. The flight wasn't too long, and she went to stay with her grandmother. She had intended to catch the earliest flight down to Bergerac Airport the next day and drive the rest of the way to the cottage, but her grandmother insisted she stay and attend her doctor's appointment with her.

What Grand-Mère wanted, Grand-Mère got, and giving up on her weekend with Arno, Chilli sent him a text letting him know she was staying in Paris and that she'll see him next weekend instead.

He'd replied, became all concerned with her plight, told her he missed her and asked after her grandmother, which Chilli thought was sweet.

She spent a lovely afternoon with the seventy-six-year-old woman, who ruled over the entire family from her apartment in Paris.

After the doctor's appointment, Chilli treated them both to a mini spa break, and they had facials and got their nails done in bright red. It was lovely, and Grand-Mère was happy.

Chilli took her for burgers and told her a little about Arno. Just the fact that her lover was French made her grandmother happy, and she was sent off to catch the next flight to be with him. Grand-Mère was a bona fide romantic and liberal with her views once Chilli had come of age.

Curiously, Chilli wasn't able to contact Arno with her new arrangements but went it alone, anyway. She knew the way and could be at his cottage by two o'clock at the latest.

Her flight was uneventful, but calamity struck at Bergerac Airport. Charlotte, the young lady at the rental desk, whom Chilli had seen on her previous visit, gave her the bad news. There were no cars available because of a château having their annual ball. The winemakers came from all over the region to wish them a bountiful season.

Now, she was stuck in the middle of the night in Southwest France.

Chilli wheeled her furry suitcase outside. It was warm, and she pulled off her grey faux fur jacket.

She was wearing black skinny jeans and a black vest. Arno loved seeing her in outfits similar to this, and she liked to tease him, especially after weeks of absence.

She tried to ring him, but his phone went straight to voicemail.

"*Excusi moi? Mademoiselle?*"

Chilli looked up to see a middle-aged man. "*Oui?*"

"Taxi?"

She didn't notice the taxi rank until she looked over his shoulder. There was one old banger there.

"*Oui*," she answered, and asked how much it would cost to go to Arno's cottage, giving him the address.

"Tournier, *oui?*" he asked, looking at her, puzzled.

Thinking she may have the name of the area wrong, Chilli fished out her phone and pulled up the Maps App. She turned it to the man.

"Ah," he smiled, and they spent another five minutes negotiating the price.

When they were both satisfied, Chilli waved goodbye to the desk clerk and off she went.

The driver, Horatio, drove slowly and talked fast, and by the time they neared Arno's little house, she was exhausted, hungry and feeling the onset of period cramps.

Her period had been out of sorts recently, so she welcomed the cramps, if only to confirm she wasn't ill or anything. Besides, it would be nice to know how Arno would handle sex being off the table. She smiled at herself, picturing his look of horror and then seeing him think of ways to satisfy them both.

Chilli leaned back and shifted her bottom several times, trying to make herself comfortable against the cracked leather seat, before snuggling into her jacket to remember the previous time she and Arno had been together.

The last time she had travelled this road, she'd been full of eager anticipation and silently congratulating herself for ignoring her inner caution enough to gather some bravado and make those last-minute plans to go to France.

Chilli only contacted Arno once she'd arrived in Paris and was about to board the internal flight for him to pick her up.

They'd made and cancelled plans too often. Knowing enough was enough and thinking their relationship would fizzle out, Chilli had dropped everything and flew to France.

Arno had missed her, oh wow, had he missed her, Chilli remembered with a chuckle feeling a warmth spread through her body to pool at her sex. The kisses once they'd left the airport became increasingly urgent until he'd pulled into a side road, and they'd made out like eager teenagers. He'd eventually driven her to his house. A quaint traditional one-bedroom cottage with a blue tarpaulin secured by bricks on one side of the roof. She had fallen in love with its charm and rustic character, muddy pathway, and the shower that turned from hot to cold then back to scorching again before you could catch your breath.

However, once they got to the cottage, Arno had been called away. Feeling worn out, Chilli had gone to sleep without bothering to unpack.

It had been dark when Arno had woken her, all apologetic, but she'd been fine, merely happy to be in his company.

They'd made love on the rickety iron bed. He'd served from plastic containers from the workers' kitchen and drank a bottle of delicious red wine, gifted from his employer for taking him away.

After dinner, they'd walked along the vines, and he took her to a large, stone, barn-looking building. Laughing and sneaking around the back, Arno had jimmied open a window, and they'd stolen inside.

Chilli remembered being hit with the intoxicating smell of wine-soaked wood and looming rows upon rows of wooden barrels stacked almost to the rafters.

When she'd wrinkled her nose and remarked about the smell, Arno, his eyes darkening with seriousness, had taken her fingers. With his hand guiding hers, he smoothed it along the grain of a barrel to tell her that these barrels were made from the very best oak and made the very best wine in France and deserved some respect.

To her amused giggles, he'd lifted her on top, pushed her legs apart and made love to her.

It had been slow and tender. Arno kissed every bit of her, stripping her naked before going onto his knees and bathing her with his tongue. Even now, she remembered how hard she'd come against his mouth.

When she had drifted down to earth, she'd pushed him against the wall of barrels and kissed her way down his chest, unbuttoning his shirt with a slowness that had him gritting his teeth and fisting his hands at his side.

She remembered smoothing her hands over the heavy ridge of him, cupping him, unbuckling his belt and pushing his jeans and briefs down to pool at his ankles.

He was harder than she had ever known him to be, and she'd delighted in the feel of him and the deep pulsating heat of him, when she'd taken him into her mouth, to twirl her tongue over the smooth head and tickle her way along his length, before taking him as deep as she could.

His hands had been in her hair, trying to control her movements, but she'd pushed him away to suck him harder, pumping her hand until he had no choice but to release into her mouth.

They'd never done that before. *She* had never done that before.

He'd held out his hand to help her up, and she remembered them holding each other for long moments. So long, a spider had crawled across her barefoot, and her screams had bounced off all those barrels.

Arno had laughed so hard she'd ended up storming off in offence, but of course, he'd caught her, and held her close as they walked to the cottage, where he made love to her all night in apology.

It had been magical.

Unfortunately, her assistant Conrad had called early the next morning, and she had to fly back to sign some contracts that had arrived earlier than expected in the post. That had been five weeks ago, and she hadn't seen Arno since.

Deep into her daydreams, Chilli didn't notice that Horatio had driven down a road she wasn't familiar with.

"Horatio? You're going the wrong way," she pointed out, knowing Arno's cottage was over the hill to the right.

"No *Mademoiselle*, this is the Tournier estate. See?" he pointed to an elaborately designed wrought iron sign that read Tournier Vineyards.

They drove down a vast, well-kept private road with tall conifers on either side and rows upon rows of grapevines behind them. After about a mile or so, the road opened, and the most beautiful château lay ahead.

"See, Tournier château *Mademoiselle*," Horatio clarified. "*Monsieur* Arno Tournier and his grandfather live here."

"You must be mistaken, Horatio," Chilli said in confusion.

The house was lit up and sparkling. From a distance, Chilli could make out the chandeliers.

Cars lined the circular driveway, and uniformed valets held open the doors to women dressed in ball gowns and glistening jewellery. The men looked sharp in black-tie.

Before Chilli could stop him, Horatio drove up to the entrance and waited in line.

"No, Horatio," Chilli voiced in rising panic. Something wasn't right. This was the wrong place. "This isn't it."

Confused, Horatio looked over his shoulder. "*Mademoiselle*?"

Shaking her head, Chilli said, "it's the wrong place."

"*Non-Mademoiselle*," Horatio pointed towards the vast entrance, "*Monsieur* Arno Tournier, see."

Chilli looked towards the entrance. There was Arno, like she had never seen him.

He was dressed in a white tux jacket and slim black trousers. His hair was gelled away from his face, and he was wearing a red rose in his lapel, as well as a slender blonde woman in a long white sequined gown that clung to his arm. She was very willowy and modelesque, Chilli noted. She was playing with the ends of his untied black bow tie, and Chilli watched when she pulled him down to her, their lips almost touching as they laughed and flirted with their lower bodies fused at the hips and both holding half-empty champagne flutes.

Chilli felt a band tighten around her stomach, making her gasp in distress, but she couldn't look away.

Arno was swaying with the woman in his arms now, looking all relaxed and happy as they danced playfully with people looking indulgently on. Chilli had never seen him look like that with her. He leaned down and said something that Chilli could see made her blush. The woman put her hand on his chest, and they moved as one, turning towards each other with an intimacy that screamed. And Chilli watched as, in slow motion, they kissed. Deeply.

A sob lodged in Chilli's throat. Tears burned the backs of her eyes, and she felt hot and then suddenly cold as though she had stepped from a sauna to dive into a cold plunge pool, making her heart gallop in distress. She was going to faint. Blackness surged within her like tar, suffocating her and cutting off her oxygen as it slowly choked her.

"*Mademoiselle?*" Horatio asked with concern, turning in his seat to look at her. His passenger had dark skin, but she didn't look well. Gone was the eager, love-struck daze she'd had all the way here.

"Horatio drive," Chilli choked on a sob as Arno turned to look outside. Their eyes met for a split second before Chilli doubled over as pain ripped across her stomach. "Drive. I can't let him see me!" she yelled, fighting the blackness.

"Horatio," she cried in rising panic, "he can't see me. Please," she begged. "We need to leave!"

Her door was opened with a flourish, and a young valet held

out his gloved hand to her.

To brave it out and make a scene was not how Chilli wanted to do this. Maybe if she was all dressed up and didn't feel her stomach squeeze into a tight ball, perhaps she would get out and demand to know what was going on. And if her grandmother were nearby, then yes, maybe she would climb those marble-looking steps. But she wasn't and Chilli couldn't.

Someone was asking why the taxi was holding up the line, and people began to notice.

"No!" Chilli shouted and pushed the valet away, slamming the door on him, "Horatio drive!"

Horatio swung out of the line and almost collided with a limousine that pressed its haughty horn, making everyone turn to see what the disturbance was.

"Drive, Horatio drive!" Chilli screamed as sweat beaded across her forehead.

Horatio, bless him, drove. He drove straight off Tournier land back towards the airport.

Had Arno seen her? Chilli thought, holding her stomach. She thought he did, but she had also seen his confusion. She wasn't supposed to be there.

Her Diana Ross ringtone sang, and Chilli looked at her phone. Arno. She disconnected.

She felt sick. He had lied to her. There could be a perfectly reasonable explanation. But Chilli didn't think so.

She was going to be sick. Chilli wound down her window and stuck her head out. She was wearing one of her own wigs, but didn't care. The nausea was real.

"Horatio?" she said faintly. "I'm going to be sick." Chilli didn't know if she said it in French or English, but the dear old man slammed on his brakes, jumped out, and rushed to her door.

Horatio held her hair back as Chilli was sick on the side of the road and then gave her a bottle of water that slipped through her trembling fingers, and she fainted dead away.

CHAPTER TEN

Arno watched as the taxi roared off, almost careening into a stretch limo, before accelerating down the driveway, and he snatched in a confused breath.

It didn't make sense. Chillitara was in Paris. They had texted each other earlier today, and she'd confirmed she would come next weekend instead, he remembered, seeing the taillights of the dilapidated taxi disappear altogether, but he still looked into the distance. She couldn't be in two places and certainly not at this time of the night, well morning, he thought, flicking back his cuff to check the time. It was almost four o'clock. He frowned with a dreaded feeling but knew there weren't any flights from Paris, and he should know, he knew the flight timetable like he did the ingredients to his finest wine label.

He hadn't had a clear view of the passenger in the taxi, but-

"What is it?" Phillippa asked.

Arno looked at her and then towards the road. "Just one little phone call," he cajoled the other woman and tapped her bottom lip, where she pushed it out into a cute pout.

Arno moved to the side of the foyer, still packed with his grandfather's guests milling around, reluctant for the extravagant evening to end. When the Tourniers had a ball, it was celebrated.

Their money was on display, the château dressed to perfection, and it was the only time his grandfather shook the shadow of grief from his shoulders and socialised with France's other wine millionaires.

Walking towards a dark alcove, Arno pulled his phone out of his jacket pocket, unlocked the screen and tapped through to Chillitara's number.

The call rang out, and he tried once again before familiar

hands moved around his waist to pull him into the crowds.

***

Chilli regained consciousness in a strange room. She looked around, seeing cream walls, a row of empty auxiliary beds with white cotton sheets, folded tight and pristine opposite and smelling the distinct smell of pine disinfectant. She was in a hospital.

"Chillitara?" a gentle voice said, and she turned her head in confused disbelief to see her grandmother sitting beside her, her pale face pinched with worry.

"Grand-Mère?"

Her grandmother held her hand, "I'm here my sweetest child,"

"What happened?"

"You almost lost the baby,"

"What, baby?" Chilli asked, thinking she had misheard her grandmother. But seeing the lines of worry on her face, knew she was serious.

"The baby. Why didn't you tell me you were pregnant?" Seeing Chilli's frown of confusion, Grand-mere added, leaning forward, placing her hands on the bed beside her granddaughter. "You didn't know you were pregnant?"

"I'm not pregnant," Chilli scoffed. The idea was absurd, she thought, turning her head away. She could see the lush greenery framed perfectly by the dated window. "I can't be," Chilli whispered more to herself, thinking back to her periods. They'd been erratic, but she still had them. Besides, she and Arno had always been careful.

"Almost five months."

"Five months!"

"Yes, *mon chere*."

"But…" Tears tipped down Chilli's cheeks. It was all too much. She couldn't be pregnant, yet things started to fall into place. She was hungry all the time. The constant cravings for mushrooms swimming in butter. And oh yes, Arno had once said her breasts were overflowing in his hands. He'd spent the rest of that night using them as cushions, she remembered.

More tears flowed. Oh God, what was she going to do? Pregnant.

"I'm sorry," Chilli whispered, as tears slipped down her face, seeing the shadow of fear in her grandmother's eyes. It was fleeting, but she saw it. The magnitude of this was going to ricochet through many lives and continents. "I'm sorry," Chilli repeated.

"No, my sweetest." her grandmother moved to sit on the edge of the bed and held her hand. "Don't worry, you are a Laurent, and we will get through this together," she promised, patting her fingers. "The father?"

Chilli closed her eyes, the memories of the last few hours tumbling back. Arno had seen her, and she remembered the shock, guilt and then panic on his face. A woman in a clingy white dress stuck to his side, her body language intimate with his. The kiss. Arno had seen her, and he had lied.

"As you said, Grand-Mère, you and I will get through this."

***

Chilli stayed in hospital for ten days, as the baby had been a little restless and her blood pressure was a cause for concern.

Her doctor preferred her not to fly, ordered her to rest and gave her a prescription for prenatal vitamins, lots of pregnancy pamphlets before discharging her from their care.

Horatio, the taxi driver and his wife Celeste, visited every day and they'd all become firm friends. She was so grateful her new friend had looked through her phone and telephoned the number most called. Which had been her grandmother.

Horatio invited her to stay in his village. His daughter's two-bedroom flat was empty, and she was welcome to use that.

With only her baby on her mind, Chilli negotiated to pay her way and began life in a cute village at the base of the Pyrenees.

***

Arno couldn't find her. One week she had been missing, and now, he knew with regret, it must have been Chillitara in the taxi that night.

He had to explain things. But had to find her first.

She hadn't picked up his calls, and she hadn't been online at all. Her social media footprint was silent. No videos. No photographs on that picture app thing she was so fond of using either. Nothing.

He'd wanted to go to England the next day, but an emergency at the vineyard, plus his grandfather's ill health due to overdoing it at the ball, had put paid to that. He had to kick his heels and watch out for her instead.

It was because of those frustratingly empty days without her that Arno was forced to evaluate their relationship.

He knew nothing of her family. He hadn't formally met her friends. He knew she had family in France and a grandmother she adored in Paris, but he didn't know the grandmother's name or her address.

Had she lied and met up with a lover? Only guilt had sent her to his arms instead? He couldn't stop the thoughts of doubt and guilt from mixing, making him angry and entirely unlike himself. She was twisting him up in knots. He *felt* too much, and he didn't like it.

Arno parked his car in the short-stay car park at the airport and walked into the small terminal. The tourist season would start soon, and it would become a cattle market, he thought with distaste. Arno was as French as everyone else when it came to sharing his perfect country. He hated it.

"*Monsieur* Tournier," someone called out. "*Bonjour.*"

Arno didn't have time to chit-chat, but turned impatiently to see the young woman behind the car rental counter. What was her name? Charlotte, wave to him before quickly approaching.

"*Mademoiselle* Chilli? She made it to the ball in time?"

Charlotte inquired hopefully. She had gone home to her boyfriend that night and relayed the evening's events and how romantic it was.

Arno's dark eyebrows snapped down when he looked at the young girl. "You saw her? Last Saturday?"

"*Oui,*" she confirmed, explaining about the lack of rental cars and how Chilli had taken a taxi to the Château. "Is everything all right, *Monsieur*?"

"Do you know which taxi she took?" Arno asked urgently, remembering the old car. The *unlicensed* taxi. She had no business travelling in a vehicle like that. Putting herself at risk.

The area was extensive, although the population was small. Everyone knew everyone else and, as his family owned most of the land around here, everyone knew him.

"I'm sorry he was new," Charlotte looked thoughtfully towards the stand. "You know, I have not seen him since that night." Her eyes suddenly bulged. "You think something has happened to *Mam'selle*?" she touched her chest and then looked at her phone before quickly swiping and tapping through various screens. "Chilli has been offline for days, *oh non!*" Charlotte exclaimed.

Arno's mind was racing. It was something to suspect she had seen him, it was something else entirely to know that it was true. He pulled his business card from his jacket pocket and wrote his private number on the back of the crisp white card. "Did you see her come back?" He asked.

"*Non-Monsieur,*" she answered. "*Mam'selle* is lovely, always waves. I follow her online. She is a good influencer, yes? So talented and nice." Charlotte gushed, missing the tense look on the other man's face.

"Here," he gave her his card. "If you see her or the taxi driver, call my private number, okay?"

"*Oui Monsieur.*"

"Thank you."

He walked towards the ticket desk and then paused, oblivious to the surrounding people. The crime rate was non-existent in this part of France. It was very traditional. Although Charlotte had said she'd never seen that taxi driver before. He wasn't local. What if he had done something to his Chillitara? Arno's blood ran cold, and he took his phone out of his pocket and called his friend at the police department. She was in a foreign country, and she was beautiful. Thoughts of her mangled, dead body scorched his brain and burned his retina. His Chillitara, a victim of some hideous crime.

There had been no incidents within the community, he had been told when he'd landed in England a few hours later.

Arno drove straight to her office. She wasn't there. Her staff refused to tell him where she was or when she was returning.

Arno had almost lost his temper.

Chillitara wasn't at her flat, he discovered minutes later, gritting his teeth as he stalked to his car and slammed the door shut. The next time he would see her, he would demand his own key, he thought darkly, looking up at her windows. What was the point of having a girlfriend and not having a key to her flat? He growled roughly to himself, not wanting to look too closely into the label of girlfriend. They slept together, and he wanted it to continue, so he would damn well use that label, he fumed.

Arno waited for two days in soggy London before leaving for France. He was needed. His emotions were all over the place. Anger at her for making him worry like this and a mixture of anger and guilt at himself, for taking so long to tell her the truth. He had been stupid and arrogant.

CHAPTER ELEVEN

Arno buttoned his long black coat and pulled up the collar. The blast of unseasonally cold air when he stepped onto the train platform was frigid and didn't improve his temper.

Only one other person was going westbound to Spain like himself, he noted. What should have been a one-hour plane journey was turning out to be three and a half hours because of the series of aviation strikes going on in France at the moment. Hence another gripe being added to his already extensive list.

Travelling by rail when you had things to do was not how he liked to spend his time.

Spying a metal bench closest to the closed mobile confectionery stand, Arno made his way, knowing it would at least offer a bit of shelter from the cold air.

He was tired. Tired of this bitter feeling of hopelessness. Two months, no, he corrected, seven weeks and three days and no Chillitara. He'd eventually hired a private investigator the second week and still nothing.

He knew she was alive and hadn't ended up in a ditch somewhere, murdered by the unknown taxi driver, because she had signed several lucrative contracts electronically.

Arno huffed into the collar of his coat. What was it to live anywhere in the world and be able to sign contracts worth hundreds of thousands electronically? He snorted.

The only reason the investigator had discovered the deals was because of the series of announcements detailing her collaborations and sponsorships on her website and other social media pages.

Steering his dark thoughts away from her, because nothing good ever came from falling deeper into his self-made pit of despair, Arno watched the opposite platform shrink in size with crowds of people heading for Paris.

The rail company was making money, he calculated, seeing the crowds. However, they could spend some of the profits on decent shelter from the elements, he thought darkly, shoving his icy hands into the pockets of his coat.

There were families, tourists, backpackers and businessmen. A group of teenaged girls were huddled together, looking at something on a phone.

They could be watching an old video or something of Chillitara's, Arno thought, knowing she had followers in the millions, and wondering which clip they were watching. He had watched them all, more than once, even the makeup ones. He now knew how to do a halo lid and a transitional eyeshadow shade. *This* was what his life had become.

She hadn't uploaded anything in weeks and aside from odd clips of her sitting in a chair, with a plain, nondescript white wall behind her, she talked about the latest mascara or some other pointless thing.

Physically, she had disappeared.

How could she talk about makeup and perfume when he was dying inside? He snarled at his melodrama before glancing over to watch a woman in a bulky, purple-coloured coat walk onto the platform opposite. Hell, he was even conjuring her up; he berated himself, watching the woman.

She didn't walk like Chillitara and was rounder, but her complexion was similar. He couldn't see much of her face because of her bright green woolly hat being pulled down low on her head, and the matching scarf folded several times around her neck and head, leaving her eyes and nose exposed to the elements.

Three men dressed identically to him walked onto his platform. Knowing one of them, Arno stood to wave him over. They talked about winemaking, of course, and his friend asked after Arno's grandfather before returning to his party.

Bored, Arno returned to his seat and looked at the time. His train wasn't due for another twenty-two minutes, so he settled in to read his emails and check if the investigator had sent him any new information.

The teenagers across the platform suddenly screeched loudly with excitement and Arno glanced up with annoyance, and then his breath left him.

They had moved to talk to the woman in the purple coat.

She had pushed her hat back and her scarf down, showing her entire face. A face Arno knew so well.

They were taking pictures together, and Arno stared, not believing it was Chillitara standing diagonally to him on the other platform.

It can't be, he thought in disbelief, closing and opening his eyes, but then the teenagers moved, and he noticed what he hadn't seen before. The pink furry suitcase. They had made only twenty; he remembered Chillitara telling him proudly.

Arno stepped forward, not knowing when he had even moved. The tips of his handcrafted brogues hung off the edge of the platform. He didn't know if he said Chilli's name, but her head snapped up and their eyes locked. Warm earthy brown and deep forest green met for the first time in seven weeks and three days.

A gust of wind hit the platform then, and people surged forward.

"Chillitara!" Arno barked, but his voice was whipped away as a train, her train to Paris, came rushing in. One minute she was staring at him, her eyes wide in shock, the next all he saw was a frustrating blur of blue and yellow carriages whizzing past.

In a panic, Arno raced across the platform, up the steps three at a time, before trying to rush through a group of school children—wearing high-visibility aprons—to run over the bridge that straggled both railway lines and ran down the steps to the other side.

He got there just as the doors slid shut and the train pulled away.

***

Chilli sat down with relief and allowed the shock of the last thirty seconds to settle.

She took several deep breaths to regulate her breathing and slow her heart rate before opening her coat to smooth her hand reassuringly over her baby bump.

No stress, she thought. She couldn't afford to stress the baby. She closed her eyes, but all she saw was Arno. Arno stood there frozen, looking at her as though he had seen a ghost.

She felt the backs of her eyes begin to burn, and she was thankful her carriage was empty. She needed to be alone.

These past few months she'd struggled with herself, wanting to confront him, get to the truth, but then remembering no stress. She would deal with Arno once the baby arrived safely. The baby was all that mattered.

Grand-Mère had thought otherwise, but when she realised Chilli would not budge on this, she left her alone. The baby came first. Her grandmother couldn't argue with that.

"Arno," she whispered his name out loud for the first time in weeks, and a single tear slipped down her cheek to hover at her jaw.

He was thinner. She saw it in the gauntness of his cheeks, and his eyes looked dark and haunted. Had she done that to him? Chilli thought guiltily. Was she unfair? Yes, she was, she agreed with herself. But the baby came first.

Being pregnant for almost five whole months, drinking alcohol, eating takeout, shellfish and runny eggs and even spreading honey on her toast, essentially, doing all the things a responsible mother-to-be would never do, ensured she lived each moment in a web of guilt and self-hate.

Granted, she didn't know she was pregnant, but she hadn't listened to her body and felt guilty enough. Her baby had not had the best start in life. She had nightmares about the things that could go wrong. The damage she may have already done.

So no, she would not feel sorry for Arno. She would not feel guilty about not telling him. She was going to stay healthy and stress-free for her baby's sake and tell Arno after the baby had arrived safely. She owed it that much.

***

Arno stared numbly for a whole second and then sprang into action. He ran. He ran through the groups of children again, an apology barely leaving his lips as he stormed through the crowd. Arno knew what he needed to do. He ran to his car; thankful he'd driven himself in the growling Porsche that rarely got driven during the week.

He jumped in, and the engine roared to life.

He had about eight minutes to get to the next train station. If it didn't stop, he would drive straight to Paris. She was not getting away from him. Hiding in plain goddamn sight, he thought savagely as he made calls and threw his name about to get what he wanted, breaking the speed limit and letting the car fly along the familiar winding lanes.

Arno came to a screeching halt in front of the station that was little more than a crossing with a wooden shed.

The train was over the ridge. Still on his phone, he barked out orders, knowing those orders were raining down on the train driver's head as the train came his way.

There were at least seventy carriages and most whizzed past him as he impatiently twirled his car keys this way and that, ready to jump into his car again if it didn't stop.

Stop. Stop, Arno chanted silently, making deals with the universe and smiling when the train finally slowed and then stopped with just two carriages left.

The doors automatically opened. Arno stepped in and walked towards the last carriage as the train continued on its way.

***

Chilli hadn't used this train service before, but she was almost sure it was a non-stop service. She looked at the electronic ticket on her phone to confirm that it was, because there was no way she wanted to stop at every little village that skirted the Pyrenees and plains before getting to Paris. She would ask the conductor when he came along, she thought, slipping her coat off her shoulders to settle in and chat behind the scenes with one of her favourite followers.

Chilli hadn't met this particular follower, who went by the handle *'Doing it Right',* but they'd been online friends for years and the one follower she would throw caution to the wind and meet in real life.

The train was dated and rickety, with dark wooden panels dulled with too many layers of wax. Pea-green leather seats sagged with overuse. The train could be the perfect backdrop for a murder mystery party, she mused, making a mental note to mention that on one of her social media platforms.

Unfortunately, she was no longer alone. A young couple had joined her, but after polite greetings, they became engrossed in their iPad and shared headphones to watch a film.

Chilli was dozing when the carriage door swept open, and she gasped in disbelief.

"Arno," his name was but a whisper on her lips.

"*Oui*," he bit out, "Arno. So, you remember my name?" he said in a deceptively soft voice.

She knew him well enough to know he was angry because it was rolling off him and filling up the carriage like hot steam. He stood looking at her, breathing hard as though he'd been running. His hair was longer, hanging in waves to his shoulders, but what really caught her attention were the slashes of deep red scorching his high cheekbones. No, he wasn't angry. He was livid.

"How are you Chillitara?" his green gaze swept over her, and Chilli was thankful her coat was still bundled on her lap.

"I'm well," she answered politely. "And you?"

"How do you think?"

He had no reason to look at her like that or ask her anything, she thought, gathering what little courage she had. She did not like confrontations. Especially confrontations with a man with green eyes spitting bloody murder at her. She could tell he was barely holding on. His back was rigid, his jaw hard when he gritted his teeth. The only thing left was for him to start foaming at the mouth, but she knew, without a doubt, that he would never hurt her.

"I'm–" she began tentatively.

He seemed to have enough of the chit-chat and stepped inside the carriage with a restless shrug, only to lean against the door with his arms folded and his ankles crossed. It would have been the perfect photograph, dressed as he was in a long dark coat, open and pushed back to reveal black trousers and an off-white shirt beneath a cashmere jumper in dove grey. She was wearing grey underwear, she remembered with a chuckle.

Arno frowned, seeing no humour in the situation. She thought this was funny? He'd looked in every carriage on the train. He'd forgotten the toilets and had to go back and check those. And she was sitting looking unfazed by what she had put him through, not only today but from the moment she had fallen into his lap. On. A. Goddamn train!

And to see her sitting there beside the window, with a streak of pale spring sunlight highlighting her perfect skin, and looking so damn beautiful with her hair pulled back into a high ponytail, he'd never seen her do before, showcasing the lovely lines of her jaw and neck when he had been going out of his mind? She didn't look as though she had missed him. She looked…? He struggled to find the words, beautiful yes, but different, in a softer, almost ethereal kind of way. But she hadn't missed him. He could tell by the flash of her eyes and the mulish tilt of her chin.

"Where have you been, *Mademoiselle*?"

Chilli swallowed, resigned, turning towards him. She had to tell him. It would be foolish not to. He was here, obviously not going anywhere, and she was trapped.

"I've been living in a little village."

"In France?"

"In France."

"Where in France?"

"Certainly, nowhere near you." She scoffed.

His breath came out in a single measured huff. "Where in France Chillitara?" He gritted.

"Excuse me?" the young man across from them addressed Chilli. "Is this man bothering you?" He asked, looking at Arno, apparently picking up his tension.

The air in the carriage crackled and snapped.

Chilli looked over at Arno, who was daring her to say what she wanted to say with narrowed eyes trained intently on her face.

"No," she answered honestly, shaking her head and offering a small, reassuring smile. "No, he's not."

The man looked at them both. "It's just that he seems...?" he trailed off.

Yes, Chilli thought, she couldn't put it into words either.

She had to rescue the situation, she thought, seeing the storm brewing in Arno's eyes. He may not hurt her, but the aggressive anger aimed at the young man was another matter.

"It's okay," Chilli smiled reassuringly, "we know each other."

Without taking his eyes from her, Arno reached into his pocket and pulled out a stack of notes and his business card before turning to offer the young couple a tight smile. "My name is Arno Tournier," he introduced, handing the man his card, "I hear the restaurant is excellent. A meal is on me," he offered, holding out the wad of Euros. "On us." He added, flicking Chillitara a glance.

The young man looked at the cash, unsure. However, his girlfriend flipped the cover over the iPad, elbowed her boyfriend in the ribs, took the money, grabbed their bags, and stood.

"*Merci Monsieur*," she thanked graciously to Arno, before holding out her hand to her boyfriend. "Come."

If Chilli hadn't been so wary of being left alone with Arno, she would have laughed.

Arno threw himself into the vacant seat and pinned Chilli with a look she couldn't decipher.

"Let's start again," he said eventually, then thought better of it. Instead, he stood to lean over her, placing one hand on the panel behind her head. Using three fingers, he tipped up her chin and kissed her.

The kiss was like going to heaven, and Chilli willingly sank into it. Arno's lips moved over hers, sipping and sampling, as though kissing her for the first time, before groaning deep in his throat and moving his hand to her ponytail, pulling her head right back. He moved to brand the delicate skin of her throat with kisses and gentle nips with startling urgency.

Chilli gasped, and he took advantage, entering her mouth to take over her mind. Chilli let him, dancing her tongue around his, feeling the delicious tingles he could always evoke, blaze and burn throughout her body. It had been so long since she'd felt like this, so allowed herself the luxury of savouring him. Remembering him. She'd missed him, had craved his touch when the weeks turned into months, and pregnancy hormones had raged through her body, making the nights long, hot and restless. It was only then that she allowed herself to think about him, pressing her fingers between her thighs to relieve some of the pressure that was continuously building.

They had things to discuss and my God, she had many things to say that would ensure he'd probably never speak to her again, much less kiss her, but she selfishly needed this. He was already mad at her, the kiss punishing with his intent to remind her what she had put him through.

When her hands crept over his broad shoulders and around his neck to pull him even closer, Arno stepped back, and again flung himself into the seat opposite. He was breathing hard, his chest rising and falling as he struggled to regain control. One kiss and he wanted to lay her on the bench and lose himself in her softness. She would let him too, he knew, seeing her dark eyes at half-mast and watching when her tongue touched the spot on her bottom lip where he'd sucked too hard. He wanted to go over and soothe it himself. But not yet.

"You kiss like you haven't been kissed in a long time *Mam'selle*," he said eventually, filling the silence.

She laughed, a soft sound that skirted all around him, making his already hard body twitch when she lifted her chin with amusement.

"I haven't been kissed in a very long time, *Monsieur*," she answered truthfully. "Since you, in fact," she offered. "Is that what you want to hear?"

"*Oui*," he smirked, but it didn't last. His eyes dimmed. "Why did you leave me?"

"Where do you live?" she countered. "The tiny tumbling down cottage that had fresh flowers on the table and held sweet memories for me, or the humongous château over the hill with the military-styled trees?" she asked. "And I want the truth, Arno. All of it."

"The cottage is mine," he began with a shrug. "The château is also mine."

"Thank you for that at least," Chilli looked down to smooth her coat on her lap, not wanting him to see how much he had hurt her. She had not been good enough.

The silence stretched, the rhythmic swish and swoosh of the train the only sound.

Arno sighed. "I heard you."

Chilli looked up to meet his gaze, startled to see an accusation she didn't know about being fired at her. "What?"

"I heard what you said on the Eurostar that day," he began slowly, "and decided to teach you a lesson." His gaze was intent and unrepentant. "Only I didn't think you would mean as much to me as you did, as you *do* so quickly. You wanted to catch yourself a rich man," he revealed. His dark brows dipped when he continued. "I am rich, and I would not be caught."

Chilli couldn't believe what she was hearing. The arrogance of the man.

All this, on a single crazy conversation he'd overheard between her and her friends? A discussion that meant nothing?

Her opinion of him hit the dirt.

"You eavesdropped on a private conversation," Chilli said tightly, remembering Vinny and Candace and yes, herself, declaring they wanted to catch themselves a rich man. It was an inside joke of theirs. "And you lied to me."

Arno shrugged as though it was nothing.

Chilli felt the telltale sting of tears at the back of her eyes, and she blinked, valiantly trying to stem them off. She would not cry in front of him. The deceitful bastard.

He'd lied to her. Everything they'd had, everything he'd done, every word and action had been based on a lie and a flimsy one at that. He was not going to get away with it, she thought savagely, taking a deep breath. She would deal with him after the baby was born safely. No stress. She would not stress her baby. A baby conceived in a web of lies, by a father who thought her to be nothing more than a plaything to while away the time. *Not going to be caught*, she repeated silently, shaking her head. Chilli wiped away the tears she could feel hovering with fingers that trembled slightly. She took another deep breath and closed her eyes. Calm down, she chanted. Calm down. No stress. She would get them through this as calmly as possible, she promised her baby silently. Arno Tournier had no role here; he'd forfeited that right.

Arno watched the fleeting expressions that crossed her face. Anger, regret and then something startling, a blankness he had never seen before. Her hands went beneath the coat bundled on her lap, seemingly to hug herself. For a moment, he allowed himself to feel a touch of remorse for lying to her, but it had all been *her* fault. She'd set herself up for this, he reasoned.

Opening her eyes, Chilli found Arno's gaze narrowed with superiority, waiting for her to explain herself.

She couldn't help but laugh. She owed him nothing.

"I'm pregnant," Chilli declared, delighting in his shock before his eyes glazed over and he dipped his head.

CHAPTER TWELVE

For several long seconds, Chilli watched and waited. She had knocked him sideways, and for the first time ever, he was at a loss for words.

Arno wanted to kill her. How dare she sleep with another man after him!

He raised his head to pin her with a scathing look.

"Congratulations," He drawled, curling his hands into tight fists to stop himself from smashing something, anything. He couldn't get the thought of her sleeping with another man out of his head.

She smiled with false brightness. "Thank you."

"Is he rich?"

Chilli gasped at his callousness. "You bastard," she flung at him before leaning forward. "I'm thirty-two weeks, to be exact." She announced with delight, watching the colour leach from his face. "Can you count backwards?" she taunted. "Would you like me to help you?" she didn't care if she sounded cold and unfeeling. "I conceived the first time you were busy trying *'not to be caught!'* She concluded with a tight smile.

Thirty-two weeks? Arno repeated in his head. He thought back, remembering the night and every which way they'd had sex. He'd been hungry for her. The sex mind-blowing in its intensity and yes, he remembered the condom breaking during a particularly rough session when she was on her knees and him pounding like a madman into her from behind, aiming for her throat. He remembered going to the bathroom, seeing the tear in the condom, and then seeing her sprawled on the bed, lying face down with the alluring curve of her naked bottom, teasing him, inviting him. She'd asked if everything was ok, before making a contented mewing sound, turning over and lazily stretching her whole body. His penis had twitched, and he'd replied yes before throwing the damaged condom in the bin, forgotten, and reaching for a new one.

"And you're telling me this now?" he asked.

"I didn't know I was pregnant," Chilli admitted, tipping her chin in defiance.

His burst of laughter filled the carriage, startling them both, and he snapped his mouth shut. They'd been together countless times since that night. He'd kissed, sucked and stroked every inch of her luscious body. He would have known she was pregnant, wouldn't he? Wouldn't *she*? Missed periods and all that other stuff he remembered his neighbour's wife complaining about in the first weeks of her pregnancy.

Chilli was lying. She had to have known. The timeline was off. He looked at her stomach, now that she had helpfully moved her coat to one side and was resting her hands on top of her large bump. She was definitely pregnant, and something dark stirred within him. But by whom?

He felt a flaming hotness unleash inside him. Memories of Chillitara fawning all over another man only hours after sleeping with him. There had been those empty weeks before he had tracked her down. She could have had sex with somebody else, he thought darkly, remembering another time when, in his twenties, he'd been made a fool of. Chillitara was sensual and uninhibited and highly sexed. She'd easily kept up with his demands. Besides, she had slept with him after only a few hours of meeting him. Was he the best catch of all? Yes, he was. He was a Tournier.

"Seriously, Arno," Chilli brought his gaze back to her face. "I didn't know." She smoothed her hands over her stomach and watched as his gaze fastened there. "It's a boy." She added, just to punish him.

"A boy." Arno repeated in wonder.

Chilli was going to go all the way with this because she needed to walk away and to walk away, she had to put it all out there for him to do with what he will. He was to blame for not being there for the baby scans. All the other firsts. He had lied and taken her for a fool. He had played games with her heart, pretending to care when he had been leading a double rich-man-poor-man life and lying. It was all so sadly, laughable. So *unnecessary* and she would never forgive him.

"I'll be staying in Paris for a few days," she went on. "And then my grandmother and I will be going back to England, where I will have my little boy."

Arno finally heard what she was saying and snapped out of his daze. It was all coming at him at once. He wanted to fall to his knees and bury his head on her stomach. He had a son. He wanted to kiss her until his name fell from those delectable lips of hers. She was carrying his child. The mother of his child.

Yet he wanted to shout, pummel a boxing bag, to let out his frustrations. He wanted to punish her for leaving him. He wanted to tie her up, lock her in the cellar at the château, because he couldn't lose her again, and yet, there she sat, swollen with his child, daring to dis-clued him from his son's life. She must be damn mad. But he let her talk. She didn't know she had lost all control of her life the moment a Tournier seed began to grow in her beautiful body.

"I came to surprise you that Saturday night," she revealed. "It was Horatio–"

"Horatio?" Arno latched on to the male name with a deep frown.

"Yes Horatio," Chilli clarified, smiling softly as she thought of her friend. "Who drove me to the proper Tournier estate, imagine that?" she flicked him a cutting look. "I will always be indebted to Horatio. He was my knight in shining armour, and I love him for it.

"I saw you with that woman plastered all over you. *Kissing* her. You didn't look like the man I had *once* lo-liked," she stumbled. "Wholeheartedly." She revealed grateful her eyes remained dry and her voice even, even with her great reveal. They had never talked about love, and she was happy to declare she was over him. "Horatio got me out of there and helped when I passed out on the side of the street. I'd almost lost my baby!" she wailed, remembering the pain of that time, the uncertainty, but she went on. "And it was Horatio who has looked after my son and me ever since!"

Arno paled again and reached over. He hadn't heard much after she had said she'd almost lost his son.

"Please don't touch me," she requested, tucking her hands under her thighs. "I'd almost lost my son," she repeated, her voice quivering with emotion. "On the same day, I stumbled across his father's lies. I will never trust you again," she declared passionately, holding his gaze. "You are nothing to me." Chilli finished, proud of herself.

"That kiss was telling me differently, *mon amour*," Arno said quietly.

She pursed her lips at his audacity for daring to mention that kiss. "That was nothing."

"You will not take my baby from me," he growled, noting her seriousness and remembering how thoroughly she had hidden from him. "You will not be going anywhere without me."

"You don't have much choice in the matter," she shot back. "You still haven't told me who you really are. You still haven't apologised, and quite frankly, I don't really care." She said, stifling a yawn behind her hand. "I'm tired of talking. No stress, Dr Osier said. I will not put myself at risk because," Chilli looked him dead in the eye. "You no longer matter."

***

Smothering another yawn, Chilli looked over at Arno after a moment, trying to read the dark green gaze he had trained on her. He was making no attempt to hide his curiosity.

"It's rude to stare," she said, wishing she hadn't unwound her scarf or removed her coat.

His eyes drifted lazily up to hers. "You are carrying my baby," he whispered. "I'm in awe."

"In a good or bad way?" Chilli asked. "You didn't want this," she went on before he could answer. "I was just the girl you were having fun with."

His dark brows snapped down, but instead of the tongue lashing she thought she was going to get, he smiled instead, and his whole body relaxed against his seat. "You want to fight *mon amour*?" he shook his head and pursed his lips. "Tut-tut Chillitara, but you do not know what I want. Now all I can see is this beautiful woman carrying my son."

"That's all I am to you, though, isn't it?" As the words slipped from her lips, she wanted to shove them back in.

"Look at me *mon amour*," Arno invited, opening his arms out wide. "I'm hooked. Caught. I saw the fishing line and jumped on it myself *oui*? I was hooked from the moment you deliberately fell onto my lap."

"No, you weren't," she argued, then immediately clarified. "And I tripped."

Arno canted his head to the side to smirk over at her as though he had a secret and Chilli braced herself for what was coming next.

"I have been searching for you," he told her gently. "I hired a private investigator, scouted all of England and Paris, spending thousands trying to track you down," he revealed. He was still sprawling, but there was a tenseness about him now. "On the internet?" he shrugged. "That was easy, but then physically? No, I couldn't find you. But to know you were on my soil, in my beloved France, warms my heart. Subconsciously you wanted to be close to me, *mon amour*, where you belong."

Not being able to help herself, Chilli laughed outright. There he was, sprawled across from her, lying his head off. "Well, that's a load of codswallop."

"Codswallop?" he repeated, sitting forward to hang his hands loosely between his hard thighs. "I don't think I know the term."

"It means you're talking rubbish," Chilli explained, pursing her lips. "I was in France because my blood pressure was super high, and I was not allowed to travel home." She informed him. "And why were you even looking for me, anyway?" she thought to ask. "Last I saw, you've got somebody to warm your bed," she flicked one hand at him. "It doesn't matter now anyway, Arno," she sent him a tight smile. "Horatio suggested I come and stay in his village, get some rest and enjoy the clean air, so I did."

Arno's jaw locked. He did not like that his woman, his pregnant woman, found comfort and protection from another man.

"Who is this Horatio? What is he to you?"

"Really, that isn't any of your business."

His smile did not reach his eyes. "Continue to think like that, *mon amour*," Arno threatened smoothly.

Chilli spread her coat over her belly and up under her chin.

"You are cold?" Arno asked, watching her keenly.

"No, I'm tired."

Arno looked around the carriage as though seeing it for the first time.

"Wait here," he ordered, and then left.

As if I'll be going anywhere, Chilli mocked, closing her eyes, realising he hadn't answered or even acknowledged what she'd said about having someone to warm his bed.

Chilli only opened her eyes when the young couple entered the carriage, buzzing about the seafood platter they'd enjoyed and wishing to thank *Monsieur* Tournier.

Chilli sighed, another two had joined his fan club she mused without malice.

Arno returned a few minutes later, received his thanks from the young couple graciously and then held his hand out to Chilli.

"Come," he instructed.

"Where?" Chilli ignored his hand to snuggle deeper into her coat.

He turned to the other couple. "Sorry to be leaving you, but I have found my wife a bed to rest. She is heavily pregnant."

Chilli gasped at his outrageous words, especially when he had the audacity to wink and grin happily down at her, but his green eyes flashed brightly with strident warning. Do not embarrass him, she read.

With a tight smile, because she didn't have the energy to argue, Chilli gathered her things, which Arno promptly took from her and placed her coat over her shoulders.

Her large belly brushed against him, and he looked down in wonder. She knew what he wanted to do. But this was her body.

"No," she said, walking ahead of him and missing the flash of hurt in his eyes.

Arno escorted her to another carriage, double the size of the previous one. A made-up bed with crisp white sheets already turned down was to one side. Oh, how the other half lives, Chilli thought, spying a pot of tea.

"Please rest, *mon amour*."

"I'm not sleeping with you, Arno," she said, spinning on her heel to warn him off.

He stepped closer, the front of their bodies almost touching, and reached up to cup the side of her face in one big hand.

"Not today," he advised quietly. "But for the rest of your life? Yes, you are." Using his thumb, he stroked her cheek. "You will never get the chance to go off to some *village* where I can't find you," he began. "You will never get so distressed that you put yourself at risk and you will never be without me."

He made it sound all so reasonable, as though everything was hunky-dory and her fault.

"I did not put my son at risk," she clarified, shifting her head away and stepping backwards. "I didn't know I was pregnant," she defended. "And it was you who made me distressed."

Arno followed her steps and placed his hands on her upper arms, to capture and kiss her swiftly on the lips. Before she could object, he turned her around to ease the coat off her shoulders. He deposited it on a chair and guided her down onto the bed.

She could barely keep her eyes open, and she let him pull the zips down on her low-heeled boots.

"Socks on or off?" he asked reasonably.

Socks, Chilli mused, reliving the morning after that infamous night and wearing his socks. He'd tracked her down to get them back, she remembered fondly, fighting her tears. Stupid hormones, she scolded herself.

"On, please," she answered sleepily, already curling up as soon as he'd finished, but her eyes snapped open, feeling him touching her belly. She went to pull back.

"Please." He said gruffly.

Chilli let him touch her, leaning back a little to make it easier for him. She was wearing a V-necked jumper dress in soft oatmeal and black pregnancy leggings. She was dressed for comfort.

Chilli watched when he hunkered down in front of her, placing his large hands on either side of her stomach to starfish his fingers.

"I'm huge," she said, filling the silence as her eyes burned with tears.

"It's beautiful. My son is in there." It wasn't a statement of fact, just words echoed in wonderment.

He pressed his head closer.

"He's sleeping," Chilli told him softly as tears fell. It was a special moment.

Arno looked up at her, saw the tears, and reached over to wipe them away before placing his hands on her stomach again. Chilli's stomach rolled with movement. "You've woken him up," she sniffed and giggled, seeing Arno's look of horror and then fascination as her belly swayed and rolled under his fingers. "Sometimes at night, he pretends he's playing football or something." She explained shyly.

Arno flashed her a look of pure pain, and she slammed her mouth shut.

He moved away to stare out of the window, seeing but not seeing the passing scenery.

"I will never forgive you for making me miss my son growing without my protection."

Chilli snorted. "That's okay, Arno," she turned to lie down, curling her legs on the soft mattress and pulling the blankets up to her neck. "I never asked you to."

CHAPTER THIRTEEN

With his hand on the small of her back, Arno and Chilli exited Gare d' Austerlitz station mid-afternoon. They'd been travelling for roughly six hours.

"Where to?" Arno asked, moving to place his body between her and the hustle and bustle of the crowds surging all around. A harried-looking tourist almost pushed her over with his backpack and Chillitara would have fallen if Arno hadn't been holding her arm.

Arno clenched his jaw in growing anger, knowing if he had been in her life, if he had known about the baby, he would not have let her travel for hours on end by train, much less subject herself to this cattle market.

"Don't even think about it," he said, his mouth tightening, seeing her objection about to tip from her pretty lips. "I go where you go."

Not long after moving her to the private carriage, Chilli had fallen asleep for a solid five hours, so leaving her to rest, Arno hadn't had the chance to talk about her plans. Plans that, come hell or high water, now included him.

But for today, seeing the smudges of fatigue under her eyes, he was okay to let her lead. However, tomorrow? Tomorrow he would take charge. Nothing beats life experience with situations like this.

By the stubborn tilt of his chin and fighting fire in his eyes, Chilli knew he was here to stay.

"We get a taxi to my grandmother's apartment." She conceded with a shrug.

Arno immediately guided them to the taxi rank, entered the first car available, and listened with raised brows when she gave a very upscale address to the driver.

Twenty minutes later, they reached the area of Saint Germain, and after paying for the taxi, Arno followed her into an old but charming building, where she called the elevator.

Arno looked at her as they waited, remembering the one other time they'd waited for the elevator like this and what had happened with all that exciting sexual tension. His baby had happened. A streak of satisfaction blazed through him, but he damped it down, tracking his eyes over Chillitara instead.

She looked exhausted. He could see it in the way she held her body, her hands going to the curve of her back, now deeper, supporting the weight of his baby. The journey had been too much for her. Almost eight months pregnant and travelling on public transport! One side of his mouth turned down at the grim thought. She should have been taking better care of herself.

They entered the large apartment. In one sweeping glance, Arno took in the natural light pouring from tall French windows, which were dressed in long white billowing lace that teasingly played peek-a-boo with the view. Dark polished floors, rugs and lots of tables with round frilly things protecting the surface from every size, shape and colourful pottery ever created. The room was bright, cheerful, and chaotic.

"Your grandmother lives here?" he asked, following Chilli, who was unwrapping her scarf and walking to what he now discovered was a large slightly dated kitchen.

"Hmm-mmm," Chilli turned on the kettle before taking off her coat to throw onto the back of a chair. "She's not here at the moment." She opened a cupboard and pulled down two mugs. "Coffee? Tea?" she offered.

Arno nodded. "I will make it." He unbuttoned his coat and placed it on top of hers. A statement in itself. He was here to stay. "Please sit down," Arno waited until Chilli sat awkwardly on one of the tall stools arranged around the large island topped in what looked like marble. "Your grandmother, she will come back soon?"

"Tomorrow afternoon," Chilli admitted.

He frowned over at her and didn't bother to keep the sensor from his voice. "You would have been alone?"

"It's not a problem, Arno."

Arno turned back to the kettle that had now clicked off, to cool his temper, which had been slowly simmering. He took a deep breath before asking, "Tea?"

"Hmm-mmm," with her head bent, Chilli rubbed hard tight circles on her temples trying to chase away a headache which had been threatening all day. "Milk and one sugar, please."

Arno familiarised himself with the layout, opening and closing cupboards, finding what he needed to make their beverages.

Chilli watched tiredly on.

"Come," he helped her off the stool and led her into the living room, waited until she had settled into the floral sofa, before handing her the tea.

He was so polite, Chilli mused. Then again, there was never an issue with his manners. It was his lying that was the problem. "Thank you."

They were quiet for a moment, and Chilli waited. She knew what was coming, but would not invite the start of what could potentially be a volatile conversation. She didn't have the energy. But he surprised her, remaining quiet, hugging his mug with both hands and sipping his coffee deep in thought. His hair had fallen forward, framing the sides of his face.

She remembered the video chat of him out amongst the grapevines all those months ago, beads of sweat over his brow and the bandanna holding back his hair. He'd looked young and carefree then. Now, grooves of tension or anger–she didn't know which–bracketed his mouth. His eyes were dark, forest green and distracted. She watched the pleats between his brows deepen as he busily planned and plotted how he was going to ingratiate himself back into her life. An unplanned pregnancy with a woman he'd only been playing with? She had messed up his life *and* found him out.

For a time she had wondered what he had planned that

infamous weekend that never was. He'd probably aimed on hiding her away at the quaint little farmer's cottage and then nipping out in the evening to play posh host and master at the château over the hill.

Those weeks in Horatio's village, she had learned to put Arno in a box. It had been hard, but really, Arno's motives didn't matter.

To distract herself, Chilli had recorded several videos a day, changing her hair and makeup, knowing the days she felt tired and cumbersome, she could post a tutorial. She felt awful for cheating, but her pregnancy was all that mattered.

The silence stretched and stretched. Chilli finished her tea with several unladylike gulps, got up to pull the curtains back, and opened a set of doors to step outside to the wrap-around balcony.

The five-storied building had survived World War II, temperamental artists and passionate authors. It now looked haughtily down at the many cafes on the tourist-filled streets.

The view was as perfect as it always was, taking her breath away. The river Seine danced along the riverbank, delighting the many tourists bundled in their coats, with its open secrets of love and war. A luxury cruise liner glided past, and she waved like she always did at the people on the terrace. They waved back, and she knew they were probably wondering who she was. Not Beyoncé this time folks, she chuckled to herself.

Chilli felt Arno come beside her to lean against the wrought iron rail.

"Before you say anything," he began with care, purposely moderating his voice. "I want you to know I will be here for you and the baby and–"

"Thank you."

"No, please, let me finish," he insisted at her interruption. "I will be here for you, for whatever you need. Financially and emotionally."

"Thank you, Arno." Chilli interrupted again. Anything to annoy him and stem off this conversation he'd been plotting over his coffee.

Arno looked at her, and she turned to face him after a slight pause.

"This was not part of your life's plan," Chilli told him lightly. "But I thank you for the offer."

"I take my responsibilities seriously Chillitara," he stressed, his eyes narrowing seeing the light of amusement dancing in her eyes, knowing she was indulging him, and he didn't like it. This was no casual offer. He was Arno Tournier. The baby she carried was a Tournier. "We will officially become parents in every sense of the word." He declared, making himself clear.

Chilli didn't like the sound of his words and where they led. "I spend a lot of time in France, and of course, you can visit the baby any time you want in England, Arno. I won't stop you."

"Are you deliberately misunderstanding what I am saying?" he challenged instead, crossing his arms over his chest.

"Yes," Chilli admitted without prejudice. He was the one with a long record of game playing and lies. "But I am the one carrying this baby, and I don't want to be having this conversation. No stress, the doctor warned, and I will not be coerced.

"So forget about us being parents *in every sense of the word,*" she parried. "Whatever that means, because right now I don't want to know. Another few weeks and we will discuss where we'll go from here, but I'll tell you this," she smoothed her hands over the top of her bump, watching as he followed her movements, "you are under no obligation towards my baby or me. I don't expect anything from you, and I don't need anything from you. I can manage on my own."

"Like you are managing now?" he banked the anger her words ignited, but only because she was tired and vulnerable, and she was right, she should not be stressed. While she'd slept on the train, he read everything he could on pregnancy at thirty-two weeks and what to expect in the coming weeks. They needed to have this conversation, just not yet. "Go to bed, *Mam'selle*," he ordered. "You are dead on your feet."

Chilli was dead on her feet and moved to the small wrought-iron chair to sit down and awkwardly toe off her boots. Arno immediately knelt on one knee to help her, pulling off her boots and her socks.

At his gasp, Chilli looked down, seeing what he was seeing. "My feet have been swelling," she admitted, wriggling her swollen toes and rotating her puffy ankles. "it's perfectly normal and looks worse than it is."

With a grimness she didn't want to think about, Arno helped her from the chair, bent and then scooped her up into his arms.

"Which way to your bedroom?" he asked, and followed her directions, walking down the long corridor, his shoes a soft tap on the expensive tiles.

"I need to go to the bathroom first," Chilli said when he placed her on the edge of her four-poster bed. "The baby is pressing on my bladder again." She explained, with a tinkle of laughter, rubbing the small of her back and knowing her walk was more like a waddle when she moved towards the en-suite.

When she returned, she tiredly opened a drawer, and dragged out the first T-shirt she touched, before disappearing into the bathroom again.

When she re-entered the room, Arno had pulled the sheets back and was standing stiffly beside the bed, one arm coiled around the bottom bedpost, watching her. Maybe the way he was holding the ornate mahogany post was his way of keeping the words he wanted to say at bay. She knew Arno was dying to say something. Object about the conversation of 'parents' but was keeping it safely in, which was no mean feat. Arno liked to express himself and be heard right away, whether it be softly spoken poetic lies when making love to her, or now when he wanted to impose his outdated views. But tough. He could keep his opinions to himself until after the baby was born and if she had anything to do with it, way after.

"I'll rest for an hour," she said, making herself comfortable, throwing several frilly pillows to the floor, adding one between her legs, before settling in. She could barely keep her eyes open. "Just pull the front door shut behind you when you leave." She finished with a yawn, closing her eyes.

***

It was early evening, and Chillitara was still sleeping.

Arno disconnected the call to Agnes, his housekeeper, at the château and looked out at the tourists and locals walking along the street below.

For the first half an hour, he'd prowled around the apartment trying to find something of Chilli in the opulent space. But there was nothing. No photographs. No trinkets.

One bedroom had a vase of silk flowers and a half-empty bottle of lavender-scented water on a long, beautifully carved dresser.

Otherwise, there was nothing personal in the exclusive four-bedroomed apartment in an old, but respectable area of Paris.

Sitting idly waiting for Chillitara to wake up, Arno couldn't help but think about what he knew.

She was a social networking influencer who ran a lucrative business online. Yet, personally, what did he know? She was beautiful. Her body was sensational, and she was articulate and expressive. But what was her favourite colour? What did she study at university? Arno knew none of those things. He'd been hung up on her body and was obsessive about being deep inside her like a hormonal teenager. He liked her, liked her company and the way she laughed at herself, but did he know her? He'd been planning on taking their relationship to the next level, that is, telling her who he was because she was around more than any other woman in years. She meant something to him, and it was unfortunate she'd seen what she had seen and derailed his careful plans. He'd wanted a key to her flat in England. But none of that mattered anymore. She was carrying his baby. A Tournier.

They were going to become a family.

***

"You're still here, I see."

Arno jumped out of the doze he must have unconsciously slipped into at the sound of her voice and sat straighter in the chair he'd been lounging in.

"*Oui Mam'selle*, no place I'd rather be," he answered, noting the roll of her eyes, but didn't rise to the bait her tenacity provoked. He smiled instead. She looked so cute, so round and soft, with sleep creases on one side of her face, trying to look fierce but failing. "Sleep well?" he asked.

"Baby boy has decided he prefers to play football when I lie down," she said instead, giving up on trying to tie the belt of her silk kimono where her waist used to be. She sat opposite him watchfully. He looked slightly amused, like he didn't have a care in the world.

"Arno–" Chilli began carefully.

"What were you planning on doing for food? There isn't anything here," he interrupted.

"Go downstairs or order something in," she answered automatically. "Arno–"

"Order in." he picked up his phone and leaned forward to hand it to her.

"Arno–" Chilli tried again, a bit more forcefully.

"What?" Why was she always so serious? He asked her.

"Because," she seethed. "I don't know what you want. Why are you still here? I told you I expect nothing from you. You're free." She declared.

He smiled tightly. "Thank you, *Mam'selle*. Now order dinner. You need to eat. If not for you, then for the baby."

"Fine," she snatched his phone, looked through it and shook her head before reaching for her own mobile, selecting the right app to place their order in seconds. "We're having chicken." She told him, throwing her phone onto the low side table beside her. "And your phone is archaic."

He shrugged ruefully. "It makes calls."

"Why talk to people when you can pick your own meal, and

have it delivered faster than actually placing the call?"

"Why indeed," Arno drawled, not particularly interested. "As you are so good at it, how about ordering me some clothes and toiletries?"

"You aren't staying here," she told him, tipping up her chin, and resting her folded arms on top of her bump.

"I'm supposed to be in Spain completing a deal that would put my wine in every hotel along the Costas. My car is parked on the side of train tracks with the doors open. I don't know where my travel bag is, and you tell me I'm not staying here?" Arno flashed his arms in the air. He'd tried to be reasonable, and give her time to talk to him, but she was being typically stubborn.

"I've been searching for you for months, and you suddenly turn up, in my country, heavily pregnant with my son, and to this second you have not had the decency to offer me a credible explanation?" Arno moved restlessly in his chair before standing to peer down at her. "What you saw didn't warrant such a dramatic reaction," he accused, breathing heavily and switching to French in his agitation. "You disappeared. We were lovers. Did I not deserve to know why you left me? The respect?" he listed tersely. "You should have contacted me. I had that right. So if you think I am leaving you here, think again," he challenged, glaring down at her. "Where you go, I will go. I will not be forced out of your life!" he blasted. "Have I made myself clear?"

With his words hanging over her head, fascinated, Chilli watched him pace about the room as he spoke, stopping every so often, his chest expanding as he tried to rein in his temper. She had only ever seen him like this once before, and that was via video link. Now, being in the same room with him, she felt the full force of his passion. His emotions sandblasted every corner and crevice of the room. He'd never once told her he loved her, but right at this very moment, she and the baby were all that mattered to him.

It was there in his fierce gaze and pale face. All of his emotions lay bare, and Chilli wanted to kiss him and bawl her eyes out at the same time. She wanted to take that tortured look out of his dark green gaze and have him smile again. She shuffled to the edge of the sofa and hauled herself up to stand.

"Arno–" Chilli began, holding her hand out to him. She wanted to comfort him and keep him close, but the intercom rang. "Dinner," she said instead, turning towards the door.

Arno raked his fingers through his hair at the interruption. They'd been on the cusp of something, something big. She had smiled, showing the first glimmer of warmth since this morning. Was it only this morning that he had been standing on that platform?

"I will get it," he said, stopping her in her tracks and knowing he may not get another chance to see her smile at him again.

CHAPTER FOURTEEN

It was still very early, and Chilli could see an entire evening stretching gloomily ahead of her.

They'd had a civilised dinner, eating mushroom-stuffed chicken breasts, topped with cheese, with heaps of steamed vegetables on the side.

Arno had been attentive throughout the meal, asking questions about her life, her degree, where she had studied and, curiously, what her favourite colour was.

When they'd finished eating, Arno had washed up and, wanting to escape his hovering, Chilli was now lounging contently in the bath, listening to her playlist via headphones.

The water was perfectly tempered, with only a slight wisp of steam drifting off the scented surface.

There was a tap on the door and relaxation went straight out the window when he entered with his shoulders stiff, his face stoic and reminding her of the first time they'd met on the train.

"Arno," Chilli gasped quickly, slipping down into the water to cover her breasts, but the bubbles still swirled around the smooth swell of her belly like an abandoned island.

"I thought you might need this," Arno offered her the glass of water he'd brought and nodded at her small smile of thanks, before moving to sit on the edge of the bath. After fifteen minutes in the tub, Chilli was probably as relaxed as he was going to get her.

The water now reached her neck because she'd slid even deeper into the bath, and Chilli reluctantly took off her headphones, handed them to him and waited. She was trapped. She didn't think he would have followed her in here, she thought, taking a delaying sip of the water and placing the glass in the convenient nook made for that purpose beside her and waited.

He was in here to push his wishes forward, she knew, but it was unusual to see Arno like this, so quiet and watchful. His long silences were making her nervous. But she waited, watching his finger idly draw a large figure eight in the bathwater.

"I want to go back to how we were," he said quietly, eventually, looking at the pattern he was making in the bubbles.

Chilli looked up at him. She had not been expecting that. Demands to be let into her life, maybe. To go back to how they were? Blinking hell, the question here, she silently wondered, was where had they been in the first place? She asked him.

"You mean back to me being blissfully unaware you were leading a double life?" He'd ambushed and trapped her in the bathroom, wanting to talk, when she had explicitly told him she didn't want to discuss it, *them*, so she would not make this easy for him.

His finger stopped moving, and he looked up to capture and hold her gaze. This was the first time in months Chilli had felt that little thrill whenever he looked at her. It was as though she was the most precious person in the universe, and it was counterproductive that he could even make her feel this way. Still.

"The weekend I asked you to come to France," he began. "Was the weekend I planned to tell you who I am."

Chilli pursed her lips, totally unimpressed. "How many months later?" she asked, then went on when Arno parted his lips to speak. "Did you even consider us a couple? What was I to you?" she questioned, feeling her throat clog with suppressed anger. "I thought of you as my boyfriend. I was faithful to you, only to realise you'd lied and cheated. I was such a fool."

Arno pushed his fingers through his hair in frustration. He didn't want her getting stressed and upset, but they needed to talk this through to move forward. He was not having this coming between them any longer, nor was he going to allow any more of her insulting delaying tactics of her leaving every room he entered.

Quietly and succinctly, he told her about his wine, the vineyard, and his grandfather.

"It was only my background I–"

"Don't even try to justify yourself," Chilli cut in, narrowing her eyes at him. "Who you are doesn't matter anymore. I saw you kissing that woman. Cheating on me."

Chilli noticed a slash of deep red quickly appear and then disappear along his cheekbones.

"She is nothing," he shrugged one shoulder. "A neighbour I've known for years."

Chilli relived the memory of the woman in his arms. The intimacy. She didn't want to ask, but she needed to know. "Have you slept with her?" She blurted.

"What you saw was nothing," he said, ignoring her question and drawing down his eyebrows into a tight crease. "You should have come inside."

Her laugh was but a scoff. "Nothing? Really?" she sneered. "All those people dressed to the nines, that woman hanging onto your arm as though you were her life-support machine and I was supposed to walk in and say 'hi, I'm his girlfriend he forgot to mention. Oh and by the way, I thought he was a grape-picking labourer?'" Chilli felt the anger and humiliation of that night all over again.

"That's precisely what you should have done," he scolded. "You should have come inside, and confronted me, but you gave up." Arno accused, levelling a gaze laden with blame at her. "You didn't fight for us."

This time, she did laugh. "You have some nerve, Arno Tournier," she began. "I don't fight for any man," she stated, tipping up her chin. "I don't need to."

Their eyes warred with each other. Neither giving in.

"Did you sleep with her that night?" The thought of him sleeping with that woman while she had been in the hospital trying to hold on to her baby had shattered her. She'd committed the ultimate sin in naivety. Chasing romance and living her life through rose-tinted glasses. Arno, a grape-picking labourer who travelled to England at the drop of a hat, rented cars and stayed in a high-end boutique hotel in the middle of Paris Fashionista Week. His clothes were dull and conservative, but of top quality. She had been naïve and stupid and very much aware history was repeating itself.

"Well, did you?" she prompted.

"No."

"Have you ever slept with her?"

Arno dipped his arm into the cooling water, searched for her hand, and laced their fingers together.

He swallowed back the words he would have said if a lover had dared question him about his past. "Yes," he finally admitted. "A long time ago," he added. "We were young." He clarified quickly, hating to see the shadow of hurt in her eyes.

"Okay." Chilli didn't know why she said it was okay. It wasn't okay. Wasn't okay at all. They'd been tangled up in each other's arms, she remembered painfully, feeling a sharp pain jab her heart. People all around, smiling at them, comfortable seeing them together. "What's her name?"

Shaking his head, Arno sighed, "Chillitara,"

"I want to know."

"Phillippa."

"Did you love her?"

"As much as a teenager could."

She pulled her hand away and smoothed it over her stomach.

"She means nothing, is nothing and I'd been drinking," Arno clarified into the lengthening silence. "You and the baby are all that matters." A tear slipped out from under her lashes, and Arno watched it with regret. "I'm sorry."

"It hurt me to see." Chilli sniffed.

"I know."

"I can't think past you and her together," she admitted, her voice almost a whisper. "The image of you kissing her." Chilli drew in an unsteady breath. "It's like it has been seared into my brain."

"Chillitara," Arno drawled, his mouth turning down on one

side. "That's not healthy."

Her eyes flashed at the tinge of pity she picked up in his voice, and sat up straighter in the bath, her nipples barely covered by the water. "Oh yeah," Chilli started. "How would you feel seeing me in the arms of another man? Drunk or otherwise," she seethed. "Kissing and enjoying myself?" She asked. There was no doubt he had been enjoying himself. He'd been sweeping his hand across the woman's–Phillippa's–naked back, just above the curve of her bottom, pulling her tighter against his body.

His lips tightened, and Arno felt something shoot through him. It was blinding hot. Jealousy? Yes, and he was ravaged by it. But she didn't need to know she held that much power over him. He was a possessive guy, his one fault, and he would not allow her to play childish games like past lovers.

"We're talking about you and me," he dismissed impatiently. "Phillippa is nothing." He shook himself and reached for a towel warming on the rail. Standing, he held it out to her. "Come, the water is cooling."

Chilli folded her arms over her chest. "I'm not getting out in front of you."

"I've seen you naked," he smirked with appreciation. "Every lovely bit of you."

"But not like this," she stated stubbornly, sinking deeper into the bath.

Looking into the water, Arno's eyes shimmered with emerald sparks, seeing her new shape where the bubbles had dissolved. "You are even more beautiful now, Chillitara," he smiled. "And you are carrying my son." He flicked the towel as though teasing a recalcitrant bull. "Come."

For several seconds Chilli looked at him, but he wasn't moving, and she reluctantly took the hand he now held out and allowed herself to be bundled in the towel and helped out of the bath.

For a moment, she closed her eyes, breathing him in. No matter what, his arms had always made her feel safe, and she cravenly wanted that feeling again. It had been so long.

Arno's hands drifted down her arms, gently patting at her damp skin with the towel, taking his time.

"Arno," Chilli began when he knelt at her feet, opening the towel to pat her legs dry. First one, gliding over her calf muscle down to her ankle, before moving to her other leg.

A sizeable, gilded mirror was on the wall in front of them, and Chilli watched him, his head bent, his dark hair falling forward, as he concentrated on drying her. His hands weren't clinical, but they weren't intimate, either.

"Shh," he whispered, patting one inner thigh. Arno nudged her legs apart, to enable him to dry her. He could see her sex. Smell her sweet musky scent, barely concealed by the fragrant potions in her bathwater. He moved higher, concentrating on one side of her body, drinking in the changes, the long dark line that ran from her breastbone all the way down to her sex. He shifted higher still, reaching her full breasts. They were darker, the discs larger. "You are so beautiful, *mon amour*."

Arno moved down her other side, taking his time and when he reached the apex of her thighs, leaned forward to kiss her sex, almost hidden by the swell of her body.

Chilli grabbed his long hair. She didn't know when his touch had changed, she just became more aware of his hands through the soft towel, the pressure of his fingertips against her skin. Her nipples were peaking, and a delicious warmth was spreading through her body. She wanted him to touch her, to take her nipples into his mouth and suck. Hard. It had been so long since she'd felt his touch.

The towel pooled at her feet and Arno kissed along one thigh and then the other. He ran his tongue over her knees, holding the backs of her legs, keeping her steady, and taking his time while tasting her skin.

Gently, he placed one leg over his shoulder and moved in to taste her properly.

The soft folds of her sex were darker, flushed, and he ran his tongue over them again and again, encouraged by her throaty gasps. He delighted in the feel of her hands in his hair, urging him on as he nipped and sucked, coaxing the little nub out to play.

He wanted to lay her on the floor, plunge into her and lose himself, but not yet, not tonight. Tonight was about her. The only image he wanted her to remember was of the two of them like this. This moment.

The mirror, almost the size of the wall, was perfectly placed. He knew she was watching him. Watching him on his knees worshipping her body because that's what he was doing. She was beautiful. A goddess. A goddess, pregnant with his baby.

She humbled him.

He pushed his tongue into her, swirling it around her inner walls, before replacing it with his fingers, first one and then two, gently finding and caressing the rough little patch inside, giving her the ultimate pleasure.

She groaned and gasped above him, her hands no longer in his hair, but holding his ears, directing his mouth where he blew and kissed her sex.

She fell apart. Her thighs trembling, her knees giving way to almost fall to the floor if he hadn't been holding her.

Slowly, Arno stood, kissing every bit of her along the way, tonguing one breast and then the other, dipping it into the shallow vee of her collarbone, before finally finding her mouth.

He kissed her deeply, reminding her of all that they were.

"Look at us, *mon amour*," he persuaded, moving behind her to stroke his tongue along the soft skin behind her ear. Her hair was up haphazardly in a loose bun, allowing him access to her lovely neck and shoulders.

In a daze, Chilli opened her eyes to look at their reflection. His hands were on her body, palming the heavy globes of her breasts, skimming over her darkened nipples, stiff with arousal, to eventually roam over her large tummy. Chilli felt the sting of tears behind her eyes as she felt so beautiful.

"Look," he whispered into her ear. "This is us," he gently kissed the curve of her shoulder, catching her gaze in their reflection. "You and me," he traced the dark line over her stomach in wonder. "And baby makes three." He caught the single tear that fell onto her cheek with his fingers. "We are a family Chillitara."

CHAPTER FIFTEEN

Chilli stuffed the pillows behind her back and wriggled about on the bed, trying to get comfortable. But it wasn't working. It hadn't been working for the past ten minutes.

"Here, let me help," Arno offered, coming into the room.

They'd reached a new understanding after the bathroom incident. They had watched a French comedy and had now moved to her bedroom. His eyes had shimmered with amusement when she'd given him a pile of bed linen for another room.

"Thanks."

Arno fluffed several pillows and then lifted her legs to place one under her knees.

"How's that?"

Chilli gave him the laptop to place on the bedside table before smiling. "Much better, thank you." She watched him settle onto his back alongside her, his hands going behind his head, from under her lashes. "I think you need to know what my plans are," she said eventually, into the comfortable silence.

Arno shifted to face her, his neat brows lifting in enquiry.

"I'm booked on the late afternoon Eurostar tomorrow."

"Travelling alone?" he asked.

"That was the plan," she answered before adding impishly. "But I guess you'll be coming along?"

He returned her smile in agreement.

Chilli told him about her doctor's appointment and her birthing plan in England. "I want a natural birth. No pain relief," she told him. "The welfare of the baby will come first," she grabbed his hand, clasping it tightly. "No matter what, Arno, promise me the baby will always come first."

Arno wondered at her strange wording, seeing a fleeting shadow of fear in her irises before lowering her eyes. He'd read about the fear many first-time mothers felt.

"I can't stand by and watch you in pain, Chillitara," he warned. "But okay, the baby comes first. No pain relief in the delivery room." He confirmed.

"That's another thing." She let go of his hand to smooth it over her tummy instead. "I'm not sure you'll want to be in the delivery room."

"Why not?"

"Well, all that blood and gore, for one thing."

Chilli watched him pale, but he reached for her hand and weaved their fingers together again. "I will be there for you. For you both," he promised, kissing her fingers. "Or maybe, perhaps, you don't want me there?"

Chilli bit the corner of her lip. "It's pretty personal, Arno," she admitted. "And not something you signed up for."

His brows dipped. "Neither did you," he challenged. "And besides, I watched a birthing video online," Arno admitted, grimacing at the memory of the forty-minute video online he'd watched on the train. He believed in being prepared and was thankful he was a man. After that video, he had a new respect for women.

Chilli looked at him in amazement. "You did?"

"It was enlightening."

She squeezed his hand, chuckling. "I'm sure it was," she agreed, her dark eyes dancing.

"Why not have the baby in France?" Arno asked, wanting to get the image of that video out of his head and talk about something else.

Chilli unlaced their fingers and turned away. "No."

Arno frowned at her statement. "You don't trust our system?" The French healthcare system was one of the best in the world. "Chillitara?" he prompted.

"I just prefer the good ole NHS, okay?" she said, pressing her lips together before turning away.

Her tone of voice and body language ended the discussion, and he wondered about it, but she was carrying his child, and for that, he was grateful. If she wanted to have their baby on the moon, he would find a way.

With his fingers under her chin, he turned her to say, "*Oui*, okay. We will have a little British son, who will speak French first, *mon amour*." He teased, watching the shadows of fear he saw in her eyes melt away when she laughed.

They laughingly joked about how French or British their son was going to be, both carefully avoiding where they were going to live. It hadn't come up. It had never come up when they were sleeping together all those months ago, either.

"Is it possible to order some clothes for me?" Arno asked. Now that he was staying was a given fact, he still needed clothes and toiletries and would prefer them to be delivered to him. He didn't know Paris well enough to run a quick errand, and besides, he would not leave her. Not even for a toothbrush.

Chilli pointed to the laptop, and he handed it to her. "Only if you let me order for you."

Arno nodded. "I am yours to do with what you will," he declared, shrugging.

She laughed outright. "You just might regret that, *Monsieur*," she teased.

They settled in. Arno was relaxed and content because Chilli was relaxed and busily shopping on his behalf. He handed over his credit card when she asked, her eyes dancing with laughter when he'd asked if it was safe to purchase things online.

He made her a mint tea later, and they chatted on, reaching a place of understanding, ease and friendship. They were about to share one of the most monumental experiences that any two people could experience, and they were both aware of it.

With her fingers pressed to her mouth, Chilli giggled at his outrageous suggestions of names, and he cried when he saw the first grainy image of his son at five months, and then the months that followed, looking at them in wonder.

Chilli told him about her blood pressure, and only now

being cleared to travel. She said she didn't have any symptoms, but she'd had more than the average amount of antenatal care because of her health issues.

Chilli threw several pillows on the floor to snuggle under the covers. She was telling him about Dr Osier, the village, Horatio and his beautiful family when she paused.

"Ow!" She touched the top of her side. "Phew, what was that?"

"What is it?" Arno asked, sitting up in concern.

Chilli rubbed her side. "It's passing," she said, more to herself. "Must be those Braxton Hicks things I've been reading about," she reasoned, settling against the pillows.

"You sure?"

"It's gone now," she confirmed. "Probably just my body getting ready for baby," she told him, gently tapping the bump. "A lot is happening in the third trimester."

Arno observed her quietly, as they talked, and when she eventually fell asleep, left her bedroom door open, before settling in the bedroom next door, content for the first time in months.

***

For a moment Chilli wasn't sure what woke her until a sharp pain moved across her stomach and she gasped, riding the wave until it disappeared.

She held her breath and smoothed her hands over her tummy before looking at the clock. It was a little after three.

Feeling better already, she closed her eyes, knowing the next seven weeks were going to be filled with moments like these. Braxton Hicks was supposed to feel like contractions and if that were a contraction, she would be fine, Chilli told herself.

She sighed, stroking her bump, feeling the baby stretch before settling. She had never thought about being a mother, well, not yet anyway. And even though she had missed the first few of months, had been stuck in France, and after all the re-assurances from her doctor, she was looking forward to motherhood.

Her team in England had been real troopers, keeping her pregnancy a secret at her request, and still able to increase her following and endorsements without her physically being in the country. When items were sent to the office, they sent them on, and she did the reviews as usual. It had all been straightforward. As an influencer, she was still part of the game and had top rankings and a steady increase of followers and subscribers on all of her platforms. She just felt removed from it, though.

Arno had left her bedroom door ajar, she noticed, and the hallway light on. He was taking this all in his stride, Chilli thought generously. He'd been right, she had overreacted. Maybe if she had been in her right mind, and not, as she now knew, hormonal and pregnant, she might have climbed those grand steps at the château. Actually, she knew she would have. Her grandmother had once told her she was like her mother in that respect. Fiery. Her temper came out at any injustice. She was not to be played with.

Chilli laughed at her wild thoughts, imagining herself marching up those steps, throwing back her shoulders and putting Arno in his place as the beautiful people looked on.

Feeling another wave of Braxton Hicks, she breathed through it. Easy peasy, she thought, moving to go to the bathroom. She could do this, and naturally, too.

In the semi-darkness, she used the toilet, and feeling the fuzziness of fur in her mouth, turned on the light to brush her teeth.

Chilli looked at herself as she brushed. It always surprised her with the changes in her face. She hadn't put on a ton of weight, but looking at the edges of her jawline, there was a softness there, her nose slightly rounder. Her hair had never looked so healthy, and her skin barely needed any help with foundation either. She'd been leaving her natural curls out, although pulling her hair away from her face, using colourful silk headscarves. A few weeks ago she had made a video on the many ways to tie a headscarf, which had received a rising number of views and an offer to collaborate with a well-known headwear designer.

Rinsing her mouth, she splashed cold water on her face, and then patted it dry. Another Braxton Hicks hit, but this time it was stronger, and she held onto the edge of the basin, trying to breathe through it. It lasted longer, stealing her breath for almost fifteen seconds she counted.

Just when Chilli turned to switch off the light to make herself a cup of tea, she felt a warm gush of wetness between her legs.

"No," she gasped in fright. "Not labour," she spoke to herself in fear, looked down, froze, then screamed. A pool of dark red blood was at her feet. "Arno!"

CHAPTER SIXTEEN

Arno woke with a start, and hearing his name surged naked out of bed and ran into Chillitara's room. She wasn't in bed, and for a split second, he stared at the colourful pillows all askew.

"Chillitara?" he called but was already moving towards the bathroom, seeing the light on. "What is it?"

"The baby," she gasped, her eyes wide with fear as she bent over, clutching her stomach when another contraction hit. "I'm bleeding."

Arno remembered little of the next few minutes. He'd called an ambulance, settled her gently on the bed, dragged on some clothes, picked her up, and waited at the entrance of the building with her in his arms.

She'd been crying, clinging to him, praying to God not to take her baby, making promises, begging and pleading, bargaining incoherently about history, Java and her father, and screaming when contractions hit.

Now, at the hospital, Arno repeated what little medical history she had told him just a few short hours ago. Thirty-two weeks. High blood pressure, but otherwise a healthy twenty-six-year-old woman. What was her date of birth? He didn't know, barely able to remember the name of her French doctor.

"*Non, Monsieur*," the nurse said, looking down at her tablet once the patient's full name was confirmed. "She is younger, and this is a high-risk pregnancy."

Arno paled. High risk? What did that mean? Younger? What did she mean? Everything was coming at him at once, and he was losing himself in the maelstrom of questions.

"Please wait here." The nurse told him when he turned to follow Chillitara, who was curled up tightly in pain, crying, and shouting his name as she was being wheeled on a gurney through a set of doors for an ultrasound.

Arno stood there, lost, in the middle of the emergency room, surrounded by organised chaos.

People sat slumped in chairs, sniffling. An old man's head was bleeding. There was a row of vending machines. A woman protectively holding her wrist high on her chest. Arno saw all of it, but computed nothing, not even the nurses behind the circular desk, busy tapping into computers, looking up charts or on the telephone. He felt removed from the entire scene.

"You are a relative, yes?"

He didn't know why the nurse was speaking in English, but it pulled him out of the numbness he was feeling and made him concentrate on her words. She was standing in front of him. "Yes, her fiancé," he lied smoothly. "Arno Tournier."

She frowned, looking down at her chart.

"Is there a problem?" he asked.

Her smile was tight, her eyes unreadable. "Please wait here," she moved away, and Arno watched her pick up the phone to make a call. When their eyes connected, she turned her back on him.

Arno ran his hands through his hair. What the hell was going on? Where was Chillitara? She'd been gone too long. He stalked to the desk.

"Where is my fiancée?" he demanded to everyone in the vicinity.

The nurse who'd been speaking to him replaced the phone, looked over his shoulder, and then at him.

"This way, please," she preceded him through a set of double doors. "Miss Laurent is in here."

Arno rushed to Chillitara's side. Her eyes were red and swollen from crying, and she was in obvious pain.

"It'll be okay *mon amour*," he told her gently, looking at the two nurses hooking her up to several machines.

"Turn her onto her left side please," a smooth-faced, dark-skinned doctor with a cloud of curls ordered, striding into the room. "Miss Laurent, I'm Dr Dumas," he introduced. "Your blood pressure is very high, but we can monitor that—"

"My baby?" Chilli interrupted, on a stuttered breath.

"Has a strong heartbeat, listen," he glanced at a nurse who pressed a button, and the baby's heartbeat filled the room.

"Please turn up the volume," Chilli asked, fighting through another contraction to listen with relief, the steady heartbeat, music to her ears.

"He's holding on," the doctor confirmed.

"But?"

"But your placenta has pulled away from the uterus slightly. Placenta Abruption," he explained. "It is rare." He walked to the side of the bed and looked at the monitor. "Any falls in the last twenty-four hours? Strenuous exercise?"

The doctor was pressing down lightly on her abdomen. A stoic expression on his face.

Chilli grimaced when the nurse pricked her skin to take her blood. "I stumbled earlier today," she explained, remembering being bumped into at the train station. "But I didn't fall or anything." She tensed, feeling another contraction coming. They were awfully close. She knew they were too close. They needed to hurry up and give her something to stop the labour.

"No matter," he carried on briskly. "At thirty-two weeks, we want the baby to stay where he is. We'll be monitoring you both closely for the next few hours now that the bleeding has stopped. The baby is stable. However, bed rest and–"

Whatever else he was going to say was interrupted by a small woman with pale blonde hair bursting into the room like a pink tornado. "Chillitara!" she wailed, pushing the doctor out of the way.

"Grand-Mère," Chilli cried through her sudden light-headedness. "They called you?"

"I am your emergency next of kin," she explained, quickly flapping her hands away. "The baby? What happened?"

The doctor left the room. A nurse was busy setting up an intravenous drip in Chilli's hand.

"He's," Chilli tried to talk. The words were there, but not coming out how she wanted them to. They seemed to hover above her lips, in dancing childish script. She wanted to laugh and vomit at the same time. "He's–" she began again, turning her head to avoid her grandmother's all-seeing stare, to look at the monitor. "He's stable."

The electronic graphs blurred. The pink and green lines morphed into a scattering of crying emojis. "No, no, no!" Chilli cried, fighting with the image, and reaching to turn the monitor off. "My baby!"

The nurse grabbed her arm, but she fought on. Fighting the pain and fighting the hands holding her down.

"Arno," Chilli implored with wide frightened eyes. "You promised!"

Arno stepped forward, frowning. She had beautiful golden skin, but it was pale, and her lips pinched white with pain. "I'm here," he soothed when he really wanted to shout and demand they ease her suffering. "I won't let them–"

"*Non!*" Grand-Mère screamed, making everyone in the room jump. "This is my granddaughter, and I demand you take the baby now." She shouted at the nurse.

"The baby is stable," Arno said respectfully, carefully. He didn't even know her name. "The doctor said–"

The look levelled at him across the bed made him snap his mouth shut.

"My daughter," she told him, unwavering, her face almost as white as the bedsheets. "Her mother *died* during childbirth."

In the stunned silence, the long pauses between the baby's heartbeats could be heard.

"The baby has gone into distress!" Grand-Mère shouted, clutching her throat and swaying on her feet. "Oh my God! Take the baby! Take the baby!"

"Get the doctor!" The nurse shouted, moving swiftly, seeing blood seeping from the IV at the needlepoint on the patient's hand, and the rapid drop in her blood pressure on the monitor.

On another horrific scream, one that made the hair on the

back of Arno's neck stand on end, Chillitara's eyes rolled to the back of her head, and she lost consciousness.

"Get her up to surgery now!" The doctor ordered.

***

Arno watched in frozen horror when Chillitara was rushed out of the room, and into a large elevator with medics frantically shouting at each other, using terms like distress, haemorrhage, blood clots and DIC. What the hell was a DIC?

"Please come this way." A nurse urged gently, showing another elevator.

He shook himself out of his numbness, moved to follow her, but stopped, looking into the room.

Chillitara's grandmother was leaning against the wall, looking tiny and frail, her lips pinched and white. Her fingers, claw-like, dug into the wall behind her, as though hanging off a cliff.

Arno walked into the room. "*Madam?*" he said, finding something to say. "We must go."

The old lady was silent. She was looking blankly at the floor, and Arno followed her gaze, seeing the dark red stain of smeared bloody footprints going in all directions.

He stepped in front of her, blocking her view. "*Madam?*" he bent at the knees.

"*You,*" she shrieked, suddenly seeing him, her eyes widening. "You got my granddaughter pregnant." She sobbed, pummelling his chest. "It's all your fault. All your fault," she accused, with tears streaming down her face. "She's just a baby." She cried, her small fists gathering the damp fabric of his shirt as she suddenly collapsed against him. "Just a baby."

Arno held her shaking body close, supporting her as she let out her grief, and he tried not to wince as her words lacerated his heart.

When she was calmer, Arno gently peeled her hands from his shirt. "*Madam, we must go.*"

She looked up at him then, her eyes a piercing light blue, and drew in a deep breath. "Yes," she said, exhaling slowly, stepping away, and pushing her shoulders back. "Yes, of course."

With his hand holding one of hers, they quietly followed the nurse into the waiting elevator, where they were then escorted to a waiting room decorated in earthy tones and told to wait.

They waited. They waited, hearing nothing but the hush of a dozing hospital. They waited, only lifting their heads when footsteps walked down the corridor, sometimes rushed, oftentimes unhurried, but always continuing.

With the silence becoming unbearable, Arno turned to the old lady beside him. "I'm sorry," he began. "My name is Arno Tournier." He introduced.

She didn't look at him. "I know who you are."

Her statement didn't invite further conversation, and Arno collapsed into his seat to wait.

"You have blood on your sleeves." She said, a moment later.

"What?"

"You have blood on your sleeves," she repeated, indicating his shirt sleeves. "My granddaughter's blood."

Arno looked at his shirt, seeing the blood for the first time. It was on his sleeves and smeared down his front. "I'm sorry, *Madam*," he didn't know why he was apologising. "I will take care of it." He made to move, but her hand shot out to stop him.

"No, it is okay. Don't go," she rushed. "I need to thank you for being with her," she began, a glimmer of a smile in her eyes. "I'm sorry for what I said earlier," she held out her hand. "I'm Meredith Laurent."

Arno grasped her small hand and re-introduced himself. Together they sighed, the only sound bouncing around the beige and brown room, with orange-striped chairs along each wall, and wooden tables dotted between every six seats.

"My granddaughter is very stubborn," Meredith stated, filling the silence once again. "Much like me," she mused. "And her mother."

"I'm sorry," Arno consoled, remembering what she'd

said downstairs. This woman was suffering, doubtlessly remembering her loss. "About your daughter. I didn't know."

She patted his hand where it lay on the wooden armrest between them at his words. "Chillitara will be fine," she said with conviction, more to herself. "She is strong and loves life," she nodded, and breathed in deep, before smiling. "Yes, she will be fine." Meredith turned in her seat to speak to him. "Everything she records." she looked to the ceiling, rolling her eyes. "As a little girl, she had diaries and recordings of her day," she chuckled outright. "She shares her life with everyone. Most things are viewed," she shrugged. "But not everything." She shook her head, unaware the bun on top of her head had slipped down, becoming loose. "People love her. Do you know she calls her camera, Frankie?"

Meredith talked and talked, and Arno was very much aware this was how she was coping. Despair came with endless silence. She told him about Chillitara as a little girl, always talking into her hairbrush, pretending she was a journalist. She'd been four.

Arno listened keenly, getting more insight into the woman fighting for her life from the woman who meant the most to her. Their love for each other was clear, and Arno envied their closeness. He and his grandfather had mutual respect, but nothing like this. The bond between the two women was strong.

Both Meredith and Arno turned towards the open doorway, hearing the double swish of the door opening and closing at the end of the corridor, and then brisk footsteps. They didn't go past.

A woman in navy scrubs and a mask pulled down to her neck entered the waiting room with an air of regret about her.

Both Arno and Meredith surged to their feet, their hands searching and bumping together before their fingers entwined in support.

"*Madam* Laurent?" she asked, pulling off her surgical cap to reveal short grey curls. "I am Dr Moreau, head surgeon. May I have a word?" Her gaze slid to Arno, standing stiffly beside the older lady before flicking away.

"Yes," Meredith said, walking beside the doctor into the

corridor.

Arno waited in frustration. Something was wrong. He knew it. He paced into the corridor, seeing Meredith hunched over with her forehead pressed against the wall, the doctor with her hand on her shoulder, talking to her softly.

Chillitara was dead.

CHAPTER SEVENTEEN

She was dead. The baby was dead.

Arno stumbled into the chair behind him, racked with guilt. It was his fault Chillitara was dead. He should never have touched her. He should have told her about the condom breaking. It was all his fault. A sob bubbled and throbbed in his throat, and he let it out. Then another and another. He'd killed her. He'd killed his family.

"*Monsieur?*"

Arno felt a small hand on his shoulder, shaking him, and looked through his tears at the concerned face of Chillitara's grandmother.

"She's dead." He whispered.

"*Non,*" Meredith shook her head quickly in denial, a watery smile wobbling into place. "Did I not say my granddaughter is a fighter?" She sat beside him, taking his hand to curl her fingers over his. "The doctor said she had lost a lot of blood and needed a transfusion. Seventy-five percent of the placenta had broken away," she explained. "The baby was not getting enough oxygen. By the grace of God, Dr. Moreau and her team were still here. The baby–," she bit her lip and looked away. "They did an emergency caesarean."

"How is she now?"

"Still in surgery. She's bleeding." Meredith wrapped her arms around herself. "They will have a long recovery."

His head snapped up. "They? The baby?"

Meredith's smile was small. "We can go and see him."

It was too much. The overwhelming feelings of worry and relief made Arno light-headed. He'd been through every emotion known to man today, each one rolling desperately into the other like a boulder rapidly gathering speed down a craggy mountain.

Chillitara was still in surgery, and his son had been born eight weeks early. What was the survival rate of a baby delivered eight weeks early? He didn't know.

Arno scrubbed his hands over his face several times and stood to hold out his hand to Meredith. "Come *Madam*, let's meet your great-grandson."

***

The neonatal intensive care unit, NICU, was two floors up, and when they arrived, a junior nurse dressed in yellow and green scrubs met them.

"*Madam* Laurent? *Monsieur* Tournier?" she inquired, obviously expecting them.

"*Oui*," Meredith and Arno answered in unison.

"Hello, my name is Aimee," she introduced, handing over two visitor passes. "You will be able to access the floor if you wear these." She advised, watching when the visitors placed the bright orange lanyards over their heads. "Swipe the pass here," she swiped her pass, the door clicked, and holding the door open, let them through. "And here." She swiped the pass again, allowing them to leave what could only be described as an inner security chamber with cameras.

The security was tight, but Arno was too tired to be impressed.

"Please always sanitise your hands," she pointed to the sanitisers dotted beside every doorway. "And wear these." '*These*' being white cotton, tie at the back, hospital gowns with hearts and stars on them.

Dressed and hands dutifully sanitised, she nodded and moved on.

"Baby Laurent," she flicked a glance at Arno from under her lashes at the name, but went on. "Is our only guest in NICU at the moment, so he's enjoying the facilities," she said, over her shoulder. "Such a handsome baby."

"How's he doing?" Arno asked belatedly. He still couldn't

believe his son was actually here. His heart tripped over with a potent mixture of elation and trepidation as he trailed behind the two women down a dimly lit corridor.

The area was tranquil, with softly painted walls. Playful motifs with life-sized farm animals were stuck along the corridor it. This floor was opposite to the traumatising ward downstairs.

Aimee walked into a room in front of the nurses' station. "He's doing well," she told them. "The doctors have been and are thrilled." She advised quietly. "Here, he is."

The nurse stepped aside, and Arno stepped over to his son.

His heart jumped and squeezed at the first sight of his little boy. The baby was tiny, lying on his back wearing a nappy that looked too big for him, and with a blue woollen hat pulled low on his head. Brightly coloured wires connected him to various medical machines. A mask covered his mouth and nose, with tubes going into both. One foot had plastic paddles holding an IV and other needles in place. His poor son.

"With him being premature, his lungs need a little help," Aimee explained. "We're monitoring his heartbeat and oxygen and giving him fluids and nutrients to help him along." She walked around the incubator and pushed the nest of blankets surrounding the baby a little closer. "Talk to him and touch him gently," she encouraged, running her fingers along the baby's arm. "Contact is vital for preemies," she said, before leaving the room. "I'll be right outside if you need me."

"He's so small," Meredith whispered in wonder through her tears.

Arno remained quiet, feeling a wealth of love and protectiveness surging through him. Changing him. He may have only known of his son's existence today, but seeing him now, tiny and bird-like, his eyes closed, and needing so much help, Arno knew he would give his little boy his life.

"I'll give you a moment," Meredith said gently, squeezing Arno's shoulder before leaving the room.

Arno pulled his chair closer to the incubator, not bothering to hide his tears. His baby, his son, had almost died today. Arno had heard his heartbeat stop himself and felt the terror all over again.

"Hey, baby boy," he choked in French, using Chillitara's nickname for the baby. It was only a short few hours ago that he'd been lying on the bed beside her, and she'd told him to talk to the baby so that he would recognise his voice once he was born. Not knowing where to start, Arno had spoken about the fermentation process of winemaking. Chillitara had rolled her eyes and laughed at him. Now, he was trying to remember if he'd spoken in English or French. Would it even matter? No, it would not, he told himself.

"Hi son," Arno began again in English. "Remember me?" he gave in to the urge and reached through one hole in the incubator, hovering his finger above his son's tiny arm. It looked so fragile, as though a single touch would break him. The baby's foot looked no bigger than his little finger Arno compared. "I'm your daddy, and I'm going to love you and protect you with everything I have." He promised, finally daring to stroke his son's arm. His skin was petal soft.

The tiny fingers on the baby's hand moved at his words, and Arno believed his son heard him. "I love you, baby boy. Your mother is going to get better. She is going to love you and hold you, video you, and take many pictures of you. So, get ready." Arno chattered away, encouraged when the baby's fingers or toes moved every so often. "I'm going to take a picture of you now for your mother, yes?" Arno told him, fishing out his phone. His archaic phone, he remembered Chilli labelling it. He was going to buy a phone. Today. One better than hers. He had a video diary to maintain.

He was still talking to the baby when Meredith arrived. "Chillitara is out of surgery and in recovery," she informed him. "You can see her."

Arno stood but kept his hand on the side of the incubator, needing to stay connected to his son.

"You're not coming?" he asked.

"No."

Arno looked at her then. She looked worn out. "You'll remain here?"

Meredith slid into his seat. "I'll keep my great-grandbaby company until you return."

He may have just met her, but they had gone through so much together today, and Arno bent to kiss her cheek. "Thank you, Meredith, for everything." He acknowledged, before leaving the room.

Arno swapped one hospital floor for another. Chillitara was on a less manic ward this time.

"This way, please." Wearing a new plain blue hospital gown, Arno followed. "You can only stay a few minutes. Miss Laurent is heavily medicated and groggy." She opened a door and let it slide closed when he entered, leaving them alone.

Arno walked to the bed and picked up Chillitara's hand. "Hi," he said, and watched her eyes flicker drowsily open. "How are you feeling?" Arno was aware it was a stupid question the moment the words left his mouth. She'd gone through so much, and he silently repeated the same promise he'd made to their son. He owed Chillitara.

She blinked several times, trying to focus. "The baby?" she asked.

"We've got ourselves a little fighter," Arno told her, pulling a chair closer without releasing her hand. "Three pounds, two ounces, and quite long. He's going to be an Olympic high jumper." He teased, liking the glimmer of a smile on her lips. Arno pulled out his phone. "Look."

Arno showed her the pictures, his face softening when she smiled and cried at the same time. "He has your nose," she laughed through her tears. "He's beautiful."

"Just like you," he pressed a kiss on her forehead and smoothed her hair away from her face.

"I want to see him." She tried to push up from the pillows, but fell back.

"No, don't move," he said. "I'll ask." Arno made to move, but she held on to him.

"Thank you for being stubborn," she slurred, fighting the grogginess. "And not listening to me." Her eyelids finally fluttered closed, and she lost the battle to stay awake.

Arno kissed her forehead again and pulled the blankets up to her neck. He spoke to the nurses who advised Chillitara will sleep for several hours now. Her body went through a lot of surgeries today, including a caesarean.

Arno wondered what other surgeries, but decided he'd ask about that later. He went upstairs, and Nurse Aimee advised both Meredith and him to go home for a few hours. She'd looked pointedly at his bloodied shirt, again on show now that he'd taken off the hospital gown.

They left the hospital in agreement and blinked at how bright, loud and chaotic the morning rush hour was. Life had continued, Arno thought sombrely.

Meredith said she will pack a bag for Chillitara as her clothes were there. They were to meet later.

Arno frowned at that. Where did Chillitara live? He had a lot of questions, but he needed a shower and coffee first. Flagging down a taxi, he smiled. He had a son. He had a family.

Arno was leaning against the wall waiting for the elevator in Chillitara's building when a tall skinny man with spots on his forehead approached him.

"Excuse me," he said in English. "You are Miss Chilli's guest, Mr Arno Tournier?" he asked, looking Arno up and down, his dark eyes flaring, seeing the dried blood through Arno's opened coat. "The princess is okay? The baby?"

"They are both fine," Arno happily repeated the baby's weight to the stranger. "Fighters, the both of them."

"Congratulations," the young man's face lit up. "Come, come," he showed his open doorway. "Deliveries came a few minutes ago." He informed Arno. "Miss Chilli sent me a text to look out for them last night."

Arno followed the young man into the ground-floor flat.

"Here you go," he threw his arm wide, and Arno could see

why. Chillitara had ordered enough clothes to last him the rest of his life. He shook his head in amusement. "Thank you," he said, reaching into his trouser pocket for his wallet. "What's your name?"

"Kylian, Mr Tournier," he accepted the wad of euros.

"Call me, Arno."

They shook hands, and together they loaded the elevator with all the bags and boxes. Arno didn't notice the young man pull out his phone and make a call.

Wedging the door open to the apartment, Arno made several trips, stashing the deliveries in the hall.

He cleaned up Chillitara's bathroom, changed her bed, found the bag of toiletries and grooming equipment she had bought, had a quick shower and much-needed shave, before making himself a coffee, and went through the bags again looking for something to wear.

She had thought of everything. A full wardrobe, including underwear, and Arno chuckled at the silk boxers. Arno had never worn silk boxers in his life. He pulled on the first pair of black jeans he came across. He put on a white T-shirt under a dark green sweater. The sweater was long with several zips. She'd bought shoes, trainers and boots. Choosing the boots, laced them up. How much did she spend last night? He chuckled to himself.

He re-heated their leftovers, and while eating, thought to pack her a few things. Meredith was taking care of her clothes and personal items, but her handbag and gadgets were here.

With the plate in his hand, he walked into her bedroom again, placing her laptop, phone, and her precious camera on the bed. Then, looking around, spied her handbag on a chair. With one hand, he picked it up, only for it to fall on the floor, scattering the contents everywhere.

Shaking his head, Arno put the plate down to re-pack the bag. A packet of tissues, a bunch of keys, a hairbrush, a purse, a metallic pink makeup bag, mints, a tube of wig glue, several portable phone charges, an adaptor, and a fancy sparkly cardholder.

Her British driver's license was at the front of the holder, and giving in to his curiosity, slipped it out to flip it front and back. She hadn't aged a bit, he thought, seeing her bemused expression that only Chillitara could get away with on an official ID. Arno looked at her date of birth, remembering the nurse had asked him earlier, and he stopped breathing. Closing his eyes tight, he opened them again, looking at the year in disbelief. She was twenty-two! That couldn't possibly be right, he thought, feeling sick to his stomach. Twenty-two!

Arno remembered the night they'd met at the hotel. He'd asked her age. What had she said? He thought back, going over their conversation, trying to remember.

Damn.

She had echoed his words.

Arno scrubbed his hands over his face as guilt rolled over him like an avalanche. She was so young! He had been too wrapped up in himself to think beyond his own pleasure. She had almost died. Arno swore, disgusted with himself. Her life as an adult had barely begun, and she could have died today.

He was going to make this right.

CHAPTER EIGHTEEN

Arno returned to the hospital in under two hours. Chillitara was still sleeping. With instructions to contact him when she woke, he went up to NICU to be with his son.

The doctor was there doing her checks, and much to his delight, said the baby was breathing on his own. Gone was the scary mask over his mouth and nose, replaced by a soft tube attached to his nostrils and taped to his cheek to hold it in place. She introduced herself as Dr Dupuis, a neonatologist.

"One tube down," she advised with a smile, adjusting the feeding tube in the baby's mouth. "Another to go."

"Would you like to hold him?" she asked, and Arno swallowed. He'd never held a baby in his life, much less one as tiny as his son.

"I'll help," Nurse Aimee, who was still on shift, advised, picking up a folded blanket in the incubator and shaking it out. "Sit over there, and I'll pass him over."

Arno watched keenly as she swaddled the baby loosely in a blanket before picking him up. She settled him in the natural cradle Arno made and gently pressed the newborn into his chest.

"There," she stood back, her hands going to her hips. "Nothing to it."

Arno gazed down at his son and listened to the doctor and Nurse Aimee discuss the baby's care, consulting the tablet held between them.

"When can his mother come and see him?" he thought to ask, wanting to reunite Chillitara with the baby as soon as possible.

"Once she has rested, and her doctor gives clearance, we can bring her upstairs," Nurse Aimee answered. "Have you thought about using our Daisy Suite?"

"Daisy Suite? What's that?" he asked, gently rocking his son.

"We were supposed to leave for England today, but our baby boy had other ideas, and we aren't prepared at all." He admitted, feeling as though he had betrayed his beautiful country.

"Lucky for you," Dr Dupuis said, handing Nurse Aimee the tablet to address him. "Our health care is much better than England," she said proudly. "We have several suites for our special babies and their parents. You pay for the cost upfront and may be reimbursed."

"I'll take it." Arno rushed. Money was not an issue.

"I'll speak to her doctors and see if we can move her upstairs, hopefully later today." Dr Dupuis said. "Do you know if the mother is planning to breastfeed?"

They hadn't discussed it. "I don't know."

"Not to worry," she went on. "Any questions?"

"So, he's okay?" he asked, looking at his son. It seemed a lot less scrunched-up and more like a person.

"Yes," she confirmed. "For thirty-two weeks and four days, he's doing well. Those four days have helped with his development and made a tremendous difference in the neonatal care he requires." She looked at the tablets Nurse Aimee held out for her. "His weight is a little low, and that's normal for a preemie. He needs colostrum."

"Colostrum?" Arno asked, ready to go to the pharmacy. "What is that?"

"It's the first milk, clear and nature's way of giving the baby the best start in life," she advised, stepping into his personal space. "It comes before the milk is produced and is full of antibodies and protein," she went on, looking down at him. "Even if the mother doesn't want to breastfeed—and I prefer she does—I do want the first few feeds to be colostrum."

Arno noted the pointed look Nurse Aimee shot the doctor and realised the physician was a staunched advocate for breastfeeding.

They left him alone soon after, and Arno spent the next hour talking to his son and holding him close. Sometimes the baby responded by kicking his little legs or flexing his fingers, but most times he slept. He even yawned around the tube in his mouth once, and Arno captured it all on his phone.

"Meredith?" Arno gasped, when Chillitara's grandmother appeared in the doorway, making her way towards them. Like him, she had changed her clothes, he realised, noticing a panel of a bright yellow skirt beneath the hospital gown and black biker boots. Her blonde hair hung over her shoulder in a long braid, and she wore long shiny earrings that almost touched her shoulders. Her relaxed bohemian attire was the antithesis of the pinched and pale look on her face. "What is it?" he asked, alarmed. Her eyes were red and glassy with tears, although she tried to blink them away. "Is Chillitara all right?"

"Yes, yes," she reassured him hurriedly, pinning a smile on her face. "I was just with her. She's awake."

Arno nodded, but wasn't convinced things were okay. She looked a wreck. Something was wrong. He felt a lightning rod of fear lash through him. "How is she?" He asked again, unconvinced.

"As good as can be expected," Meredith replied, bending at the waist to stroke her finger along the baby's soft cheek. "How is my great-grandson?"

Arno repeated everything the doctor had said, before slowly shifting in the chair. "Would you like to hold him?" They looked at the wires attached to the baby. "Maybe you should get Nurse Aimee first?" he suggested, wanting to check on Chillitara himself.

Meredith went to do just that. The three of them moved around until Meredith was sitting holding the baby.

"I'll go down to Chillitara now," Arno advised, taking a few more photographs of the baby in her arms.

She looked up at him then, her eyes flooding with tears. "Tell her I'm sorry."

Arno frowned, his eyebrows dipping low. "Why?" he asked. "What did you do?"

Meredith's lips tightened, but she shook her head. A tear fell onto her cheek, and she wiped it away. "She'll tell you."

Arno stared down at her for several seconds, but she avoided his gaze, so after touching the baby's head in farewell, he left deep in thought.

***

Chillitara was in another room when Arno went downstairs. Unfortunately, she shared the space with another woman. Not liking the lack of privacy, he spun on his heel to speak to the nurses.

They informed him Chillitara was going to be moved upstairs to the Daisy Suite if her vitals remained stable over the next few hours, so this set-up was only temporary.

"Hi," he said a moment later, entering the room. She was sitting up but looking straight ahead and didn't acknowledge him. "Chillitara?" Arno prompted, moving into her line of sight. Even then, she didn't look at him.

"Chillitara, what is it?" He caught her hand, but she pulled it away, tucking it under her blanket. Chillitara was a firecracker. She was always animated and chatting away. He didn't know her like this. Had never seen her look like this. Blank. There was nothing, no emotion, her dark eyes dead. What had happened? Did Meredith have something to do with it?

He looked around in frustration. The patient opposite was making no bones about watching them. He smiled tightly before pulling the curtain around them with a loud swish, giving them a modicum of privacy.

Dragging a chair to her bed, Arno sat as close as he could, rummaged under the blankets for her hand, and held on tight when she tried to pull away again.

"Talk to me," he encouraged quietly. A single tear escaped, quickly followed by another and another down her face. "You're scaring me, sweetheart," he admitted, waiting for something from her. When she remained silent, he pulled out his phone with one hand to pull up pictures of the baby. "Look at our baby boy, Chilli," he encouraged, putting the phone under her nose, but she closed her eyes and turned her head away.

Alarmed, Arno pocketed his phone and ran his hands through his hair. "Please Chillitara, what is it?" he asked again, taking her hand. "No matter what, I'll make it right, I promise."

She looked at him then, her eyes drenched with tears and her bottom lip trembling. She looked tortured. Totally ravaged. But at least she was looking at him and Arno realised with a jolt that it was Chillitara who filled his world with brightness. Her smile alone brightened his day. He didn't like her like this. "I swear to you, whatever it is," he swore. "I'll make it right."

"Not this," she hiccupped, trying to keep the sobs silent but failing, turning her face to the wall again.

Had they told her something was wrong with the baby? Arno thought silently. Was that it? Yet that made little sense. He'd just been in NICU, and the baby was fine. "Is it the baby?" he pressed anyway. "I was just with him," Arno told her. "He's a little fighter, like you," he teased, trying to get a reaction from her. "And already needing less help to breathe. He's doing us proud *mon amour*," he said, wanting to reassure her. "Your grandmother is with him now and—"

She stabbed him with a look that could only be called hate. "You get that woman away from my son!"

Arno rocked back under the force of her words. "What?"

"I don't want her anywhere near my baby!" Chillitara shouted, trying to sit up.

"I don't understand," Arno said.

"Do you know what she did?" she asked him savagely, wiping away the tears and falling against the pillows in defeat. "Were you there?"

"Chillitara, I promise you; I have no idea what you're talking about."

"Just answer the question," she gritted, trying to sit up again. "Were. You. There?"

"Chillitara, calm down."

"I won't calm down. Don't tell me to calm down. I want to know if you were there!"

"Where?"

"When she did what she did."

Abandoning the chair, Arno moved to stand over her to ask. "What the hell did she do?"

Chilli sobbed into her hands, and he pulled them away, leaning forward and getting into her face. His heart sank when he saw the pain in her eyes. "*Mon chou?*"

"She let them take away my uterus." Chilli sobbed in a small voice.

"Uterus?" Arno puzzled, his brows dipping low, "I don't understand."

"I can't have any more children," she cried, wiping her eyes quickly with her fingers, only for more to fall. "And she let them do it," she sobbed. "The baby could die."

Arno leaned back, frozen with guilt, mentally listing everything he had done to her. He hadn't bothered to tell her about the condom breaking, got her pregnant, and now he had wrecked her entire life. No more children. She was only twenty-two. Arno had done this to her. He was the one to blame. He didn't know what to say, aware she was watching him through tear-stained eyes. He needed to think.

"I'm sorry," he whispered, knowing the words were wholly inadequate, and searched for more, but she beat him to it. Her next words took him by surprise.

She cut him off. "I need you to go upstairs and make her leave."

He stepped back. "What?"

Arno thought of the old woman upstairs. She had so much love and strength for her granddaughter.

"Chillitara, she is your grandmother," Arno placated gently. "You don't mean that."

Chilli's eyes flashed. "If you don't make her leave right now, I'll get security to remove her."

"She loves you, she–"

Chilli's laugh was akin to a huff. "What kind of love is that? She takes away my right to have more children? She had no right.

No right!" she shouted on a fresh wave of tears. "What if the baby dies?" She repeated, scrubbing her knuckles into her eyes.

Arno remembered the surgeon speaking to Meredith earlier this morning. The surgeon had probably advised her of the hysterectomy then. Now that he thought about it, Meredith had looked haunted ever since.

"The baby will not die," he charged, taking her hands, unable to comprehend such a thing. "He's fighting and–"

The curtains moved, and a nurse came in, cutting him off. "Miss Laurent has just had major surgery and needs to rest," she looked pointedly at Arno. "She should not be upset."

"He was just leaving," Chillitara prompted, peering at him and slipping her fingers free of his.

Arno pulled himself up to his full height when inside he was crumbling. What should he do? He didn't want to ask Meredith to leave. It wasn't right, but he couldn't have her this upset, either. Chillitara and the baby came first. They were his priority.

"I'll speak to her now," he conceded, mentally preparing himself for the unpleasant task. He liked Meredith. "Please calm down."

Chilli nodded and just when he reached the doorway stopped him. "Can I see the photographs, please?" she asked softly.

Arno relaxed slightly and gave her his phone.

"Thank you." She looked at him from under her lashes, standing awkwardly at her side. "You look nice."

Relieved, this was the Chillitara he knew, uncomplicated and playful. He had never seen her this angry before. "Yes, well, it seems I've got myself a new wardrobe." He picked up her hand, and smoothed his lips over her knuckles, glad to see her small smile, although her eyes were still shadowed with pain when she looked back at him.

"If the doctors are happy, you can go upstairs later, but only if you rest, and your vitals are stable." The nurse advised, interrupting their moment.

"She'll rest," Arno informed the nurse, without looking at her. "Won't you?" he declared, arching a single dark eyebrow at

Chillitara.

"You'll do what I asked?" she challenged instead.

It pained him, but he conceded. "I will." Then added with a teasing wink, sweeping his arm over her bed and all the machinery she was attached to. "Don't go anywhere *mon amour*, I'll be right back."

Then he was gone.

Chillitara looked after him, stunned, completely unaware Arno even had a sense of humour.

CHAPTER NINETEEN

It was later in the day.

"Guess what?" Arno asked, walking into Chillitara's room and swishing the curtains closed behind him.

When Arno returned to the NICU earlier, Nurse Aimee introduced him to another nurse as she was about to go off shift. He'd thanked Aimee for everything, and she said she would be back later tonight, and hopefully, fingers crossed, they would be in the Daisy Suite. She'd also informed him Miss Laurent had departed, leaving him a note, which she retrieved from her pocket. Meredith had written her phone number for him.

Arno had been relieved to hear Meredith had already left. He still needed to find out what had happened, and relay Chillitara's request to stay away. However, he had a strong suspicion Meredith was already aware of Chillitara's stance, by her absence.

Arno stayed upstairs for a while, keeping the baby company. He stroked the tiny body and explained the fermenting process of wine making to him. The baby seemed more responsive and appreciative of his efforts, with all the enthusiastic leg kicking and arm movements he was doing.

Arno wondered what his personality would be like. Chillitara had said he was active, and Arno pictured him running about the grapevines, much as he had done growing up.

Then, because he could feel himself flagging, found a cafeteria and had a strong black coffee, before going to see her.

"Has she gone?" Chillitara asked instead.

Arno didn't skip a beat. "Yes."

She nodded. "So, what am I guessing?" she prompted, sipping her mint tea, which was supposed to help relieve the cold feeling in her shoulder, an apparent side effect from the anaesthesia.

"You can come upstairs," Arno declared with a smile, pulling up the chair to sit beside her. "If you're feeling up to it, that is." He tacked on.

Her smile reflected his. "Really? Right now?"

"Right now," he confirmed. "I was just outside talking to your doctor and asked for ten minutes. If you feel up to it. And for only ten minutes," he warned. "And we're not to push it."

"I do. We won't," Chilli promised, before adding. "Thank you, Arno."

"Come on," he said, unable to hide his eagerness. It wasn't fair that she had spent almost eight months carrying their son, had suffered tremendously, and at the final hour had been knocked out, and yet to see him, not to mention the devastating news that had followed, and her belief the baby could die. Chillitara deserved a break and needed to see their baby was a fighter. "Finish your drink. The orderlies will be here soon."

Chillitara finished her drink in a single gulp and pointed to her pom-pom-enhanced, multi-coloured handbag he'd brought in earlier.

"Can I have that please?" she asked eagerly. "I need to do my hair."

Arno handed her the bag. "He can't focus on things properly yet."

Chillitara rolled her eyes at him and dived inside to pull out a brush and a makeup bag. Arno watched as she reached up to brush her hair but winced, and quickly held her abdomen instead, closing her eyes.

"Okay?" he asked in concern.

Chilli held up her hand, silently requesting a moment. She breathed in and out slowly before opening her eyes and answering. "But he'll see the photographs for years to come, won't he?" she chided, brushing off his question. Because of the medication, she wasn't in pain, but felt a strong pull across her belly when she reached up. A potent reminder to be careful.

"Can you do it for me, please?" she begged, holding the paddle brush out to him.

Arno looked at it, at her thick curls, then at the brush again.

"It won't bite," Chilli scolded, aware European people really didn't know how to handle her natural curls.

Arno reached for the brush and moved to the top of the bed. "What do I do?"

"Take out the clip," Chilli began tongue in cheek. "Brush my hair up into one hand. Put the clip back in." She instructed drolly.

Arno tugged gently on a curl. "I can think of many things to do with this paddle brush, *mon amour*," he warned without heat, "if you continue that tone with me."

She laughed, not expecting him to say such an outrageous thing. He was so full of surprises, and she wondered at his many layers, not least the ones he'd shown in the last twenty-four hours.

"You have beautiful hair," he said, stroking the brush through it. It was dark brown, shot through with bright auburn streaks.

"Thank you."

"Why do you wear wigs and hairpieces?" Her hair was thick, shoulder length, and he didn't see the need to cover it up.

Chilli bit back the '*because I can*' retort she would have usually said. Hair was a sensitive topic for many women of colour, including her. "Variety," she said instead. "And to protect it from the environment and chemicals."

Arno continued to brush it for longer than was necessary, enjoying the small sounds of appreciation she made with each lazy stroke.

"What colour is his hair?" Chillitara asked suddenly, thinking about her son. She remembered asking Arno when she'd come out of surgery, but at that point, he hadn't checked.

"I don't know," he admitted. He hadn't dared lift the baby's hat to look.

"Arno, seriously?"

"Ten fingers, ten toes, two of what he's supposed to have, and one of everything else."

She shook her head and looked heavenward.

When he finished, Chilli rubbed a wipe over her face, opened a small jar of Vaseline, and smoothed some along her lips. She had once done a vlog on the many uses of petroleum jelly and did it now. Smoothing it over her eyebrows, eyelids, and cheeks to give her a fresh, dewy look. Then she applied a little to her eyelashes for definition. "How do I look?" she asked critically.

Arno smiled indulgently. Chillitara must be the only woman on the planet who, after an emergency caesarean, massive blood loss, and a hysterectomy, would enquire about how she looked.

"Sensational," he replied honestly, feeling a tightness in his throat. She didn't need makeup, and he regretted never telling her how beautiful she was, with and without the wigs, mascara, and contouring.

He hadn't told her the things that mattered. He'd been caught up in the sex. God, he'd been shallow.

It might have been different if they spent more time outside of the bedroom. She may be much younger than him, but her level of maturity and the strength she had shown today outstripped him his any day. He leaned forward and kissed her forehead. "Sensational." He repeated.

"Please?" A nurse came in and swept her arm towards the door, with eyebrows raised in expectation.

Arno reluctantly left, although returned on the heels of two orderlies who brought a wheelchair.

The nurse opened the curtains, and Arno watched keenly for any sign that they were hurting Chillitara. She had been disconnected from the IV and monitors, and they eased her into the wheelchair. She winced several times, and held her abdomen, but soon settled, smiling, and giving everyone a thumbs up.

Arno was so proud of her and again admired her strength. He was in awe and indebted to her for the rest of his life.

The orderlies introduced themselves to him, and with Chillitara's handbag slung over his shoulder, together they entered the elevator.

They'd already made space for Chillitara's wheelchair beside the incubator, and Arno tipped the orderlies discreetly when they promised to collect her in ten minutes.

"He's so small," Chilli whispered.

Arno knew what she was feeling. The wonder and amazement at their little boy. He still felt it.

Unlike him, Chillitara immediately reached through the hole, and touched the baby, running her fingers lightly along his leg while he slept.

"Hello little man," Chilli said through her tears and began talking to the baby, who twitched slightly at the sound of her voice. "He knows me."

Arno took pictures and recorded the moment. "Do you think I can hold him?" Chilli asked, looking up at him, her eyes glassy yet hopeful.

"I'll ask."

Arno returned with the nurse, who fiddled with the tube and bag attached to Chillitara's abdomen, moving it to the side.

"We are advocates of parents being with their babies here at St. Mary's," she told them, moving to the incubator next, gently picking up the baby with his blanket, and laying him in Chillitara's arms. "Just for a few minutes," she warned. "We don't want you tiring or upsetting your stitches. Your body has been through a lot today." She left them then.

Arno playfully took more pictures at Chillitara's instructions.

"The three of us," she ordered, and with his arm extended and crouching down beside the wheelchair, they took their first family portrait.

"We need a name for him," Arno said, looking down at his family.

Chilli looked at her baby. She had a list of names. Arno showed no sign of liking any of them until she suggested.

"How about Stirling Arno Mylo Tournier?"

Arno tipped his head to the side, saying it all out loud.

"Mylo Stirling Arno Tournier?" Chilli continued with raised brows.

Arno repeated the name out loud.

The baby squawked and yawned, and with his parents

looking indulgently on, cracked his eyes.

"Mylo Stirling Arno Tournier, it is."

They both laughed when the baby made another noise and closed his eyes again.

***

Chilli was returned to her room, and Arno, flagging again, had a coffee and spent time with his son.

The new nurse, Sophie, he finally remembered, showed him the Daisy Suite. Although nice, Arno wanted to make it unique for his family, being as they were likely to stay at least three weeks, depending on the baby's progress and weight gain, they had warned him. With Nurse Sophie's help, Arno ordered several things online using his phone.

She also told him to go home and rest. Any move would happen much later in the evening, she advised at his objections.

Seeing his new family settled, Arno made his way to Chillitara's apartment, picking up some food along the way. Fortunately, there was a plethora of cafes and restaurants within Saint Germain. There was also a phone shop, and with a spring in his step, bought a new phone, similar to Chillitara's. The clerk updated and transferred everything for him. He tipped the clerk one hundred Euro.

He ate, checked in with Agnes, his housekeeper, to see how his grandfather was, made some more phone calls, and pulled in favours from his neighbours.

Then he reluctantly called Meredith. They'd surprisingly had a good chat. Knowing her granddaughter as she did, she thought it best to make herself scarce until Chillitara had calmed down. She and her granddaughter had clashed many times, he was told, so he shouldn't feel uncomfortable. He asked about the hysterectomy and agreed with the choices made. Ending the call with promises to keep her updated and to send photographs, he set his alarm clock and finally allowed himself to relax and fall asleep.

***

It took another four days for them to move into the Daisy Suite, because of Chillitara not feeling well, the baby needing the UV light for his jaundice, and to monitor his sleep apnoea.

Arno spent most of his time between the two floors, with a quick excursion to the apartment to pick up the things he'd ordered - with Nurse Aimee's help - to make the suite suitable for his family.

Sitting beside Chillitara one evening, they ordered premature baby clothes to be delivered to the apartment for him to pick up.

Nurse Aimee and Dr Dupuis had taught Chillitara how to encourage her breast milk production, and every few hours, night and day, Chillitara pumped milk for Mylo.

The baby had lost a little weight, which they said was normal and on one occasion he even latched onto Chillitara's breast, but his sucking reflex wasn't developed enough yet, so was still being tube fed.

Arno wheeled Chillitara into the suite, proud of his efforts. The hospital bed linen had been exchanged for a bold black-and-white pattern similar to what she had in her flat in England. He'd added a mountain of textured cushions, pillows, and a thick throw for her comfort.

The nurses showed him how to order prints of his photographs directly from his phone with frames, and he had scattered them around the suite, with the first photograph of the three of them larger and holding pride of place beside the bed.

"This is wonderful," Chilli said, looking around the room. "Are all the suites like this?" she asked, taking in the modern space. It looked more like a swanky hotel room, with a massive flat-screen TV and plush en-suite.

"I did a bit of an upgrade for you and Mylo, *mon chou*," Arno revealed, proud of his efforts. She'd been through so much, and he wanted to ensure she was as comfortable as possible. "You have Wi-Fi so can work from the bed, or over there," he pointed at the small living room area with three chairs surrounding a glass table with a white vase filled with a bouquet of crystal roses and stars. Fresh flowers were not allowed in the unit. "Although not too much work." He warned.

With his help, Chilli stood, only slightly bent over. She'd been encouraged to walk around, and typical of her drive, spent a lot of time walking the corridors and had even gone up to NICU on her own once, much to his disapproval.

"When is Mylo coming?" she asked.

"Here's your handsome young man," Nurse Aimee said, wheeling in the baby, hearing Chillitara's words.

She parked the cot, and with the help of another nurse, busily set up the monitoring equipment, which wasn't as intimidating as the previous ones.

Mylo was regulating his body temperature now and, thankfully, didn't need the incubator either.

"Okay, Tournier family," she turned to address them all with a bright smile. "Let's get you settled."

CHAPTER TWENTY

Mylo was doing them proud, reaching every milestone, and putting on weight to what he would have been if he hadn't arrived early. He was getting used to sucking and breathing, although sometimes couldn't manage both at the same time. Hence them not being allowed to go home.

Arno watched with pride as Chillitara settled their son in his cot. If Mylo went another forty-eight hours without the breathing alarm sounding and pass some sort of car seat test, then they could take him home.

Arno sighed, knowing they had avoided all conversation of where home actually was.

"Okay?" he asked, watching her button her shirt, then walk over to the sitting area. She looked exhausted, with dark smudges under her eyes, and he wanted to help her, ease some of the responsibility. Still, until man started producing milk, there was nothing he could do. He kept her company during feeds and helped settle the baby. But wished he could do more. Chillitara was adamant breastfeeding was just easier.

Her mood wasn't as vibrant as it used to be, and Arno worried about her. They hadn't talked about anything but Mylo, and to be honest, he didn't know where to start. She'd done so much already, and he didn't want to press her, but he needed a plan. They needed a plan and couldn't go on in limbo like this. Tucked away in the Daisy Suite, where their world was only about Mylo.

Her shoulders looked tense where she sat, and she leaned back, closing her eyes and yawning.

"I think I'll take a quick shower." She said out loud.

Arno didn't like it. Didn't like her despondency. She was running on empty, and he knew he needed to think of something to snap her out of it before it consumed her.

She hadn't spoken to Meredith, although he rang her grandmother daily, keeping her updated, and sending pictures of the baby. It was sad, and he knew Chillitara had pride, a proudness that was even more rigid than his own, but enough was enough. She needed her grandmother, even if she didn't say so.

Arno made some calls when she left the room. He had been gone for three weeks. Agnes, his housekeeper, said his grandfather was asking questions and wanting to know what the hell he was playing at. The old man wasn't aware of the baby. Knowing his grandfather was a traditional man, Arno knew it best to tell him face to face.

Thankfully, Arno had a second in command who was reliable enough to keep the vineyard ticking over, and until they gave Mylo the green light, and Chillitara well enough to travel, he was staying in Paris.

He finished his calls, happy, things were at least running smoothly, when, tipping his head to the side, realised the shower had switched off. Chillitara stayed in the bathroom as he knew she would. She got changed in there, and spent long minutes doing God knows what, but he didn't push.

Chilli wiped the steam from the mirror and stared at her body, sweeping past her full breasts to go straight to the scar, shaped like a mocking smile on her abdomen. It was a vicious reminder that she couldn't have any more children. She touched it and ran her finger along the thin line. It was numb in parts and stinging in others.

Chilli knew she should count her blessings. She had Mylo, her beautiful baby, but she had never wanted to have one child. Being an only child had been lonely. She'd wanted four children. Three girls and a boy. She even had names at the ready. Her eyes filled with tears. Mylo wasn't one of them.

Her grandmother had raised her, and she had two other cousins, but she'd still been lonely with more things materially than all of them. She'd been sent to boarding school in England from the age of seven and had spent every holiday in France over the years, but the loneliness was horrible. Funny, she thought, sniffing loudly and turning on the water to muffle her sobs, it was funny how lonely she still sometimes felt, yet perversely, she needed space right now. Time away from Arno, who was always hovering over her, trying to stay one step ahead of her needs. She was grateful he was here, but he was always here. They were still tripping over each other, despite the spacious suite. She needed a moment to think, to digest everything that had happened to her.

The nurses were great, especially Nurse Aimee, and Chilli had access to the hospital pastoral care, even though she wasn't particularly religious.

She should be grateful she had her son, she knew that, and the pastor had told her that in a gentle, biblical, story-telling way. But it wasn't fair. She had done everything right her entire life and had never questioned the choices made on her behalf. Yet the swirl of punishment, guilt and fear was always within her like a torrid tornado, picking up speed, because history had a bad habit of being repeated, and the chaos of Mylo's birth was proof of that.

"You okay in there?"

Chilli jumped at the tapping on the door. "I'm fine," she called out, switching off the tap. "I'll be out in a sec."

Giving the scar a final hard look, she dressed quickly in jeggings, and a loose chequered shirt, finger-combed her hair, twisted the curls around themselves, and secured them with a narrow yellow ribbon on top of her head out of the way. She could do with a few wigs, she thought, looking at her hair.

Bracing herself, she pinned a smile on her face while opening the door, and pretended not to notice Arno hovering and trying to hide his restlessness.

***

Chilli was nursing the baby when there was a knock on

the door. The nurses were always coming and going, although the frequency was becoming blessedly less now that Mylo was maturing, and they had a routine.

Arno glanced at her before opening the door, and she wondered at his veiled look.

"Grand-Mère?" Chilli whispered, stunned for a moment, then held out her free arm to her grandmother who, gloved and gowned, quickly crossed the room at the invitation.

Trying not to smile too widely, Arno watched the two women hug and cry, knowing he had made the right decision by inviting Meredith to come to the hospital. Pride aside, Chillitara needed her grandmother. He quietly picked up his phone and left the room.

"Grand-Mère," Chilli cried into her grandmother's shoulder. "I'm sorry."

"Shh," Meredith soothed. "It's okay," she moved back slightly to hold Chilli's face with both hands. "You are okay?" she asked with concern, moving again to smooth Chilli's hair and skim her eyes over her granddaughter.

Chilli sniffed and nodded, before looking down at Mylo. "Look," she encouraged, now smiling through her tears.

"What a big boy he has become," Meredith exclaimed, clapping her hands. Mylo jumped at the sound, stopped sucking, and turned at the noise. "He is looking right at me!"

Laughing, Chilli recounted the moment her son opened and focussed his eyes for the first time, and all the other milestones. It was a pleasant visit, and they seamlessly reverted to the closeness they'd always had.

"He'll hear about it," Meredith said quietly, once she settled into her seat with the baby sleeping in her arms, when all baby-related conversation had been exhausted. "Have you thought about what we're going to do? Where you will go?"

Puzzled, Chilli looked at the older woman who had given so much of herself to protect her, seeing the lines of worry around her eyes, and wishing she could smooth them away. But those lines ran deep beneath the surface, and Chilli felt the guilt she always felt, wanting to take the burden of responsibility away from her. That's why she was an influencer. It put her out there and made her visible with views, likes and algorithms. If she disappeared, should be missed.

It was upsetting to see the tears pooling in her grandmother's eyes, and Chilli rushed to kneel in front of her, taking her free hand. "Please don't worry, Grand-Mère," she soothed, pressing her lips to her grandmother's knuckles. "He has never expressed any interest in my life. I am going to return to England as we planned."

The tears fell. "They are powerful people."

"And I am now a mother," Chilli declared, looking at her son through softly narrowed eyes.

"But–"

"*Non!*" she squeezed her grandmother's hand. She would not live in fear ever again, remembering what it was like to look at everyone with suspicion. "I promise you I won't let—"

A soft knock at the door interrupted her next words, and Nurse Aimee popped her head inside. "Chillitara?" she began cautiously.

"Yes Aimee, everything all right?" Chilli asked, returning to her seat, secretly relieved the heavy conversation had come to an abrupt end.

Nurse Aimee glanced behind her before hugging the door closer to her side. "There is a man here wanting to see *Monsieur* Tournier."

Chilli frowned, wondering who it could be. They didn't have visitors.

"Do you know who he is?" she asked.

Nurse Aimee bit the side of her lip and flicked a quick glance at Meredith before replying. "*Monsieur* Tournier."

"What?" Chilli questioned in confusion.

"He is much older." Nurse Aimee clarified.

Chilli and Meredith looked at each other.

"His father?" Meredith suggested.

Chilli shook her head, at least knowing Arno's father was

dead, but not much else of his family tree. "No, it must be his grandfather."

"Show him in," Meredith said.

Nurse Aimee nodded; thankful she didn't have to send the old man away. He had already shouted and demanded to be let onto the unit, and she had broken the rules, and would more than likely receive a disciplinary for breaching protocol. Still, in her own defence, she couldn't leave the old man out there, barely able to stand.

The man who entered the room looked nothing like Arno. He was much shorter for one, slightly bent over, a large cloud of frizzy grey hair almost but not quite distracted from his pale eyes. With the distance between them, Chilli couldn't tell if they were blue or grey. He was wearing classic tan brogues, and she could see several inches of his brown trousers peeping out from under the hospital gown.

With her hand extended, she walked towards him. "Hello," she introduced herself in French. "I'm Chilli, and this is my grandmother Meredith."

Wintry grey. His eyes were so cold when they settled on her she stumbled to a stop, her arm frozen mid-air.

He ignored her hand to sweep his gaze around the room, skimming over Meredith and the baby, before frowning deeply. "Where is my grandson?"

"Would you like a seat?" Meredith invited.

"I am Timon Tournier, and I want to know where my grandson is."

"He's not here," Meredith replied.

"I can see that."

"You can wait in the waiting room if you prefer." Meredith invited with a small smile, yet matching his offensive tone.

He apparently preferred not to and walked past Chilli to the vacant seat beside Meredith, where he sat with his back rigid to look straight ahead.

Chilli glanced at her grandmother, and a text to Arno, before pouring the old man a glass of water. He didn't thank her when she placed it on the small table.

Then, to keep herself occupied, Chilli reached for Mylo and sat down, holding him protectively against her breast, thankful her grandmother was holding court, and discussing the weather with their obnoxious visitor.

"What the hell is going on?" Arno bellowed, seeing his grandfather sitting stiffly in a chair. The baby squawked at the interruption.

CHAPTER TWENTY-ONE

"See what you have done," his grandfather accused, turning towards him. "You made it upset." He scolded.

It? Arno mentally sighed, stepped inside and closed the door with a telling click. He'd rushed from outside where he'd been sitting on a bench, surfing the internet for something special to buy Chillitara, when he'd received a text from her, and even then, he thought she was mistaken.

"Grandfather, what are you doing here?" he asked tightly. Chillitara was rocking Mylo in her arms, and Meredith was looking pale. "How did you get here? Where is Agnes?" He listed.

His grandfather had not left the vineyard in almost fifteen years. Arno watched as the old man—who had practically been on his deathbed—throw his shoulders back, and haul himself to his feet to face him.

"You leave for Spain to return in two days and two days become weeks," he accused in French, glaring at his grandson. "Your bag is left on the platform. I thought you were dead. You speak to Agnes, but not me." He ranted, his voice rising steadily. "And then you think I would allow some hired hand to run my vineyard?" he stepped towards him. "You are a Tournier, you have responsibilities!" He charged, his face turning a deep, mottled red. "And then you turn up looking like a labourer dressed for the end-of-season festival!"

Chilli felt the tension in the room ramp up several notches. Timon Tournier had yet to acknowledge her or the baby. He had rudely directed his enquiries to her grandmother. Her grandmother skilfully ignored his blustering and stuck to mundane topics. Thankfully, Arno had arrived before they lapsed into another awkward silence.

"As you can see, I have responsibilities here," Arno returned tightly. "And you haven't answered my questions."

His grandfather tipped his chin up and narrowed his eyes at Arno. "You impregnate some woman I have not heard about and disappear," he snarled. "Did I not teach you anything? You are a Tournier, and Tourniers do not behave as you do. A child out of wedlock, with some random girl who speaks French with a British accent!"

Chilli gasped at the venom the older man was spewing.

Meredith stepped between the men. "I think you have said enough," she told Timon, with a soft voice that bellied her stance of hands-on-hips and jutting chin. "That is my granddaughter you are talking about, and I will not have you throwing your weight about upsetting her. Kindly leave." She pointed towards the door.

Gently, Arno placed his hands on Meredith's shoulders and shifted her away. He was used to his grandfather and knew how to deal with him.

"It's okay Meredith," he said gently, looking over her head at his angry grandfather. "I will not have my future wife spoken to like that," Arno growled, going toe to toe with the old man.

Taking them all by surprise, Timon flung his head back and laughed, glancing at Chillitara before looking at Arno. "So, you finally decide to get married?"

"Yes,"

"Well, that changes everything." Timon returned to the chair with a spring in his step. Even so, he didn't acknowledge Chilli or the baby.

Arno sighed before giving Meredith a quick reassuring smile. "Grandfather," he began. "This is my future bride, Chillitara Laurent, and my son—"

The old man's head snapped up. "A son!" He beamed.

"Yes, my son, Mylo Tournier."

"But he's not yet a Tournier, is he?" The old man latched on quickly.

"He will be."

"When?"

"When it can be arranged."

"And when is that?"

"When we leave the hospital, and Chillitara is feeling better."

"Is there not a chapel here?"

"Grandfather–"

"Bah, my great-grandson is a Tournier!" he yelled, going red in the face once again. "You will marry the girl and bring him home."

"Excuse me?" Chilli interrupted, getting angrier by the minute as the two men talked about her, arranging her future, as though she wasn't even in the room.

All eyes turned to her. Arno's green, weary and apologetic, his grandfather's grey and calculating and her grandmother's blue and anxious. An emotional rainbow in the room. Chilli knew what her grandmother was thinking and didn't care about the thoughts or plans of anyone else.

"Please stop," Chilli said, seeing Timon about to open his mouth. "I am not *the girl*, my name is Chillitara Laurent," she then turned to Arno, to state frostily. "And I'm not marrying you either."

"Chillitara," Arno began gently, knowing he had been pushed into a corner with his grandfather's untimely arrival. He wasn't prepared and hadn't had time to propose or persuade. "*Mon chou.*"

"No," she interrupted, putting up her hand and standing. "This is not the dark ages, and I will not be spoken to as though I'm not here." She wanted to shout, stamp her foot, or even leave the room, but settled for rocking the baby instead. "I'm going home to England."

Timon slapped the arms of his chair. "You will not be taking my great-grandchild out of France!"

"Enough!" Arno charged at his grandfather and waited for several beats for him to nod in acceptance before appealing to Chillitara. "I'm sorry," Arno said, walking to where she was now standing by the window. "Please don't get upset," he cajoled, pressing his hand to the centre of her back. "We will do whatever is best for Mylo." He turned to his grandfather again. "Chillitara lives in England," he started. "We have been seeing each other," he explained in a tone that brokered no further discussion. "She is important to me." He finished around the gritting tension in his jaw.

If Chilli could stab him with her eyes, she would see him dead on the floor with that list, she seethed.

The old man settled his eyes in Chilli's general direction, before eventually saying, "I apologise."

Chilli waited for more words, but none were forthcoming. Their eyes locked across the room. Thankfully, the baby moved and made a noise, giving her the best excuse to bring this family get-together to an end.

But Arno got there first, taking the baby from her, and presenting her precious bundle to show his grandfather. If she could snatch her child from Arno she would, she thought meanly, disliking the older man.

"If you hurt my little boy, I will kill you myself." Chilli declared calmly, hating the old man for making her feel as though she wasn't good enough. Obviously, a Tournier trait.

"Chillitara!" her grandmother gasped into the silent bomb of that statement.

Strangely enough, the older man looked slightly amused if the softening of his chin and brightening in his eyes were anything to go by.

"Good, she has spunk," smiling, he turned to Arno, moving closer to the baby, and shifting the blanket to get a clearer look at his face. "She will make a fine mother to my great-grandson." He praised.

Arno sighed. He wanted to rub his neck in frustration, but his hands were full. This was not how their first meeting was supposed to be, but knew his grandfather had, in his abrupt way, just given his blessing to their union,

"Where are you staying?" he asked, taking the baby and

settling him in on his back.

"I came straight here."

"So back to my original question, Sir," Arno said, straightening and going to stand beside Chillitara, taking her hand. "How did you get here?"

"I drove."

Arno's brows almost hit his hairline before snapping down low in suspicion. He owned a lot of cars. Not one of them was suitable for an elderly man who hadn't driven in years. "Drove what?"

"Your car," Timon shrugged with a smile, leaning back into his chair to steeple his fingers on his chest before continuing. "That little red car."

"You drove my Porsche?" Arno gritted, incredulous over his grandfather driving himself, and in the Porsche no less.

"Yes," Timon confirmed with amusement, looking into the distance as though he were still behind the wheel again, enjoying himself. "You weren't at the château and the police thought it had been stolen. I took possession, put the top down, and came to Paris to see what you were playing at. You have a vineyard to run, boy," he looked towards the cot. "But I will forgive you this time." He shook his head at himself before bursting into yet another incredulous speech. "You had a baby out of wedlock, with a child no less," he turned to Chillitara, taking in the bright blue nail polish on her toes, long baggy shirt, and childish ribbon in her hair. "Just how old are you?"

"She's twenty-two," Arno cut in, feeling as small as his grandfather intended him to feel at his words.

Chillitara gasped. "How do you know?"

"You certainly didn't tell me."

"You lied to my grandson, young lady?" The old man sputtered, interrupting them. "What kind of a—"

"Grandfather, that is enough," Arno said sternly. He could feel the dull throb of a headache coming on. "You will leave Chillitara alone and show her the respect she deserves. I am to blame for all of this." He waved his arm in a wide arch.

"It takes two, Arno," Chilli whispered.

His smile was but a ticking to his lips. "We'll talk later," he assured her, and they would. He'd put it off for too long, and with a single snowflake, an entire avalanche had just ensued. He turned to the old man, who had turned eighty-three last month, had not driven in years, yet drove himself for hours to find him in Paris. A little of his temper eased. They didn't do emotions, yet his grandfather had shown how much he cared by tracking him down. "Grandfather, I will take you to a hotel."

"That is not necessary, Arno," Meredith said, joining the conversation. "He can stay at the apartment."

"The apartment in Saint Germain?" Arno asked, barely able to believe Meredith's generosity. His grandfather had insulted both her and Chillitara and had yet to apologise for his disgraceful behaviour.

"Yes," she shrugged. "You are here. It is empty. Why not?"

"You are sure?" Arno looked at Chillitara. She was trying to convey her objection to her grandmother telepathically.

"Yes." Turning to Timon, Meredith held out her hand. Arno looked on in amazement when his grandfather stood, took her hand, bowed, and graciously kissed it. "You can take me home along the way," she ordered. "And apologise for upsetting my granddaughter."

"It will be my pleasure, *Madam*," Timon replied gallantly. "Or is it *Mademoiselle*?" he asked with a twinkle.

They both said their goodbyes, leaving a stunned silence behind them.

CHAPTER TWENTY-TWO

"What was that?" Chillitara asked, reverting to English. The language swept all the emotional French away like a cool, welcoming breeze.

Arno chuckled. "You have just witnessed the Tournier charm in full force," Arno stated, easily switching to English. His grandfather was a pleasant man, but he hadn't seen him this flirtatious in a while.

Chilli huffed, not at all impressed. "What happens now?" she said seriously.

Arno sighed and pulled his chair close to hers so that their knees were touching. "I'm sorry for what he said. He is a dinosaur, and to have a baby, a Tournier, out of wedlock, is hard for him to understand, *oui*."

Chilli nodded. She understood, but that didn't excuse his rudeness and said as much.

"When I left the château, he was in bed," Arno explained, taking her hands. "He'd been in bed for eleven days, with the curtains closed, waiting to die. So, to see him like this," he smiled, remembering his grandfather's fire. "So alive, it warms my heart, so please forgive him, *mon chou*." He encouraged, sweeping his thumbs back and forth across her fingers.

It had been horrible to meet his one other relative this way. However, Chilli knew with absolute certainty, Timon Tournier did not get a second chance to make another impression, and she didn't care how old he was, which reminded her. "How do you know how old I am?" she asked, removing her hands.

"When you were admitted, I brought your things."

"You snooped in my handbag?"

The acerbic look Arno levelled at her made an embarrassed

heat surge into her cheeks for questioning his integrity.

"Your handbag was open when I picked it up, and your things fell out," he explained, before flashing his hands in irritation. The pounding in his head was magnifying. "The fact remains, you didn't tell me."

"You didn't ask."

He tipped up an enquiring eyebrow. "*Non*? I distinctly remember asking."

"Does it really matter?" Chilli avoided knowing she had been guilty of lying and not wanting to be called out on it. Everything that happened since that night was insignificant in the grand scheme of things.

"I would never have touched you if I had known."

Chillitara looked at him, unable to keep the knowing gleam from her eyes. "You sure about that?" she asked, her lips tipping up into a confident smile. She may be inexperienced, but she was very much aware Arno couldn't keep his hands off her and needed very little encouragement to indulge himself.

Arno's jaw locked, but his eyes dipped to the enticing vee of skin at her neck. He wanted to lean forward and lick it. He settled for reaching for her hands again instead.

"I need to tell you something," he began, forcing himself to look into her eyes, and not the swell of her breasts. Her skin looked so smooth and soft there.

"What?"

He swallowed before confessing. "I knew the condom had split."

It took a second for his words to sink in. "Excuse me? I distinctly remember asking you if everything was all right," she tried to pull her hands away, but he held on. "You knew I could have got pregnant, and you said nothing? You lied?"

"Yes," he admitted quietly.

Chilli gasped. "Do you have any idea what you have done? What you have started?"

He shrugged. None of it mattered anymore, and he said as much.

"You are so selfish!" she stormed, managing to pull away and stand over him.

Everything that had happened, she thought, her entire life being derailed, the worry she and her grandmother faced every moment of every day, all of it, could have been avoided if he'd had the decency to tell her about the broken condom and not lie about it. She could have taken care of it and not been in this mess.

The baby made a small cooing sound. It sailed across the room to reverberate into her heart. She walked over to him, feeling the heavy guilt of her thoughts. Her perfect baby boy. She would have lied about her age and gone up to that hotel room with Arno a thousand times if the outcome were going to be Mylo, she knew, feeling the warm love for her child overflow from her heart.

"I'm sorry," Arno said into the silence, picking up the water jug to pour himself a glass, wishing it were a measure of Hennessey instead.

Chillitara sighed, touching Mylo's tiny fingers, before turning to Arno. "It doesn't matter. You gave me my son."

About to drink, Arno asked. "What have I done?"

"Pardon?"

"You said I'd started something," he said, turning over her impassioned words in his head. "What?" he prompted, replacing the glass, his drink untouched. "What did I start?"

"Nothing," Chilli avoided, moving to the set of drawers at the other end of the suite. She opened a drawer to look at the array of tiny clothing.

"Chillitara," he warned. "I have the right to know what you are keeping from me."

"Look, Arno," she began, unable to hide the irritation from her voice. She was so tired of him talking, *hovering*. "You are the man who accidentally got me pregnant." She stated dismissively. "You have no role in my life."

Arno all but growled, stalking over to her, crowding her into the tall chest of drawers. "We were lovers before you even knew you were pregnant," he reminded her fiercely, "so yes, we may have done things backwards, but we had a relationship."

Chilli pursed her lips, looking up at him. "Really now?" she said. "Is that how you want to remember it?" she went on, pushing against his chest, but he wasn't moving. "We had sex, and you thought nothing of lying to me the whole time we had a *relationship*." She made bunny ears at his words.

"None of it counts." She scoffed. "You're a liar." Chilli laughed up at him. "Will the real Arno Tournier please stand up?" She invited, clapping her hands slowly.

"I lied?" he snarled. "What about you?" he moved even closer. "Let's start with your age and go from there," he suggested with light menace. "You took off without telling me where you were. Not to mention the apartment in Paris. Who owns that, hmm? Some other wealthy bastard you've been having sex with?"

"You mean some other wealthy bastard who can't keep his hands off me?" Chilli countered scornfully. "I have men waiting in line, Arno, didn't you know? I have apartments all over Paris and London. Did you think–"

His dark brows dipped even lower at her words. "*Cesser*! Stop," he ordered into her outrageous tirade. He made a valiant effort to get their conversation back on track. "Did you even think to tell me your mother died giving birth to you? The risk?"

"And that would have made a difference, because?" she challenged.

"You could have died!" he shouted, inflamed just thinking about it. "Who owns the apartment?" he asked again, not wanting to relive that God-awful day both she and Mylo had touched death.

"None of your business," Chilli replied.

Arno's eyes became slits, and for a wild moment, Chilli thought she had pushed him too far, and he was going to explode, but he breathed in so deep the buttons on his shirt pulled taught.

"Why doesn't Meredith live there?"

"You need to ask her."

"I'm asking you," he'd had a good snoop over the weeks, and aside from a few essentials, there was nothing of either of them in there. "Why doesn't it look lived in?"

"What does it matter?" she asked, stalling.

"Where is the rest of your family?" Arno caught her hands at his chest, where she was trying to push him away. "Your father?"

Chilli swallowed. Too close. He was getting too close. Chilli didn't talk about her family to anyone and scrambled for something to tell him, anything to send him off track.

She licked her bottom lip and tipped her head to look into his eyes. As she knew it would, the air shifted, and his eyes went from dark stormy green to glimmer and swirl with sexual awareness.

"I have my grandmother," she whispered, walking her fingers over his chest, up to his neck, to stroke the warm skin behind his ears, before plunging into his long hair, tugging at the soft strands. "Like you, I was raised by the only person who mattered."

Arno didn't know how it happened, but one moment they were savagely snipping and snarling at each other, and the next kissing wildly. She felt so good, her lips so damn sweet he couldn't help pushing his tongue inside to take over her mind.

Chilli thought she had the upper hand, but in seconds Arno had her pressed against the drawers, her hands held above her head out of his way, to lean his entire body against hers, making her feel the blatant length of his need for her.

Arno smoothed one hand urgently down her body and up again, frantically cupping and squeezing her breasts, and Chilli gasped into his mouth at the pleasure of it.

Arno stilled before scrambling backwards, as though she had sprung spikes all over her body. A tide of fierce red drenched his cheeks.

"Damn it," he swore, flinging himself away and turning his back. "I hurt you."

"No," she assured him quickly, ashamed of herself for starting the kiss in the first place. She was not the type of person to play games like this. Chilli quickly re-did the buttons he had opened and watched him take several deep breaths. "I liked it."

"You're right," Arno said eventually, looking out of the window. Nurse Aimee was talking to an orderly. Arno recognised him as the one that wheeled Chillitara between floors. He was friendly and always available to them.

"About what?"

He turned then, his eyes tortuous as they tracked over her, taking in her swollen lips and her shirt buttoned haphazardly. She looked like she had been thoroughly ravished, he thought in self-disgust. He was ashamed of himself. She was still recovering from surgery. She was still a patient. "I can't keep my hands off you."

Chilli smiled and walked towards him, one arm outstretched, inviting him into her embrace. "It's not a problem, Arno."

"It is for me." He asserted with a grimness that rooted her to the spot.

Avoiding her hand, Chilli watched him stride towards the door.

"You're too young to be going through this. All of this," Arno stated without turning. "It's not fair. It's not right." He took a deep breath, but it didn't make him feel any better. "I should never have touched you." He declared, with his hand on the doorknob.

Dumbfounded, Chilli watched him, hearing all that he was saying, and all that he was not. "Arno?"

If anything, his back became even stiffer. "I promise I will not touch you again."

Then he was gone.

**

He'd forgotten his coat. The coldness of the air finally penetrated through his clothes to seep into his bones, but Arno kept walking.

He couldn't believe what he'd almost done. His hunger for her was bordering on obsession, and he didn't appreciate the total lack of control he had around her. He had never been like this with anyone. Ever. She tied him up in so many damn knots he could no longer trust himself.

At some point, misty rain had started because his hair flopped like long rat tails into his face. He raked it back impatiently and walked on.

Paris, he scoffed internally, the City of Love. Or was it the City of Lights? He couldn't remember which, maybe both, but whatever it was, it was mocking him. All the lovers holding hands. Oblivious to the light rain and the cold. Simply happy to be with each other. The lights, Paris was a pretty place, he thought, slowing his pace, noticing what most Parisians probably took for granted, the Eiffel Tower, standing as an altar to the city, enticing couples to commit to a lifetime of happily ever after.

It mocked him, the whole damn city mocked him, especially when he stopped, and the tower flickered a thousand dancing lights at him. The lovers turned to watch, and he forced himself to move on. To escape.

He knew what he had to do and allowed the cold air to freeze his thoughts. He didn't need to overthink it, to give himself excuses. This was what he had to do. Wasn't it? Damn it! He couldn't think, yet he couldn't help the messed up iridescent swirl of indecision forcing him to do the right thing. This had to stop.

A young couple walked towards him, laughing and clinging to each other, only parting at the very last second to go around him, before continuing to smile and giggle without a care, not bothered by the stranger blocking their way. They just flowed, like water, around him.

Had he been like that in his twenties? So carefree? He thought about what he'd been doing. The partying, staying out all hours for days on end, the lies and manipulation. Doing the right thing had backfired into the worst situation. Twenty-two? Hell, he'd been an irresponsible, self-absorbed fool.

Arno swore at his stupid, self-deprecating thoughts and turned around. Only the subdued lights of a side street drew him, and he walked towards it. It wasn't very late, and the road was deserted in that discreet, wealthy way that only the privileged few would recognise. The addictive air of exclusivity.

Seven shops in total, he counted, walking down the narrow street with cobbles glistening like iced buns. Some shops were closed, and he slowed to appreciate the creative displays. He didn't want to think. He didn't want to feel. The darkness of guilt was what he wanted to consume him. He welcomed it. Instead, he opened the door to one shop, sat in the black leather chair with gold piping, placed his feet on the footrest, and waited.

****

"What have you done?" Chilli gasped when Arno entered the suite hours later. It was not the curiosity of the bags in discreet colours and famous logos that he was holding, or his rain-sodden clothes that had her gobsmacked.

He'd been gone for hours, hadn't answered her calls or texts, and she had become increasingly worried, knowing he wasn't as familiar with Paris as she was.

Fortunately, Dr Dupuis had brought her a new pump to try, and it was magical. Chilli had distracted herself for about an hour, filling several bottles with breast milk so Arno could feed Mylo.

She moved towards him, not liking the watchfulness in his green eyes where he remained stiffly by the door, looking beautifully familiar, yet undeniably different.

"My hair?"

"You cut it," Chilli stated simply.

"*Oui.*"

"Why?"

Arno shrugged and waited.

Chilli stopped in front of him, feeling tears burn behind her eyes. He was a handsome man and losing his hair didn't distract from that. Over the weeks he had let his beard grow through, not really having the time or inclination for a full shave, he'd said. Now the hair on his face was neatly trimmed and shaped close to his skin. His eyes looked larger, rimmed by thick eyelashes, and framed by dark eyebrows that had been partially hidden behind his long strands. He now had less than an inch of hair on his head.

Arno stepped to the side, being careful with his proximity. He didn't want to touch her or brush against her, Chilli realised, turning to watch him place the bags on the table, and stride to the en-suite, where he washed his hands, and donned a clean gown, before going to Mylo.

"How's he been?" he asked, peering down at his son, who was sound asleep on his back. Chillitara had changed him into a T-shirt that read '*As handsome as my Daddy*' on it.

"Great," she gave him an update on what the doctors had said while on their rounds. He hadn't missed any of their visits before.

"I have a present for you," Chilli said into the silence when he stood to stare at her, his hands in his back pockets. She took a bottle from the fridge. Arno wasn't himself. He was too quiet, too watchful, as though keeping himself removed in case he might break. Or maybe keeping himself removed in case she might make a play at him, she thought with disgust. She will never forget that look on his face when he'd swung away after the kiss.

Arno looked at the bottle. "You pumped,"

"We can share feeds."

Arno stared for a moment before nodding.

Silently, he walked to his bags. "Here." he gave her the small pink box with the flamboyant script of a famous bakery.

"Thank you," Chilli lifted the lid, "It's too pretty to eat." She giggled, taking out the elaborate cupcake to lick at the mountain of swirling white cream icing decked out with silver stars and pearls. "I need to take a picture." She said, taking a nibble, and closing her eyes, appreciating the sultry sensation of sugar dissolving on her tongue.

Arno watched her beneath hooded eyes and swallowed hard before diving into the next bag.

"Here," he said solemnly, balancing the square velvet box in his palm to her.

Chilli stilled, apprehension skittering through her as she looked, frozen in place, at the box. He had asked her to marry him on several occasions, and biting the corner of her bottom lip, she reluctantly lifted her head. He looked the same, yet so different. Sombre. His entire face was stark without his lovely hair.

Chilli placed the cupcake carefully on the table and tucked her hands behind her back. "Arno, you know I can't–" she began awkwardly, stopping as his brows slowly pleated. "I don't expect–" she tried again.

Arno shook his head in understanding, feeling like a fool. He opened the pale blue box to reveal a pair of halo-cut diamond earrings nestled inside. "These are a thank you for my son." He said quietly, against the raging furnace burning inside him. When had the flames replaced the ice?

"Thank you," she said, when he handed her the box, tipping it this way and that, for the earrings to catch the light. "They're beautiful." She choked, feeling her throat tighten. Chilli didn't know why she felt like crying. She'd told him enough times, especially today, that she wasn't getting married.

Arno took her hand and pulled her to the chair. Sitting opposite, he quickly opened another box to reveal an eternity ring. The diamonds were cut to match the earrings.

"I know you're supposed to get this the year after you get married," he began carefully, balancing the box on his thigh to take the ring out. "But we have never done things the right way." His lips twitched but didn't quite make it into a smile. "I want you to wear this ring, knowing that I will always be here for you and our son." He reached for her hand and looked into her eyes. "I promise you I will love him and protect him for eternity," he vowed. "And I will cherish your friendship until the day I die." He slipped the ring onto the middle finger of her left hand.

Chilli allowed the tears to fall, watching him slide the ring solemnly into place. It was beautiful.

"Arno?" she sniffed. Something had shifted. Something had changed within him. When he looked at her, his eyes were the deepest green she had ever seen, and his features stronger and more angular.

He leaned forward and reached for both of her hands, clasping them tightly. "You are the bravest, most selfless person I have ever known," he began quietly. "You have your whole life ahead of you, a business to run, and you need to influence the world." He smirked, knowing he still didn't understand what she did. He raised her hands to his lips and kissed them both. "You have given me my son, and I won't ask any more of you." He drew in a long breath before saying his next words. "When you are both discharged, I will accompany you to England and see you settled."

"What are you saying?" She asked.

He dipped his head and took a deep breath before capturing her troubled gaze. "I'm letting you go."

CHAPTER TWENTY-THREE

She wasn't settled. Chilli stood at her window and looked out. It was gloomy and wet with a prediction of unseasonal thunderstorms to add to the never-ending greyness. Would England ever have a proper summer, she mused, turning to close the curtains against the dreariness. Her new ring caught the light, and she paused, still not used to seeing the circle of diamonds on her finger.

They had been discharged two days after he had given it to her. With the advanced warning, Arno could arrange their travel itinerary.

They were chauffeured in obscene luxury, accompanied by a private nurse, from the hospital to her doorstep in England.

Even the ferry crossing at Calais had been smooth. So, what could have been a traumatic journey wasn't. She'd been dreading the journey for weeks, thinking and dismissing ideas for the best way to travel to England with a premature baby.

Returning to the UK still seemed surreal. She was home, yet it didn't feel like home. The original plan was to find a new house before the baby was born. She'd had several viewings lined up, but obviously, Mylo's early arrival had put paid to that. However, her grandmother was coming tomorrow to help her hunt for something more suitable.

At Arno's insistence, both Mylo and herself were now registered at a private medical facility.

He had upgraded her old car to a new family-friendly SUV. Chilli had only accepted it because he'd been threatening to hire a chauffeur for her use at all times if she didn't.

They got on well, and for the first time, with the distraction of sex, resentment, and pregnancy out of the way, they became friends under the guise of normality. He slept in the spare room with no complaints.

With Arno looking after the baby, Chilli went to work for a few hours. Her staff were still very dedicated, and her businesses were ticking over nicely.

Arno had formally met Vinny, who had declared himself Mylo's godfather. They'd also lunched with Kerry and Noah before they returned to America.

Then Arno was gone, and she still felt his absence. He called several times a day and video-called every evening. She filled him in on how their son was progressing. He was right on target. Mylo was feeding on demand and now had lovely fleshy creases on his arms and legs and smooth, chubby cheeks.

Chilli was doing a lot of work and had apologised to her followers for not sharing her pregnancy with them. From the many positive comments, she hadn't damaged her brand.

She introduced Mylo via a picture. Skimmed on the difficulties of his birth and promised to share more when she was mentally ready. Chilli had gained three million views in under thirty-six hours after that post.

Marketing opportunities came flooding in, and she and her staff were picking through the more lucrative ones, where she was paid handsomely for doing nothing more than reviewing a baby product or nursing bra.

Yep, things work wise were booming. But she couldn't settle.

***

Chilli was wondering if she was doing the right thing. With her grandmother in the back seat beside the baby, they had driven to France two days ago, stopping overnight in hotels along the way as they made their way slowly south.

Her grandmother had arrived in England, looking worried and stressed, and within a few hours, they were on the road to France.

To appease her and listening to her valid arguments–it wasn't about her anymore, she had Mylo to think of–Chilli packed up what could fit in the car, locked up her flat and left.

She had never seen her grandmother this pale and suspicious, and she had caught it, looking into the rear-view mirror every so often to see if anyone was following them.

Chilli couldn't relax and had a tension headache that had been hammering away for days, and because she was nursing, she refused to medicate herself.

Her grandmother had said she was being followed around Paris. She'd told her about being with Timon one evening at the theatre, and how she had noticed a tall, dark-skinned man watching her and being obvious about it. She thought she had seen him at the hospital, too. Fortunately, Timon had returned to the vineyard that night, and after donning a short black wig, pearls with a grey conservative twin set, and low court shoes, she had left Paris for England that night. When Chilli had picked her up from the airport, she hadn't recognised her.

Chilli's phone vibrated where it lay in the middle console. She knew it would be Arno. He usually rang about this time of the day, but she ignored it, knowing Tournier Vineyards wasn't far.

Chilli recognised the turn that led to her beloved little cottage and the sweetest of memories. She slowed, tempted to see it, but continued on, driving for another mile. It wasn't long before she saw a wrought iron sign announcing Tournier Vineyards. The last time she had seen that sign, disaster had happened, she remembered grimly turning her thoughts to the views.

The scenery was stunning. She could see miles upon miles of bright green vines in every direction as she drove on. The landscape differed from her previous visit, where it had been pretty, but stark, and she wondered if she would ever witness a full vine-growing calendar.

She drove over a short incline and saw the entire Tournier estate spread below. It took her breath away. Without the distraction of cars, pomp, and ceremony, she could really appreciate the beauty of the château.

Built from local stone, it glowed soft yellow in the summer sun. Three floors, a wealth of floor-to-ceiling windows–Chilli counted twelve on the third floor alone–several chimneys, and two tall turrets sat proudly at both ends. Each capped with glistening slate.

She was a modern, clean-lines kind of woman, but could appreciate the beautiful architecture and history of the château.

Blooming hell, she thought, not wanting to re-visit his lies, but Arno really had hidden who he was from her.

Would he be happy to see her? Uninvited? In his territory. His *real* territory. Doubt swamped her again, and she thought about what he'd said when he'd told her goodbye over a month ago.

She'd made him scrambled eggs and toast for breakfast, and afterwards, quietly helped him pack, dreading the moment he said goodbye. He'd been her pillar of strength all these weeks, and for the first time in her life, her grandmother aside, she'd relied on someone other than herself. Yes, he'd annoyed her, but really, his hovering wasn't all that bad. It showed he cared.

He'd been standing in the doorway of her flat, his back to the stairs, his bags at his feet.

"My home is your home," he'd said. "It is simple, *oui*?" he hadn't wanted an answer. "You come home."

"Oh yeah, remember the last time I did that?" She'd teased, wanting to lighten the moment, but the tears still escaped. "Stupid hormones." She remembered saying and dashing them away with her fingers.

Arno had tipped his head to the side, searching her eyes with his, capturing and holding her gaze. It was as though he'd been looking for something. With a small smile, he'd reached over and cupped her face, wiping away her tears with his thumbs. It had been the first time he'd touched her in weeks.

"It will be nothing like that," he'd said, those lovely green eyes of his shining fiercely, a slight pleat between his brows. "I promise you."

With a last look at Mylo sleeping soundly in his cot, he had kissed her forehead and left.

Chilli drove to the entrance of the château, stopped and turned off the engine.

The elaborate wooden doors were shut tight. That infamous night they'd been welcoming and flung open with beautiful people pouring out.

"What should I do?" Chilli asked quietly, trying not to let those dreadful memories of that awful night overwhelm her.

He'd promised, she silently chanted. My home is your home, he'd promised.

"Timon said only three of them lived here," her grandmother advised, looking about.

A lot of her grandmother's sentences now began with 'Timon said' these days, Chilli realised with amusement. It was Arno who'd told her their grandparents had spent several days in Paris together.

"Including Agnes."

"Agnes?" Chilli asked over her shoulder.

"Their housekeeper."

"Oh."

"You can't stay here," Meredith urged impatiently. "Go out and ring the bell."

"What if Arno isn't here?" Chilli asked instead, biting her lip. This was ridiculous, she scolded herself. She was never nervous, yet somehow, seeing those marble steps again, and that unwelcoming closed door, had her feeling sick to her stomach. Not to forget, her life would change forever once she knocked on that door. It was too much.

"Someone was at the window."

Chilli peered at the house. "Where?"

"It doesn't matter where, Chillitara," Meredith snapped. "Just go and knock on the door."

Chilli jumped at her grandmother's harsh tone. She was guiltily aware she had been dallying and delaying the inevitable. It was hot, and they were both worried, tired and travel-worn.

She got out and closed the car door gently, not wanting to wake Mylo and again thanking God he was such a quiet baby. The heat was oppressive in the blazing sun, and she quickly climbed the steps. There were eight, she counted. She could feel sweat already trickling from the underside of her breasts and was glad she was wearing a floaty strapless maxi dress in shades of red, with slits on each side.

Just as she looked for something to alert the occupants of her presence, the door opened, and a beaming older lady with cropped grey hair and rosy cheeks greeted her.

In rapid French, she introduced herself as Agnes and told Chilli to drive to the rear of the house, and she would meet her there.

Strange, Chilli mused, Agnes hadn't asked who she was.

She returned to the car, thankful for the air conditioning, and drove to the back.

The château was spectacularly dramatic at the front, and warmly enchanting at the back. There were multiple buildings built in the same stone, but they were unseen from the front. A vast gravelled courtyard, with a fountain with four prancing fish spewing water, stood off-centre. Strange, there was a fountain at the back, she mused curiously, parking the vehicle in a patch of welcoming shade thrown from a building.

The beaming Agnes came to a doorway and waved them inside.

Chilli helped her overly tired grandmother down from the large vehicle, and with her hand on her elbow, gently escorted her inside. The journey was too much for her. Her grandmother looked every bit of her seventy-six years.

She saw her seated at a large table in the centre of a vast kitchen, before going back for the baby and his bag. Everything else could wait.

With the car door open, the bulky baby bag over her shoulder and being careful not to wake him, Chilli picked Mylo up, not bothering to use the carrier as she found it too big and cumbersome.

Mylo had been a trooper. He'd slept through most of the journey and nursed comfortably. Placing a cotton blanket over his head–to protect him from the sun–Chilli turned, hearing rapid galloping thundering towards her.

A huge black horse was storming across a field, its rider wearing dark jeans and a white shirt that caught the wind to bellow sail-like behind him. Chilli could only stare. They tore into the courtyard with a loud clatter of hoofs and came to a dramatic stop, kicking up gravel beside the fountain.

The rider jumped off and tapped the horse's flank without acknowledging the beast obediently trotting off.

Chilli was caught. She couldn't move. Never had she seen such a beautiful sight as Arno riding that horse and stalking towards her as he was now. His stride was long, sure, and possessive, his eyes bright green, where they tracked over her and the baby in her arms.

He didn't stop, just wrapped his arms around them both and brought them into his chest.

"Welcome home."

CHAPTER TWENTY-FOUR

With Mylo held loosely in his arms, Arno walked him up and down the room after feeding and burping him.

Chillitara had once explained how difficult it was to adjust her way of thinking. Mylo was three months old, but really, if he'd been born on his due date, only just reaching his milestones as a newborn. Arno understood, and what counted most for his little boy was for him to gain weight. He'd catch up with his peers when he was ready.

Arno still couldn't believe Mylo was here. He'd spoken to Chillitara multiple times each day, even this morning, and she'd never said they were in France or coming to the vineyard. It was a puzzle, and he may ask her about it, but really, he didn't care. She'd come to him of her own free will. That was all that mattered.

"Where is the mother?"

Arno looked at his grandfather, who had quietly entered the room. He rarely ventured from his suite, yet here he was in the main living room, leaning heavily on his cane.

"She's resting,"

"Where?"

"In my bedroom," Arno didn't like the look his grandfather sent his way and read precisely what the older man was conveying, with the disapproving tilt of his chin and steely glare in his eyes.

"I'll sleep elsewhere," Arno conceded before his grandfather silently mimed something else using his expressive face.

After refreshments in the kitchen, Arno had taken Chilli and the baby upstairs to his rooms. He really hadn't thought anything more than having them close.

Timon sat down on the nearest chaise lounge. "Tomorrow, you will bring in the decorators, and transform the west wing for Chillitara and my great-grandson." He ordered.

"Transform?" Arno repeated, unable to keep the amazement from his voice because his grandfather resisted change and concentrated solely on the vines.

"Modernise, refurbish, transform, call it what you will," Timon brushed aside. "You will make sure she has every luxury," he advised. "Every floor is for her," he ordered. "Convert it to fit her needs. Bedrooms, office, kitchen, nursery. Everything."

Arno looked at his grandfather in growing disbelief. "You've always said to leave it as it is." Nothing had changed in the west wing since his grandmother had died. It had been her favourite part of the château, and at her death fifteen years ago, his grandfather had locked it up and moved out. No one had lived there since.

"Bah," his grandfather exclaimed, flapping both hands at him. "That was before. Chillitara is a princess, and you will treat her as such."

Arno laughed at his grandfather's outrageous order. However, he was going to follow his instructions to the letter and make damn sure Chillitara had no desire to live anywhere else.

"When are you getting married?" Timon asked next.

Arno didn't even flinch. He was used to his grandfather's straight-talking. "You were there when she refused, remember?"

"You are a Tournier!" Timon banged his cane. "Are you going to let one little refusal stop you?" he challenged. "Court her. Make her fall in love with you and secure my great-grandson's legacy. Another generation of Tourniers."

"Grandfather," Arno began slowly. He didn't want to be having this conversation. "It's not that simple."

"Why not? You made a baby with the woman. Make more." He banged his cane again. "Do you want another man to raise your child?"

Another man with his family? Arno fought the urge to throw

something.

"I need to respect her decision not to get married." His mouth tipped down.

"Bah! You've done nothing. She loves that child you're holding and will give you many more babies." Timon smiled in satisfaction. His eyes glazed over at the thought.

"I've done enough to her." Arno closed his eyes, feeling the festering guilt that was always there gush to the surface. He picked up a chair with one hand and placed it in front of the only father figure he had ever known. "Grandfather, I need to tell you something."

Arno told him about Mylo's birth and the complications. He told him about them both almost dying, and all that Chillitara had lost. He spoke quietly and succinctly, trying, but failing, to keep the emotion from his voice.

When he finished, his grandfather held out his arms for the baby, and Arno gently placed Mylo there.

"My great-grandson deserves to have all that we have, Arno. He is a Tournier," Timon stated solemnly, kissing the baby's forehead. "We will have a welcoming party for his mother, and you will make sure she wants for nothing. We owe her, Arno." Timon said aloud, although silently plotting and planning his own agenda. Tourniers were bright, but not in love.

Arno nodded in agreement but took responsibility for himself. He owed her.

***

After a light tap, Arno entered his bedroom. His enormous bed was empty where he'd left Chillitara resting, but he could hear movement in the adjoining bathroom.

Kissing his son's forehead. He looked at the bomb that had exploded in his bedroom. Evidence of Chillitara and his son was everywhere.

A lion-themed travel cot was beside the bed. A mechanical rocking thing on the floor. Bags of nappies piled in one corner.

Chillitara's furry suitcase, as well as two others, a travel bag in another corner, and two plastic heads with her wigs on it sat on his dresser. One wig was long and wavy, the other was straight and blonde. He loved the colourful chaos of family life in his room.

Hearing the door open behind him, he turned to see her standing shyly in the doorway. They had lived together in the hospital for weeks, and then at her flat. The air crackled and snapped with heavy emotion.

"Hi," Arno said.

"Hi," she replied, holding the lapels of his robe together at the neck. "I hope you don't mind?" Chilli apologised, indicating the long heavy gown. She'd forgotten to take her clothes with her into the bathroom.

Arno smiled with appreciation. "It looks better on you than me," he said, trying not to think of her nakedness beneath his robe. She must be getting hot though, he thought, as he only ever wore it in the winter months.

They looked at each other. The silence stretched awkwardly before Chilli walked into the room.

"Is he sleeping?" she asked, standing on tiptoe to peer at their son in his arms.

"He finished the bottle, had a manly burp that raised the roof, and now he's out like a light," Arno laughed. "I need to put him down." Arno kissed his son again. He couldn't get enough of him. "But I don't want to."

"He'll sleep for longer if you put him down," she advised, guilty of ignoring her own advice on numerous occasions.

They looked at the cot. It was a lot lower than a conventional crib, and Chilli moved to take the baby from Arno's arms, but he shook his head.

"It's okay," Arno said, bending at the waist. "On his back or front?" he asked.

"Hmm, on his front for now," she said. "He'd spent a lot of time in the car seat today."

Chilli watched Arno lay their son down and when he

straightened, moved to loosen the blanket. Mylo liked to sprawl out when he slept.

"Are there any mosquitoes?" she asked.

"Too windy," Arno advised, and watched indulgently when she covered the cot with a mosquito net, anyway.

Satisfied, Chilli stepped back and, side by side, they gazed lovingly at their little boy.

"I can't get over how much he's grown," Arno said, unable to keep the awe from his voice. "And so much hair."

Chilli chuckled. "He definitely has your hair and long limbs," she agreed. "And he's only interested in eating and sleeping."

Arno chuckled alongside her and when it ended, lapsed into an uncomfortable silence when they looked at each other.

Arno's eyes dropped. The robe had gaped at her neck, and he could see inches of smooth skin. His body instantly clenched, as he knew it would.

To distract himself, he sauntered over to the window. The sun was still shining and brushing the lower clouds with pink light.

He felt Chilli come beside him. She'd used his shower gel.

"The château is beautiful," she admired, looking out. She could see the fountain and grapevines. "Is this all yours?" she asked.

Arno traced his land through the window. "As far as the eye can see. I'll take you on tour tomorrow."

"No, please," Chilli jumped in, putting her hand on his arm. "I don't want to monopolise your time."

He looked down at her. Her face was scrubbed clean, and a brightly coloured headscarf covered her hair. The large bow turned jauntily at an angle. The style reminded him of the African women he saw in Paris. His eyes lowered, taking in everything about her. She looked so young and sweet. Too young for what had happened.

"You won't be taking me from my work, Chillitara. I have a team. Sometimes I even let them show me what they can do," he teased. "Tomorrow I'm yours, yes?"

She smiled up at him. Arno delighted in seeing the dimple

beside her mouth appear. He swallowed.

"You're looking well." Arno didn't understand why their conversation seemed so forced. Yes, he could, he acknowledged to himself. It was the crackle and snap. The air laden with sexual energy. A sexual force that was going to go unfulfilled if it killed him, he swore to himself.

She tipped her head to the side. "What were you expecting?"

He shrugged his broad shoulders and smirked at the same time. "Oh, I don't know," he began, his eyes dancing over her. He needed to move. Get out of the room. Leave the chateau. Instead, he went on automatic pilot because if he'd had his wits around him, he would have stopped his hand from reaching out, and ran his finger gently down her cheek. "You are beautiful," he said, feeling his heart squeeze. "Even more so since becoming a mother."

"I don't feel it," she stepped back and looked down at herself. "I've not lost any baby weight."

Arno's eyes blazed over her. The thick fabric of his robe muted her curves, but he could still see them, and they were still as luscious and mouth-watering as he remembered. Luscious, he laughed to himself, realising he only ever used that word to describe her.

"You looking for compliments?" he joked with a wink.

Her head whipped up. "Oh, my goodness no!" she exclaimed, one hand going to her chest. "I don't feel like myself. I've been so busy I've not been to the gym," she explained. "My diet hasn't been great these past few days. And the long drive didn't help."

"Why didn't you tell me you were coming?" Arno asked, only because she had brought it up.

Chilli moved away from the window. With her back to him, she picked up her suitcase and placed it on the unmade bed.

"I wanted to surprise you," she said.

They'd never done the couple 'surprise' thing. Their relationship hadn't been that intimate. Her words didn't ring true. "You wanted to catch me out," Arno stated instead, after several grim heartbeats.

Chilli opened the case, shocked at his words. "What? No," she shook her head in denial. "I really wanted to come."

Something was off. Her words were there to placate him, yet she hadn't said them to his face. Arno's eyes narrowed, watching as she suddenly took great interest in the contents of her suitcase, unfolding and unrolling clothing to place on the bed.

"I don't believe you," he said into the silence and voiced his the one conclusion. "You wanted to catch me out. Cheating," he charged. "You will always hold that one night over my head!" he said, narrowing his eyes at her, "I told you, that *kiss*," he gritted. "Was nothing."

"Why are you getting angry?" Chilli asked, unrolling a long skirt and placing it on the growing pile she had already unpacked. "I'm here, aren't I?"

Arno drew in a deep breath, frustrated she still had her back to him. "Yes. But why the cloak and dagger stuff?"

"We can always leave," Chilli snapped, having enough of his dog-with-a-bone attitude, and picked up the skirt, and rolled it back up to repack it.

When Arno realised what she was doing, he grabbed it from her and threw it across the room. "Don't you ever say something like that to me again."

"I think this was a mistake," Chilli picked up another dress. The white dress he said she looked like a prostitute in. A timely reminder, she told herself. She should never have come.

"You will take my son out of this house over my dead body," Arno warned quietly.

"That won't be a problem, Arno," Chilli promised, turning to face him, slamming her hands on her hips. "You can't make us stay."

"Really?" he cautioned, stepping closer. "Try it," he leaned over her, "and see how far you get."

Chilli could not believe how or when their light teasing had disintegrated into this ridiculous debacle. She didn't need this or him, she told herself, storming past the rigid block of wood called Arno, to pick up the dress she'd worn earlier. It was still in a pool on the floor, and she stepped into the centre, to drag it up her body under his robe.

CHAPTER TWENTY-FIVE

"What are you doing?" Arno asked in confusion, watching her wriggle her hips and keep the robe from slipping off her shoulders at the same time.

"What does it look like?" she pursed her lips, then snapped. "I'm leaving."

In frustration, Arno snatched her up to throw her down onto the bed, where he immediately covered her body with his.

"Get off," Chilli screeched.

"Shut up," Arno growled. "Just. Shut. Up!"

"I–"

He kissed her, cutting off her words. She got in his head, made him say things he didn't mean, tied him in knots, and to top it off, was so damn mouthy, he made a vow there and then, to kiss her every time she opened her mouth to shut her up.

Chilli's resistance lasted all of three seconds. It had been a long time since she had been kissed. His lips weren't hard or punishing. No, they were much worse. Lethal weapons skimming over hers, his tongue nudging and pleading to be let inside.

She sighed against him, opening her mouth to let him in.

Chilli could kiss him forever, she thought, loving the feel of his short hair tickling her palms, and the strength of one thigh insinuating itself between her legs. His hands gathered her closer, making her feel that hard part of him, branding her centre.

Arno kissed her like he'd wanted to kiss her for months. He couldn't get enough of her sweetness and completely lost it, feeling her rock her hips, inviting him to press into her.

He groaned against her, rolling his hips urgently, kissing her deeply, before releasing her mouth to kiss and nibble his way down her neck. She still had on the heavy robe and the long dress underneath, and he growled in frustration, desperate to feel more of her skin.

Using his ears, Chilli guided him back up to her, kissing and sucking on his bottom lip, before quickly opening the robe and pulling the dress down under her breasts. She then placed his hand on her chest and smiled against his lips at his groan of appreciation.

Arno swooped down, urgently raining kisses over her face, neck and chest, moving to lift and cup her beautiful breasts in his hands.

Chilli felt divine. A delicious warmth had spread throughout her body, and she opened her legs wider.

Arno smoothed one hand down and then up under her dress to skim over her leg. Up and down, up and down he went with his hand, while his tongue licked her breasts, swirling around and around each nipple, before pulling a stiff pouting peak into his mouth.

Chilli shot into mega sensation. She needed to feel him deep inside right now. With an urgency she had never shown before, she bucked against him and coiled her legs high around his hips, telling him with her body what she desperately wanted.

Arno caught her mouth and lifted off her long enough for her to get to his belt.

She quickly undid the smooth leather and pulled it through the loops to throw it onto the floor. As soon as she had the top button undone, and the zipper down, she burrowed her hands under his briefs to cup the hard muscles of his hair-roughened glutes, dragging him closer and urging him on.

Arno had lost every bit of sense the moment he kissed her. It had been so long. He'd wanted her for so long and couldn't control his thoughts or actions.

She tasted better than he remembered, her skin smoother, her delicate scent more intense, and he was pulsing with a hardness to reclaim her and make her his. The need elemental, organic, in its intensity.

In a rush, he gathered up her dress, quickly bunching the fabric over her hips out of his way.

Her sex was bare, and just the thought of knowing she'd been so naked under his robe had him roughly grabbing himself and lining up at her entrance.

He teased her, taking a moment to bathe himself with her juices, to slow them down, wanting to treasure the moment she became his again.

"Arno,"

It took a moment for him to realise she was calling his name. The hands on his shoulders were pushing against him.

"Arno,"

"Hmm," he went to kiss her. To stop her from thinking.

"We can't," she said, moving her head aside. "The baby."

He stilled, her words infiltrating his fogged mind, and leaned away from her. "What?"

"Mylo, he's crying."

"Damn," Arno quickly moved away.

Chilli scrambled up, pushed the robe from her shoulders and pulled the dress up and over her breasts as she went to the baby, picking him up.

"I'm sorry sweetheart," Chilli apologised to her son, rocking him gently on her shoulder at his slight, stuttering whimpers.

"Is he okay?" Arno asked, adjusting his clothing, but guilt making him fumble. He hadn't even heard Mylo cry out.

"He's fine," Chilli said, gently patting the baby's back.

"I'd better go," Arno said, rubbing his hands over his head, wishing he had long hair, as it was more satisfying to stab his fingers through when he was feeling frustrated like this.

"Okay."

"I'm sorry," Arno said.

Chilli looked at him then, hovering by her shoulder when she gently lay Mylo down. "For what?"

Arno flicked his gaze to the bed and then back at her. Her

headscarf had slipped off, and her curls were a messy cloud about her shoulders. He remembered another time she had looked like this and felt the guilt lacerate his conscience.

"I should not have touched you."

"Really?" Chilli asked with a raised brow. "Are you going to take off again and come back with more guilty diamonds?" she inquired sarcastically, and to help him out, suggested, "A bracelet would be nice," she said, stabbing him with her eyes. How dare he stand there looking at her like that? Again.

"I didn't mean for it to go so far," Arno mumbled, pulling himself up to his full height. "I lost my head."

"We can have sex Arno," Chilli told him candidly. She didn't know why he was so serious about it. They had a satisfying sex life and then a thought occurred to her. "They gave me the all-clear."

Arno shook his head. "No," he stated grimly. "We can't have sex."

"Why not?"

He gaped at her as though she had lost her senses. "Because you almost died!"

"Are you stupid?"

"Call me stupid one more time, Chillitara, and you will regret it."

"I regret it already," she charged, glaring at him and then at the messy bed. "And stop threatening me."

"I apologise."

"And stop apologising!" she yelled, incensed at his higher-than-thou attitude. "So, because I had a difficult birth, I can't indulge myself?"

Good, she got it. "You have to be careful."

"Says who?"

"Says me," he folded his arms over his chest. "I'm the cause of everything happening to you. I won't sleep with you." He said stubbornly. "I almost killed you!" he blurted.

"You're an idiot."

"Call me–"

"Yes, yes, I know," she cut in. "I'll live to regret it." She rolled her eyes at him. "So, I have to live a life of celibacy because you have issues?"

"No. Yes." Arno knew he sounded crazy, like the idiot she called him, but he had to lay down the rules. She was young, and he knew best.

"And what about you?" she raised questioning brows at him. "Do you have to live like a monk, or am I the only one having to suffer a life without intimacy?"

"Of course I will."

"How very disciplined of you," Chilli sneered. "But I'll tell you this," she went on with a tight smile. "I'm very much alive, and if you don't want to touch me, well..." she left that sentence hanging, and by the deep red tide sweeping up his neck to surge into his face like a violent riptide, knew he'd received her message loud and clear.

"Go near another man and see where that gets you." He warned with a calmness that belied the blaze of verdant fire in his eyes.

Chilli tipped up her chin. "I'm twenty-two years old."

"I'm well aware of how old you are, Chillitara," Arno breathed in deeply, not wanting to be reminded of her age. Her age was precisely why he had to take charge and look after her. "Make yourself comfortable tonight. I'll be sleeping in another room."

"Of course you are." Her words dripped with icy sarcasm.

"Not because of this," he shot back. "Respect for my grandfather."

"Oh,"

"Did you bring the baby monitor?"

"Yes," she frowned at his question. Still steaming from his attitude. "Why?"

"Put it on and come with me."

"Where?"

"Grandfather has given you the use of some rooms," he advised. "I'd like to show them to you. Get your input."

"Are you sure?" Her body was still throbbing, reminding her of an intimacy that hadn't been fulfilled, and she wanted to thump him, even though she'd never been violent towards anyone in her life. "I don't want my proximity to be a challenge for you."

Arno narrowed his eyes at her but didn't rise to the bait. "Just put the damn monitor on." He stalked swiftly to the door. "And meet me at the top of the stairs." He snapped, opening and closing the door behind him.

"And that, Mylo baby," Chilli said, looking down at her sleeping son, "is your father."

CHAPTER TWENTY-SIX

"Where's Mylo?" Arno asked, watching Chillitara take a selfie between the kitchen doorway and a window.

She was angling her camera above her head and deepening the curve of her back. She playfully posed, pouted, and smiled as she touched the rim of her hat like a professional model.

They'd planned to meet at the fountain after breakfast to tour the vineyard. Well, he'd intended to take them both.

"He's with the greats," Chilli explained, stashing her camera away when she reached him.

Arno's brows pleated. "The greats?"

Chilli tugged the peak of her hat down lower on her head. The day was already promising to be a scorcher, and she reached down, twisted the hem of the off-white T-Shirt she was wearing into a knot, and secured it under her breasts when she reached him.

"The great-grandparents," she clarified. "It'll be too hot for him, so I thought it best to let them dote on him for a bit," Chilli explained. "We're playing golf?" she asked, seeing the golf cart parked nearby.

"I thought we could take that for our tour."

"I'd rather ride."

"You ride?"

"Hmm-mmm," she confirmed with a nod. "Boarding school basics, horse riding one-on-one, along with bread making and elocution lessons."

Arno looked at her, seeing the hat, the shirt, and the skin-tight white jeans. Yesterday she said she hadn't lost the baby weight, and he appreciated every delicious new curve she now had. "I didn't know you went to boarding school," He said out loud, realising he still knew little about her and come to think of it, she was very private and unforthcoming with him, which contradicted her online influencer persona. "Where?" he asked.

"England. St. Ann's for Girls," she explained. "In the Peak District, Derbyshire."

"I know it."

"You do?"

"I spent a few years at the boys' school," he acknowledged with a shudder. "And hated every minute."

Her mouth dropped as she looked at him, floored. "Seriously? Oh wow," then she smiled. "Maybe we were there at the same time?" She suggested with a chuckle.

He shook his head while reaching out to tap the peak of her hat. "That's doubtful Chillitara."

"Oh, that's right," she rolled her eyes in the face of his seriousness. "Old fuddy-duddy that you are."

At his deepening frown, she winked and looked around. "So, where are the stables?"

"Not today," he said. "I'll need to see how you ride and choose a horse accordingly."

"I ride just fine," she told him, lifting her chin haughtily. "I would love to ride the black one you were on yesterday. He's beautiful."

"Sebastian?" Arno tipped his head back in surprise. "Not happening."

"A bit territorial, aren't you?" she teased.

"I don't share." He reached out again, pulling one of her curls which ended just above the slope of her breast.

"Horses?" she asked cheekily, knowing but not caring about the verbal prod she'd just poked him with. "Or other," she paused for effect, rising a single eyebrow. "Things?"

He smirked. "I'm an only child, Chillitara," he explained, knowing he wasn't going where she thought she was taking him. "I've never had to share anything in my life," he clarified drolly rising from the edge of the fountain. "Come, let's go." Arno took her hand and escorted her to the cart.

"I heard you went downstairs to the kitchen early this morning," Arno said conversationally, steering the cart away from the house and down a wide grassy path.

"Mylo was a little fussy," she told him, bouncing along the path and having to hold on tight. "I'd already fed him, so I went for some hot chocolate for myself. I hope you don't mind."

"Why would I mind?"

"It's your house."

"And now you live in it," he said with a careless shrug of his shoulders. "Do what you want."

They drove on in silence for a few minutes, and Chilli lost herself in her thoughts.

When they'd met on the stairs yesterday, Arno had had a complete personality change. He was cordial and pleasant, the epitome of good manners. He showed her what was going to become her wing, and oh, what a beautiful space.

Yesterday, she swore she was a modern, clean-lines, uncluttered kind of girl. Yet by the end of the tour, she was head over heels in love with the distressed furniture, feminine pinks and chintz. Softly coloured paintings of tropical scenes and dark-skinned children adorned the walls. Apart from updating the bathrooms, converting a room to a nursery, and re-arranging the current office, she was going to leave everything as it was.

After dinner, she took her grandmother to see the suite and choose a room. However, her grandmother said she was happy on the ground floor in the east wing, and besides, she and Timon planned to watch movies at night, and she didn't want to go traipsing back and forth, disturbing the baby.

Remembering the soft blush on her grandmother's cheeks, Chilli smiled as romance was definitely in the air.

Her grandmother had devoted her entire life to make sure she was safe, and Chilli was happy to see her relaxed and enjoying herself without needing to view everyone with suspicion.

"Why the smile?" Arno asked, seeing the dreamy expression on her face.

"Oh, nothing," she replied playfully, twirling a section of her hair with her fingers. "Where's the cottage from here?"

"Not far," he answered. "Want to see it?"

"No, not really."

"It's just over there," he pointed to a small hill on their right, "about five minutes," Arno clarified. "You know," he went on conversationally. "It was rumoured to have been a secret love nest for one of my married ancestors."

It was no wonder the food he'd brought had been piping hot in the plastic containers that night, she thought, preferring not to revisit his lies.

Blooming hell. He'd been playing with her feelings back then. Galloping all over the vineyard on that horse of his, no doubt to keep her ignorant of his wealth, and being just as deceitful as his married ancestor.

It was a pleasant morning. She learnt a bit about the process of winemaking, took several photographs she was going to keep private, and some she was going to share on social media.

She met Arno's foreman, and a few other people working the fields, and they returned to the château just as Mylo woke from his morning two-hour nap. Their son had a predictable internal clock.

With apologies, Arno left to speak to his workmen.

Chilli spent time with her grandmother and Timon, surprised Arno's grandfather wasn't like the unpleasant man she had met in the hospital.

Now, she put it down to worry. He'd been beside himself, not knowing where Arno was.

Timon was as old-fashioned as her grandmother was liberal. Yet, he was making it his mission to see them settled. He was surprised when she didn't want to change the décor.

Alongside Meredith and Timon, Chilli went for a walk around the château after dinner, with Mylo in his pushchair, only to excuse herself soon after and take the baby upstairs because he'd started fussing.

Within the hour, Mylo was crying uncontrollably. Chilli became increasingly worried as Mylo was warm to the touch.

He refused to eat and wouldn't settle. She burst into tears when Arno came.

"What's the matter?" he asked gently, taking her and the baby into his arms. He couldn't hear what she mumbled into his shirt, but after hearing Mylo's crying when he returned to the château, figured their son was the source of her distress.

"I'm sorry," she sniffed, moving away. "I don't like to see him like this," she confessed.

Arno's heart flipped seeing his son's red face, and tears pooling then streaming into his hairline, his little bottom lip trembling. "What's wrong with him?"

"I don't know," she placed her lips on Mylo's forehead, not for a kiss, but to check his temperature. "He's warm, but not too warm." she worried.

"Have you got a thermometer or something?"

"I can't find it," Chilli confessed tearfully, looking at the open cases on the floor, the contents strewn messily about in her search for the digital device. "I phoned Gabriel, and he said to give him some medicine I have first and then to wait. He said babies are susceptible to bugs, especially preemies, and I'm not to worry just yet." Chilli drew in a deep breath and sniffed, trying not to worry, per Gabriel's instructions, but it was hard not to, Mylo had never cried like this before. "I'm to ring him back in another ten minutes." Chilli looked at the large digital numbers counting down on the face of her mobile phone.

Arno sat beside her on the bed and accepted their precious son when she held Mylo out to him.

"I'm going to ring Gabriel now." She grabbed her phone and swiped it on.

"It's not time yet," Arno said, stopping her. "Let's wait."

She sniffed again and looked at her phone. Barely a minute had past since Arno entered the room.

"Who's Gabriel?" Arno asked to distract her.

"A close friend of mine," she told him. "He's a paediatrician."

"In England?"

"Hmm-mmm," she confirmed. "He's a gentle giant, built like

a rugby player, with tattoos on eighty per cent of his body including his neck," Chilli told him. "You would never think he's a doctor by looking at him," she chuckled. She hadn't seen him since the night they shared a taxi. She explained his relationship with Vinny, whom Arno had met.

When she paused, they realised Mylo was calming down. His little face wasn't scrunched up and red with distress anymore, and his eyelids were drooping.

"He is falling asleep," Arno observed. "The medicine is working, yes?"

"Yes, thank God," Chilli leaned over to touch Mylo's forehead with her lips again. "He's cooling down."

"Good," Arno smiled at her, and Chilli smiled back with relief.

By the time her phone flashed several zeros, Mylo was asleep in his father's arms, and she called Gabriel to tell him what had happened. It was good to get his reassurance, and he gave her the name of one of his paediatric friends in the region, to get Mylo checked out.

By the following afternoon, Mylo was registered at a French clinic and declared well. Arno bought her an ice-cream cone to celebrate, and they returned to the château relaxed and happy. Which didn't last.

There was a tall, thin woman waiting for them on the steps when they arrived, and she immediately signalled her disapproval for keeping her waiting, by the almost comical puckering of her lips, and coolness of her tone when she introduced herself as the nanny.

Chilli walked past the unsmiling woman with the crown of grey plaits around her head to go inside. She was so mad it was a challenge not to stomp up the stairs.

"That was rude," Arno accused, snapping the door closed a moment later. He'd apologised, escorted the nanny inside, and asked her to wait.

Chilli rounded on him. "You just hire a nanny without consulting me?"

"I thought you might appreciate the help."

"No you didn't," she charged, taking a clean onesie and nappy from the small pile on the dresser to change Mylo. "You don't think I can look after my own child?" She opened the snaps and carefully undressed the baby, who was alert and watching her with his lovely brown eyes. With a smile, Chilli blew raspberries on his stomach and when he laughed, did it again. "Do you like that Mylo?" she asked the baby, blowing on his belly again while trying to ignore Arno, who was hovering behind her.

"That's not it–" Arno began.

"Yes, it is," Chilli cut in, using the same voice she'd used with Mylo as she didn't want the baby to pick up any negative vibes, because she'd read babies were susceptible to different tones of voice. "Do you know what?"

"I'm sure you're about to tell me," Arno invited, crossing his arms.

"First impressions account for a lot," Chilli quickly changed and dressed the baby, who was already half asleep.

"So?"

"So?" she began, lifting the baby. "So, the battle-axe you hired didn't even look at Mylo," Chilli stressed. "She didn't come over, she didn't smile, she just stuck her hand out to you, I might add, and addressed only you. Now *she* was rude and disrespectful. I am not leaving my baby with someone like that. And that Arno Tournier," she flicked him a hard glance, "is all I'm saying on the subject."

"Your hands were full," Arno excused, uncrossing his arms to remove the mosquito net from the travel cot.

"My hands were full with a baby," she shot back. "What kind of nanny doesn't go straight for the baby?"

"I guess not this one?" he answered, trying not to laugh at the image she'd conjured. "She has years of experience."

She tipped her head to the side to sear him with her coldest look. "You know what your problem is, Arno?"

"You seem to know me better than I know myself these days, Chillitara. Why don't you tell me?" he invited, having enough of the entire conversation. She needed help, and the nanny came from a top agency, was mature, and came with glowing references. She was staying.

"You are ageist."

CHAPTER TWENTY-SEVEN

Arno rocked back on his heels, not believing he'd heard right. "*Excuse-moi?*" he asked in French.

"You heard," Chilli raised her chin, watching him and rocking the baby at the same time. "Older does not always mean wiser, Arno."

"You are being ridiculous."

"No," she denied lightly, walking around him to place Mylo, now fast asleep, in his temporary cot. "I'm not." She announced leaving the blanket off the baby before turning to Arno. "How old I am has always been an issue to you," she informed him. "From the beginning you wanted me to be." she tapped her chin, looking at the ceiling. "Hmm, ah yes," she snapped her fingers. "Twenty-six, just so you could feel better about taking me to bed, having a so-called relationship, and even a baby with me," she reminded him. "And then you dared to lie!"

"I didn't know about the baby." Arno defended.

Chilli's temper exploded at his words. That's all he had to say in his defence? *He didn't know about the baby?* She repeated silently. "You wish I were at least born in the same decade as you," Chilli accused, before going on. "But that's not even it. With this latest incident, you've treated me as though my opinion doesn't even matter, as though I don't have any sense, because I'm twelve years younger than you, and you've been holding my age against me ever since you found out!"

"That's not true." Arno denied.

"You don't respect me," Chilli continued as though he hadn't spoken, feeling her throat tighten with burning fury, and she tried to control her temper. "What were you doing at twenty-two?" she asked. "Partying? Running naked and drunk in the grapevines?" she scoffed, but didn't wait for him to answer. She was feeling cleansed with every word spoken.

"Yes, I had a meltdown last night," she admitted. "But I'm a mother. I cried because my baby was crying." She drew in a deep breath before letting out everything that had been upsetting her. "I didn't cry because I couldn't cope or anything else you've been concocting in that conniving, insulting brain of yours. I felt my baby's pain and was upset!"

"I–"

"I've not finished!" she yelled, then attempted to calm down, knowing she had let herself down by losing her temper like this. "So, do what you want with the battle-axe, but she isn't coming anywhere near my son or me."

"I'm sorry," Arno apologised, thoroughly chastised. He'd never seen her this angry, and he got it. He'd been high-handed and hadn't thought it through. Not only that, she had unwittingly given him an opening to tell her something important, and he hadn't taken it. He couldn't. Not yet. They were still on fragile ground, and sharing would make things worse. "I thought I was helping."

"Yes, well. I'm going for a walk," Chilli picked up the baby monitor and turned to him with her shoulders back and chin high. "By the time I return, that woman better be gone." She pinned him in place with her fiercest look. "Understood?"

Arno tried to stop his lips from twitching, knowing she wouldn't appreciate his amusement, but she looked magnificent, with her perfect breasts moving in time to her shuddering breaths, and the hands on her hips pulling the fabric of her trousers taut across her pelvis. He could see a slither of brown skin just above the waistband, and his mouth watered. "Understood."

With a final blistering look, meant to wither him to the ground, Arno watched Chilli stalk across the room, open the door, and leave.

Only then did he dare smile and wipe away thoughts of the chance he should have taken.

***

Arno was not smiling.

For the past few weeks, he'd watched Chillitara laugh and flirt with the latest additions to the household.

He'd come home one evening to find her with three hulking men, sitting on the floor, chatting away in her office like they'd been friends for goddamn years when, in actuality, they'd only just met.

His grandfather had thought it necessary to bring in extra staff, without consulting him. From the new chef, Benny. Rainor, the handyman, brought in to work in the house and gardens, to Rainor's identical twin brother Garen. Garen was currently holding Mylo like a rugby ball, nestled in the crook of his arm, while shouting at Chillitara to do another squat, like a drill Sergeant.

Arno watched with a slow burn in the pit of his stomach when Chillitara bent at the knees into a low squat, her arms out in front. The fabric of her silver gym leggings pulled tight across her thighs where she held the pose. The bright pink top thing she wore was nothing more than a bra, barely keeping her luscious breasts from tumbling out, when, following Garen's instructions, she started running on the spot.

He didn't understand why she was even working out so hard. It was not like she needed to. Her body was even more mouth-watering post-pregnancy. It was in the evenings when it was just the three of them, and she kept him company while he gave Mylo his last feed, and she wore silk pyjamas that covered most of her yet, showcased everything he adored–and tried to ignore–about her body, that he noticed her new curves.

Right now, her stomach was bare. Even from this distance, Arno could see the sheen of sweat covering her chest. His jaw locked. The slow burn turned into a flame, knowing Garen, the manny, was seeing everything he saw, only closer. Much closer.

Funny how she didn't have a problem with his grandfather

hiring staff, Arno thought. He loosened the fists he hadn't noticed he'd made. She'd been simpering and fluttering her eyelashes ever since the men had arrived.

From his vantage point by the window in his office, Arno, in the shadows, watched when Benny–his long dreadlocks bouncing against the backs of his legs–walked out with bottles of water for everyone.

Benny was opposite to the playful twins. He was watchful. He stayed on the sidelines, quietly observing. Then he would disappear into the kitchen to concoct exotic meals.

Benny was an excellent cook, Arno conceded, however, pressed his lips together, watching when the younger man peeped at the baby, his serious face softening into a smile.

Arno didn't want to like them. But they had already bonded with his family. The twins joined Meredith and his grandfather in the evenings, to play board games and go on walks.

Benny had put his grandfather on a special heart-healthy diet and, like now, was looking at Mylo, with heart-warming tenderness.

The day they'd arrived, Arno had grilled his grandfather where he'd hired the trio from. But Timon had merely said a friend had recommended them. What friend? Arno had asked. His grandfather had stiffly said he knows people.

The small circle was now joined by the other twin called Rainor, Arno observed. He was wearing bright printed board shorts, neon-orange trainers and his shirt was tied around his waist, leaving his heavily tattooed chest bare. The only thing that suggested he was a gardener was the secateurs he held.

Arno stared, flexing his fingers when Rainor took one of Chillitara's hands to twirl her around, his eyes sweeping up and down her body as though she were his next damn meal. The burn in Arno's stomach turned into a ferocious blaze.

They needed to go.

He would convince his grandfather. They'd managed for decades with casual workers. They could do so again. He'd vet and hire an old English butler and bring in a female au pair to help look after Mylo. He wasn't sexist or ageist or possessive, he added–seeing Garen place his hand on Chillitara's stomach–he was being practical.

"Ah, I see Chillitara is outside enjoying the evening."

Caught staring at the chatty quartet with heat in his cheeks, Arno turned to his grandfather.

"She should be working," Arno growled, turning away from the window.

"Nonsense," Timon sat in Arno's creaky chair behind the desk and leaned forward to fiddle with the neatly placed pens. "She works too hard." He stated, pushing the chair back to put his feet up on the desk, crossing his ankles. "Day and night, she is posting things on her social media, gaining subscribers on YouTube and followers on Insta and that nursery rhyme sounding thing."

With his eyes bulging. About to sit, Arno swung around to his grandfather. "How do you know what social media is?" Until recently, his grandfather had shown no interest in the internet, much less knowing the names of the different platforms or lingo.

"Meredith showed me," Timon explained, smiling. "Chillitara is a very talented young lady and will launch her podcast when she has settled. She is an asset to the Tournier legacy." Then his pale eyes sharpened. "Have you asked her to marry you yet?"

A self-deprecating laugh scraped up his throat. "I've told you before, Chillitara has no intention of marrying me."

"You want her to marry someone else?" Timon enquired, wide-eyed. "One of the twins, perhaps?"

Narrowing his eyes, Arno stared at his grandfather. "Why would she marry one of the twins?" he asked with forced lightness, against the streak of heat burning through him. "What do you know that I don't?" To ask, would be to reveal too much of himself, yet the words fell from his mouth, and he turned to look outside, seeing one twin hold Chillitara's ankles as she did sit-up after sit-up, while his brother sat crossed-legged on the grass cheering her on, and counting, with one hand on her bare stomach. Did they have to be so damned touchy-feely?

"They are fine-looking young men," Timon listed, holding up his hands and checking off his fingers. "They speak several languages, are educated, and fond of my great-grandson," he itemised. "If you won't do anything about it, the quiet one, Benny, would make a good husband and father." He suggested easily. "I don't want just anyone raising the boy. He's a Tournier. In any case," he flapped his hands again. "I like them all, and they each have my blessings."

Arno's eyebrows lowered with each unwanted praise and outrageous endorsement from the calculating old man.

"And they make her laugh." Timon continued, back to ticking off his bony fingers.

It was unfortunate for Arno that Chillitara's laughter caught the breeze and entered his office through the windows at that precise moment, filling every crevice of the room.

"Did I say they are handsome?" Timon repeated.

"You did." Arno drawled through gritted teeth.

"Have you made any headway?" Timon enquired. "Are you going to propose at the party? Have you told her you love her?"

Arno counted to ten. "Grandfather, it is complicated."

"You don't have to pledge undying love," Timon suggested. "Being a Tournier brings status."

"Grandfather, please," Arno avoided letting out his breath slowly.

"Bah," Timon flashed his hands in the air, and with surprising speed stood to stand by Arno. "You are going to lose that girl if you're not careful," he warned. "Benny makes her favourite omelette every morning. What do you do?" he didn't wait for an answer. "I saw them going into the wine cellar for longer than was decent." He added for good measure. "You are supposedly the wine connoisseur in this house, you're a Tournier, and I didn't raise a fool. Yet here you are, letting another man step onto your territory in more ways than one." He slapped the desk with his palm. "Show her you love her!"

"I don't know what love is!" Arno admitted with bite. Not

believing he'd said the word love out loud.

"You don't need to know," Timon shot back, flicking his hands around. "You liked her enough to make a baby with," he added, pursing his lips. "Start from there." He slapped the desk again. "You owe her a life of luxury and security Arno, I like her, and I don't want them living in England without our protection."

Arno frowned at his grandfather's strange choice of words. Protection? "I know," Arno answered, guiltily aware of the life he had taken from her, and the vibrancy her presence had injected into his own, as well as his grandfather's life. His grandfather would do anything to make them stay. So would he.

"You see that?" Timon asked when Arno came up beside him. Outside, Benny was now sitting on the grass with his back to Chillitara, their arms linked. Together, they pushed up against each other until they were both standing. Laughing, they high-fived and hugged like old friends. "Be very careful, my boy," his grandfather warned, turning away to leave the room leaning heavily on his cane. "Be very careful."

Arno watched. He watched them exercise together. He watched, ignoring the stiffness in his shoulders. He watched when Chillitara put the chilled water bottle to her neck to cool down and noticed the three men gazing at *her* thirstily when she drank from the bottle. All this while his son was being held in the arms of another, younger man!

The blaze in Arno's stomach turned into an inferno, and without thinking, he rapped several times on the window.

CHAPTER TWENTY-EIGHT

"I hate you." Chilli huffed through gritted teeth, flopping onto her back with relief.

Garen winked down at her. "All the girls do," he declared, his smile wide. "But the boys?" he fluttered his eyelashes and tossed his imaginary long hair. "All the boys love me Chilli." He placed his free hand on her thigh and slid it upward to rest on her waist. "Can you feel the burn?" he asked, dropping his usual playfulness.

Chilli looked up into his sky-blue eyes and held back the words she really wanted to say, clenched her teeth, and pushed through the crunch, feeling her insides squeeze and burn in objection at the abuse. "Yes, I feel the burn." She panted before falling back onto the grass.

"If you can talk, you aren't feeling it hard enough," Garen stated, sliding his hand over to her bent knee again. "Come on, Chilli, five more, and nice and slow. Control those abs when you go down."

"No, I'm done."

"Five more and I'll let you finish early."

"I've finished already."

Rainor moved to her feet, nudging his brother gently out of the way. "I'll hold your legs." he placed his hands on her ankles, and with an encouraging nod, pushed against her shins. "Only five more, honey. Hands behind your head."

"I really hate you," Chilli told Garen, fighting through another sit-up, adding when she exhaled, "and you too." She informed his brother when she was finally facing him.

Rainor laughed. "Everyone loves us," he declared, without humour. "Six more and hold for three seconds."

"You," she breathed, sending Rainor a dirty look at the top of the crunch again, "can't count." She finished quickly, flopping onto her back, breathing hard, and unable to string a sentence together, much to Garen's amusement if the knowing twinkle in his eye was anything to go by. She closed her eyes.

It had been her idea to get some exercise in when Garen took Mylo for his afternoon stroll. She had been regretting it ever since, not realising Garen would take it upon himself to be her personal trainer, with his twin interfering, and Benny taking his break to watch at the same time. Not even the esteemed SAS soldiers had this amount of training, she grumbled to herself, listening to the three men talk in rapid German above her. She tuned them out.

It was a lovely evening, the sun almost dipping low, keeping the air in the slight breeze gentle.

She was reluctant to make plans. Her grandmother was settled, obviously in love, and Chilli enjoyed living at the vineyard. But it was isolated. She felt a lot better when Timon introduced her to the twins and Benny, saying they were hired to assist her. They were always close by, but still...

She had one thorn in her side, Arno. He was being stubborn. Their relationship had evolved yet again, matching another one of his many layers.

They'd gone from a one-night stand to having an affair. They'd had a relationship and became parents. Now they were just acquaintances.

Arno spent time in her suite every evening, sharing Mylo's bath time with her, and then doing his last bottle before they both put him down for the night.

She enjoyed having him around, only he never stayed to talk to her, inquire about her day, or show any interest. He was cordial and watchful, and it was driving her mad.

She couldn't sleep having him this close. To see his boring shirts rolled up, showcasing the light dusting of dark hair on his perfect forearms when he bathed Mylo, was driving her insane. His hair was growing back, almost tickling the back of his neck now, and she desperately wanted to touch it. Touch him. But, as soon as they settled Mylo, he was gone! Anyone would think he had a curfew.

She couldn't do it. She couldn't live how Arno wanted them to live. No intimacy? She'd been fine after she and her first boyfriend had split up. The absence of touch had not bothered her libido in the past. But not anymore.

She was burning from the inside out, for Arno. She was so completely aware of him, she had to change her underwear whenever he left her wing. It was embarrassing, and it was stupid. She was angry at him for making her feel like this, for making her want him, without even trying. She'd once thought she'd been the one in control of their intimate moments. Now Chilli realised how very wrong she was. All he needed to do was roll up his blooming sleeves.

She couldn't live like this. Chilli had never played games like her friends Candace or Vinny. Either they became intimate again or—She stopped her thoughts from going where they had gone a few nights ago. An idea that had germinated as her body throbbed with unfulfilled awareness.

She peeped at the three men drinking water and talking beside her. Garen's arms were empty, so she knew Mylo had finally fallen asleep, and he'd put her son in his pushchair.

The three men were gorgeous and attentive. It would be so easy to... No! She argued with herself. She would not do it. Make Arno jealous? In his own home? No, she wasn't like that. That was too petty. Childish. Blooming hell, she could just imagine him telling her off and lecturing her about her immaturity in that aggravating superior voice of his.

She sat up and huffed. The men turned to stare at her. Benny held his hand out, and she clasped it, allowing herself to be hauled up, but he tugged harder, making her stumble against him.

He grinned and raised his eyebrows playfully.

That was the thing. The three of them flirted like mad but didn't take it any further, and Chilli appreciated it. It was all harmless fun.

"What you are wearing to the party?"

"Clothes are not a problem Garen, believe me," she replied, taking the bottle of water Benny was holding out to her and swallowing the cold drink with pleasure.

"You need to look Ascot-ready."

"What do you know about Ascot?" she asked instead, but laughed it off. "No, don't tell me. I don't want to know. Anyway, I can fly to Paris or get something delivered."

"No Paris," he dismissed with a quick shake of his head. "I like that pink polka dot dress with the matching hat."

"I'm not wearing a hat, and I need to lose more weight for that dress." Chilli declared, unsurprised that Garen knew her wardrobe as he did. He and Vinny would make great friends.

Rainor said something in his native tongue and suddenly grabbed her hand, holding it above her head to whirl her around and around.

"Hey!" Chilli laughed.

"You have a beautiful body," Rainor appreciated, stepping closer to skim his hands down her arms.

"Move off, Rainor," Chilli pushed him away. Only her hands collided with his hard-bare chest. Oh my, she thought, feeling his pecks jump at the contact before she stepped back, embarrassed. As lovely as his chest felt, it was the wrong chest she wanted to touch.

Loud knocking coming from the house made them all turn. Arno was standing at the window with his palm up and fingers beckoning, looking straight at her.

"Me?" Garen pointed at himself and then his brother when Arno shook his head.

"I think he wants me, guys," Chilli clarified, rolling her eyes at Garen's comical antics, and stepping around Benny, who had somehow partially blocked her view.

"Him?" Garen shouted, now pointing at Benny, only to grimace and hunch his shoulders, when, even with the expanse of green lawn between them, you could see Arno's eyebrows lower and his eyes narrow in temper.

Chilli turned towards the pushchair, "I'll take Mylo—"

"No, I'll take the little guy upstairs. You see what the master wants," Garen advised, already dashing ahead of her. "Don't rush back. We have plenty of bottles in the fridge, and I'll give him a bath and settle him in."

The men walked off. Benny in one direction, the twins in another. They waved at Arno when they past the window. But Arno didn't acknowledge them. He stood with his arms folded high on his chest, with eyes pinned unblinkingly on Chilli.

"Someone's finally going to get some." Rainor chuckled to his brother when they entered the house, glad he'd noticed Arno silently watching them earlier.

***

Chilli tapped on the office door twice before entering. It was gloomy inside the room after the brightness of the gardens, and she blinked several times before locating him in the shadows. His back was to her. He said something terse into his phone–that she couldn't quite hear–before disconnecting.

"Hi," Chilli said from the doorway. She didn't know why she was breathless. She hadn't run down the halls or anything, but her chest felt tight.

"You let them touch you," Arno said.

"What?" Chilli asked, unsure if she'd heard his softly spoken words correctly.

Arno turned then, tracking his eyes over her body. A body displayed to perfection. But not for him. Arno felt his blood bubble and churn through his veins like boiling mercury.

With effort, great effort, he reined in all that he wanted to say, pulled in a deep cooling breath, and with studied casualness, walked towards her, exhaling slowly, calming the poking violence, when he really wanted to grab the twins, and that damn chef, and kick them off his vineyard, and out of France.

"How are you, *mon chou*?" Arno asked as casually as he could, around the vicious coil tightening his throat.

"Huh?" Chilli couldn't keep up. He didn't look right, his face pale although slashes of deep red, streaked along his cheekbones, and he was holding himself stiffly, flexing his fingers at his side, as though wanting to go a few rounds in a boxing ring, yet he called her sweetie? He hadn't used that endearment in months. "What's the matter?"

Chilli watched Arno blink several times.

"Arno?"

Rubbing her arms against the frost rolling off him, Chilli moved from the door. It was odd seeing him at this hour. "Is everything okay?"

She watched him tilt his head to the side and stand even straighter, tipping his chin higher, so, feeling at a disadvantage, Chilli stepped within touching distance of him.

He was wearing an old pair of grass-stained jeans and a pale cotton shirt. A hat covered his wavy hair, completing his work uniform.

"Yes," he answered. "We're going for a ride."

"Now?" Chilli asked, she hadn't thought about riding since that first day, mainly because she had been busy settling in, supervising the slight renovations she wanted in her wing, liaising with her staff in England, testing products, creating content, and most importantly, establishing a routine with Garen and the baby.

Arno nodded. Looking over her head.

Chilli waited, knowing something was off. She was close enough to touch. He was cordial, but his relaxed stance seemed forced.

"Are you sure everything is okay? The grapes?" she asked, biting the side of her bottom lip.

He worked alongside his labourers trimming the leaves from the vines as soon as the sun came up. Apparently, grapes needed at least seven hours of sunlight to absorb essential nutrients, she'd learned.

"The grapes are fine. The vineyard is fine. All of France is fine." He answered with a quick frown. "Do you want to ride or not?"

Chilli tried to read the expression in his eyes when he did design to look at her, but he pulled his hat lower, casting half of his face in shadow before flicking his gaze away again.

They had lost that spark of friendship they'd cultivated over the weeks after Mylo's birth. Maybe this was his way of trying?

Something was wrong. The air was charged with it. But he wanted to ride? Chilli smiled brightly, letting excitement chase away the skittering trepidation she felt in her bones. "I'll change," she turned towards the door. "Meet you at the stables?" She suggested over her shoulder.

"No, you're fine."

Chilli looked down at herself, about to argue, but Arno grabbed her hand, weaved his fingers through hers and opened the door. This was the first time he'd touched her in weeks. Thoughts of changing clothes, even her own name, flew out of her head.

Arno pulled her towards the back of the house, through the kitchen–where Benny and Agnes gaped opened-mouthed when they passed–and out into the gravelled yard, with Chilli kicking up the pebbles as she struggled to keep up with his long-determined stride.

He walked them to the stables and once there, clicked his fingers in the air. One of the stable lads led out Arno's huge black horse in one hand and held out a black velvet helmet in the other, passing it to Arno.

Arno slammed the hat on Chilli's head, fastened it under her chin, and said, "no arguments," when she opened her mouth to object.

Chilli didn't really mind and was looking forward to riding her own horse. Only Arno had other ideas. Before she realised what he was about to do she found herself airborne, plonked into the saddle–where she almost slid off again in fright–before Arno mounted behind her, secured her against his chest with one arm, and with a flick of his wrist, Sebastian sped off.

CHAPTER TWENTY-NINE

Chilli had no choice but to slide one arm around Arno's back, and cling to his arm that held the reins, to keep herself from falling.

Always in control, Chilli had never ridden aside before. It should have been unnerving, yet it wasn't. The taste of excitement that licked against her skin in the evening breeze, and the solid wall of Arno's chest pressed against the side of her body, had her snuggling deeper into the protective curve he made.

Between the rhythm of the horse beneath her thighs, and weeks of pent-up frustration, Chilli stopped thinking altogether.

With intimate familiarity, she turned her head to touch the tip of her tongue to his warm neck. She could taste the sun and salt from his morning spent working in the fields. She tasted him as though she had every right to kiss him.

Arno's arms tightened about her, but he didn't slow down or turn his head to kiss her. He rode on.

Clenching her thighs and snuggling as close as she could to the muscled curve of his body, they rode into the small, dusty yard of the cottage.

Chilli saw little of the pretty building that held her happiest memories. It was just a blur of aged stone before Arno dismounted, quickly tugged her down by the waist. Grabbed her hand and pulled her inside.

He slammed the door shut with his booted foot, yanked off her helmet, threw it down, and crowded her into the wooden door at her back.

Arno captured her face between his large hands. His fingers went to her nape, gently tipping her head back. "You let them touch you," he growled against her lips, his green eyes glaring into hers. "When you *know* you belong to me!" He seethed, before kissing her for all he was worth.

Chilli lost herself in the feel of him. He was everywhere, storming all of her senses with his lips, his teeth and his tongue, yet still, she wanted him closer, pulling at his hair, diving under his shirt, gliding her fingertips up and down the strong indention at his spine, searching for more of that something only he knew how to give her.

Then he stepped back. Breathing hard. Watching her with eyes so dark, the green looked almost black.

Chilli felt aroused, exposed, and terrified all over again. The memories of similar scenes played on repeat in her head. She remembered the other times when, after kissing her, his lovely mouth would twist and turn down in self-disgust.

She waited. Unable to breathe. Waiting for Arno to ruin the moment by saying something obnoxious. But he surprised her, canting his head to one side, his eyes clearing slightly, and said. "Murderous."

Chilli blinked, trying to understand his harshly spoken word, thinking that maybe she had missed something. "What?"

"You once asked me how I would feel seeing you in the arms of another man," Arno clarified, his eyes pinning her in place and shoving his hands into the front pockets of his jeans, repeated. "Murderous."

"Oh." There was nothing else to add. Chilli's whole body was on high alert, her nipples pinching painfully, and she knew without looking down that they showcased her obvious arousal. She dropped her eyes and was unsurprised to see him, not faring much better. His arousal displayed long, heavy, and promising within the confines of his dark jeans.

"Should I be worried?" Chilli wanted to joke in the face of his anger, but her words sounded weary. He was still watching her, his body straight and tight as though a sudden movement would cause him to shatter or commit murder.

She watched his jaw twitch, and his eyes narrow where they blazed over her, lingering on her hair, her lips, and her breasts, dropping lower, causing her to press herself against the wooden door for support.

One side of his mouth tipped down and he nodded slowly. "Worried? Yes, you should be," he warned. "I asked you to marry me," he reminded her solemnly. "You sent me packing." His brows lowered at the memory. "You come down here, making yourself comfortable, and before you open that pretty little mouth of yours and insult me," Arno charged, seeing her about to say something he likely didn't want to hear. "I'm not complaining. I want you here." He captured and held her gaze steady. His eyes dull.

Chilli should have been scared, but she wasn't. Something delicious and dangerous flittered through her instead, making her breasts swell even more within the confines of her bra top. She was hot, burning up on the inside.

Months of waiting had culminated to this. She wanted it. She didn't dare move or speak; grateful the door was anchoring her in place.

"You were trying to make me jealous," Arno reasoned, watching her. "Letting them touch you like that," his dark eyebrows snapped down at the memory. "Right in front of me."

Arno over thought things, and she needed him to stay focused. Yes, he held a power over her, but she also held a power over him, and right now, she wasn't ashamed to use her body to get it.

Chilli watched his lovely mouth tighten around the edges, and she wanted to reach out and reassure him it wasn't true. Yet he had been jealous. She hadn't needed to make him notice her. Unbeknownst to them all, he'd been watching from his office window and coming to his own conclusions.

The twins were naturally playful, their interaction with her completely innocent, unlike his kiss with that woman, but she didn't need to defend Benny or the twins. She could have simply pointed out that she hadn't known he was in his office, but he didn't need to hear that. What he'd seen had brought them to this pivotal moment, and she was thankful.

"No, Arno," Chilli admitted, shaking her head. "I don't need to involve anyone else."

Chilli watched his chest expand before he looked at her with tortuous eyes. His exhale was long and measured. "What do you want from me, Chilli?"

He rarely called her by her nickname, and to hear it made her heart break for him. He wanted honesty, yet honesty in words would send him away from her forever, and probably regulate her from acquaintance to some other undesirable label.

She took a deep breath, wanting to share something of herself with him. She remembered those nights when, separated by an ocean, they'd opened themselves honestly, completely. Pleasuring themselves as they watched each other. That had been honest.

"I want you to ease the ache I have here." Slowly, she smoothed her hands down the sides of her body, glorying, when his lust-filled eyes tracked the seductive movement, and he swallowed when she pressed the heel of one hand into the throbbing vee of her sex, easily outlined between her thighs.

"Is that all you want?" his voice was deeper and rougher, his English words almost suffocated by his lovely French accent.

It was so typical of him to overthink and psychoanalyse everything. They were in the most perfect location and alone. Today, she intended to get what she wanted.

Chilli reached up, pulled the band out of her hair, and shook out her loose curls, before looking at him from under her lashes. Seduction one-on-one.

Chilli moved slowly, pressing the palms of her hands into the scarred wood behind her, thrusting her chest forward for him to see what he did to her. He wanted honesty. She was giving him honesty. She was showing her vulnerability.

They had been lovers before; they would be again.

"Yes Arno," Chilli finally replied, running a finger along the elasticated edge of her top, beneath the curves of her breasts. "This is what I want." She pulled the top over her head, dropping it to the floor, and naked from the waist up, stepped towards him, holding his gaze. "You are all I want."

She kissed him.

Arno took over the second she touched her lips to his.

She felt herself being lifted off the floor, and knowing what he liked, quickly wrapped her legs around his waist, anchoring herself to him, when he pressed her against the door once more, kissing her deeply.

His hands were everywhere, spanning her waist, sweeping over her chest, pinching her nipples, pushing the globes of her breasts together, urgently sucking first one, and then the other, deep into his mouth.

His boots beat against the old wooden flooring, eating up the space, where he quickly crossed the room to the stairs with her clinging to him.

Chilli moaned deeply, pulling his hat off and finally running her fingers through his hair. She had to grab the silky strands when he tripped on the steps, almost dropping her. She laughed against his mouth at his frustrated growl.

He didn't make it.

Arno stopped midway up the narrow stairs to gather Chilli closer, kissing along her neck, and frantically pulling at her leggings to touch her.

Chilli tried to help, but he was everywhere, so instead, she lifted her hips and gloried in his urgency to make love to her.

Arno placed one hand on the step above her head to support his weight and glided his hand down the smooth plane of her stomach, and into her leggings, with the other. She was hot, her panties damp, and he leaned back to watch when he finally palmed her sex.

Chilli held his gaze, touched the tip of her tongue to her throbbing bottom lip, and opened her legs wider, inviting his fingers deeper.

Arno smoothed his hand over her, pressing down with the heel of his hand on the forward motion, and curling his fingers, faster and faster still, before finally dipping inside.

It had been so long. The emotion deep. Chilli gritted her

teeth, trying to hold off the orgasm that was building rapidly under the magic of his fingers. She had wanted him with her to feel this rush of love and emotion together, but she couldn't escape it. He knew where to go, finding the sweet little patch of nerve endings that made her gasp and scream and fall apart in his arms once again, and she held him tight, wanting to cry from the emotion of it all, but didn't dare.

She held him, scared of what he might say or do next. Chilli sucked and nibbled on his neck. Anything to distract him, to stop him from thinking. And after a moment, she finally felt his whole body soften above her, and she smiled against his skin. The wooden stairs, barely cushioned by the worn carpet, dug into her back, but she didn't care. He was finally in her arms with his fingers still inside her.

Arno shifted slightly, looking down at the acres of smooth brown skin beneath him, and he slid down her body, licking a straight line between her breasts, the tip of his tongue swirling into her belly button, before trailing to her sex.

With his hands on her inner thighs, Arno pushed her legs further apart and dipped his head.

She tasted divine, and he lapped and lapped, alternatively fluttering and flattening his tongue against her folds, before sucking her swollen nub into his mouth.

She bucked against him, but he pressed on, barely wincing when she grabbed at his hair, forcing him to stop when she powered through yet another orgasm.

Arno tried to move, but Chilli pulled him closer, kissing him deeply, and reaching for the opening of his jeans to pull him out, hot and heavy, into her hands at the same time.

"Right here, right now," Chilli ordered, using one foot to push the rest of her leggings down to her ankles, giving him full access to her body.

She was naked from her ankles up, her body undulating under the blatant messages of what his fingers and mouth evoked with each touch.

She gloried in the feel of him, and pushed his denim

jeans, rough on her hyper-sensitive fingers, down over his firm bottom, to drag him into her.

Arno fumbled for a moment, unable to reach her properly, the stairs too narrow and too steep, then he stepped urgently over her leggings, and groaned out loud finding her open, glistening and ready, when she helped by climbing her legs high over his hips, to lock her ankles at his back, tipping her pelvis in readiness to receive him.

Arno had never felt such a tremendous feeling of relief as when he slid inside her. Chilli was just as tight and welcoming as he'd remembered. He tried to slow down. He wanted to savour the moment, but she wouldn't let him. Her inner walls grabbed and strangled his sex, cutting off his breath, and his control slipped.

Like a maniac, Arno thrust and surged inside her, groaning deep, chasing his release. With his free arm at the small of her back, he desperately pulled her closer still. Lifting her higher when he climbed another step to surge so deeply, she screamed and splintered around him. Arno almost lost consciousness from the violence of his orgasm, shouting his release, and collapsing on top of her, totally depleted when he continued to pulsate inside her for long seconds.

Eventually, catching his breath, Arno kissed her neck before leaning away by placing his hands on either side of her head. He smoothed her lips ever so gently with his, before searching her face and looking solemnly into her eyes.

Chilli didn't know what he found, but his beautiful mouth tipped into a slight smile, and she saw a glimmer of the humour he always tried to stifle and whispered. "Now I want more, sweet Chilli."

CHAPTER THIRTY

With Chillitara snuggled into his side, Arno stroked her silky skin from the side of her breast, down into the dip of her waist to climb over her hip, and back again with his knuckles. Like a satisfied cat, she would purr and undulate against his hand.

Their lovemaking was more intense after months apart. They had been making love for hours. Arno knew this feeling of bottomless contentment could only be achieved with her.

She made him feel like he'd never felt before, every emotion enhanced, everything he had ever felt. Maybe this was the real thing? It had to be.

"What's wrong?" Chilli whispered, feeling the sudden change in his body. The fingers he'd been touching her with had stopped, and his heart had raced beneath her ear.

Alarmed, Chilli quickly coiled one leg over his, locking him in place when she looked up at him. They had just spent the most magical hours ever together. She had missed him. Missed what only he could give her.

She refused to return to how they were. She was going to fight, and using her free hand, reached up to cup the side of his face, and turn him towards her, before he ruined it all.

Arno's eyes were shining bright green in the dim slither of light cast by the partially open bedroom door, and he was smirking as though he had a secret, Chilli noted in confusion. Instead of pulling away, he gathered her even closer, making a low, contented growling sound as he did so.

"Everything," he stated, copying her movements to cup the side of her neck, his fingers going into the curls at her nape. "Everything," he repeated, "is finally right." Arno declared, leaning down to kiss her brow.

They stared at each other and it was Chilli who broke the spell. "Shouldn't we be going back to the château?" she asked softly.

Arno gave her a small squeeze. "Not yet."

"Mylo–"

"Is in excellent hands."

Arno resumed his stroking, and Chilli, not wanting to fuss, snuggled down again, content to listen to the rhythm of his breathing.

"I have something to tell you." Arno began a moment later.

Chilli, fighting the rhythmic waves of sleep, pulled herself to the surface, already bracing herself at his quiet words.

"I have no regrets," she stated quickly before he could say any more, only to feel his chest vibrate under her face at his low chuckle.

"I know you don't," he smirked in a whisper. "I can feel the sting of your nails on my back, and my ears are still ringing from your screams." He teased, and then after pulling in a deep breath, said, "you once asked me what I was doing at your age, and I never answered."

Chilli made to move, but he gently pressed her head down until she relaxed against him.

"You were right. As a teenager, I used to get drunk and race horses through the vines with my friends," he told her. "But never naked," he tacked on, chuckling, only to suddenly close his mouth into a tight line. "I was an irresponsible idiot. Spoilt and arrogant," he listed. "The type of person too much money and minimal discipline stereotypically becomes.

"Grandfather did his best, but I was wild with no direction. He sent me to boarding school to cool off. It worked for a while.

"I worked in the vineyard, found my love and respect for our grapes, and worked hard to produce the finest Cabernet in France. We were wealthy and became more so. Suddenly a market leader and one of France's top three producers." He said with pride. "That's when things started changing. The faces around us. Me," he amended grimly, "changed. Everything was exciting, including the women," he admitted. "But you were right. I am a simple grape-picking labourer at heart. I just enjoyed an excess of everything–the women–for a while."

"Do I really want to hear this?" Chilli asked quietly, feeling something sharp jab her heart, imagining him with other women.

"You have to,"

Arno shifted them both again until Chilli was almost tucked beneath him, and one hair-roughened leg was placed over the both of hers.

Chilli lifted her hand to touch the skin behind his ear, but he caught her fingers and brought them to his lips.

"Please don't distract me," he said gravely, capturing and holding her gaze. "I thought I was in love once," he began. "I'd grown tired of the unfamiliar, the cities, and I played closer to home instead." His mouth turned down at the memories he preferred to forget. "I got her pregnant."

Chilli gasped. "You–"

"I married her."

Chilli tried to sit up. "You were married?"

"Not for long," Arno said quickly, shifting his leg higher to keep Chilli in place. "She played games and was never pregnant."

"I'm sorry, that must have been hard," she fell against the pillows. "How old were you? Twenty? Twenty-one?"

"Twenty-two," he was quiet, and Chilli patiently waited, knowing there was more.

"Both of us were the same age as you are now, and she and her money-grabbing family played me like a damn fool."

"I'm sorry," Chilli soothed again. "What happened?" It was no wonder Arno had always been so hung-up about her age. It all made sense.

"I tried to make it work. You know, be a man," he admitted, shaking his head. "I was miserable. Her family was very much in our lives, wanting money, guilt-tripping and accusing me of taking advantage of their young daughter. When they started hinting that they wanted to live at the château, I finally swallowed my pride and went to my grandfather. To cut a long, unpleasant story short, grandfather paid them off. She went overseas, and we divorced."

"Good."

"She came back," Arno told her grimly. "Tonight, I'm telling you everything, and I want you to listen and not get upset," he warned, feeling Chilli's body tense as she held her breath. "It was–"

"Phillippa," Chilli finished for him. It was obvious. Only an overly familiar woman could touch him as she had done when Chilli had seen them together.

His breath came out in a huff, and Chilli felt it bathe her face. "Yes."

"Why are you telling me now? What's changed?"

"We've changed. You and I," Arno moved yet again, although Chillitara was still glued to his side.

"She came back and wanted us to give it another go now that we're older," he shuddered. "She thought I'd forgotten what she did." His laugh was more like a scraping of his vocal cords. "I didn't."

"Suddenly she was always here, following me around, trying to make herself useful, inviting herself on my morning rides, and reminding me of the playboy I used to be." Arno paused for a moment.

"Then she changed tack," he said. "She tried guilt, saying I'd ruined her life. Forced her to live overseas. The thing is Chillitara, I don't feel guilty anymore. Back then, I was a shallow twenty-two-year-old fool. All my friends were," he revealed with embarrassment. "I was immature and spoilt, seeing only what I wanted to see," he admitted. "But I understood her games, *oui?* The rules. They were safe and familiar."

He kissed the tender spot at Chilli's temple.

"All I'd wanted was to be with you, *mon chou*. Every minute of every single day. I didn't recognise it for what it was. The feeling. Then you were gone. Vanished. For a while I was fooling myself, thinking that maybe you were–"

"If you dare say like her, I will kill you!"

He chuckled and smoothed his hand down her body to rest his palm on her hip. "You don't have a mean bone in your body to kill me," he clarified with confidence. He looked down at her, his verdant eyes dancing. "And nobody can love you as I do, so you can't kill me." he kissed her quickly and used three fingers under her chin to close her mouth. "But I'll come back to that."

"You love me?"

He tapped her nose. "*Oui*, I will come back to that okay?" he arched a single eyebrow waiting for her to be silent.

"Okay." Chilli conceded, although wanting to smile in the face of his declaration. He loved her.

"I kept waiting for your games to begin, but they never did," he said passionately. "Your actions were contrary to those words I'd overheard on the train with your friends. You were always so focused, so serious and hard-working," he chuckled. "The opposite of me at twenty-two. It took a while for me to realise you only wanted me for me, and it scared me. You were the unknown entity, so different, and as soon as Phillippa came back, I was thrown for a *tiny* bit," he admitted, holding her gaze. "I knew her, knew how she played, and I'm ashamed to say the night of the ball, I wavered."

"The kiss."

"Yes, the kiss," Arno confirmed. "I'd been looking forward to seeing you. I had everything planned. It had been five weeks and two days Chilli," he remembered. "And I missed you like crazy. I knew I had powerful feelings for you, and I began drinking myself into the barrels when you had to stay in Paris. Juvenile I know," he admitted. "Phillippa has always been manipulative. She took advantage of my state, which is no excuse on my part. But in my defence," he added in a rush, "if you had waited around, you would have seen me realise what I was doing, and immediately leave disgusted with myself. I went to bed alone that night with your videos on loop on my TV. I would never do anything to hurt you, Chillitara, believe me."

"I do," she sniffed, feeling the sting of tears behind her eyes.

"Where is Phillippa now?"

He shrugged one shoulder before saying. "Gone back to wherever she came from," he explained impatiently. "From the moment you purposefully landed on my lap, I thought of you."

"Hey," she defended, pulling at his nipple, "I tripped."

She could tell he didn't believe her from the telling look he levelled down at her. But did it matter? Not in the least.

"You and Mylo are my every thought," he said. "You make me happy," he touched her cheek. "Mylo makes me happy." The green in his eyes deepened. "But I have been so miserable." He confessed.

"What? Miserable?"

"*Oui*, you make me feel too much," he grinned down at her. "Every emotion is heightened. I go from zero to a hundred like that," he clicked his fingers, "but I am getting used to it, *mon chou*."

She smiled back, feeling a happiness she hadn't felt in months. "So, back to this love business?" she prompted, looking up at him from under her lashes.

Arno noticed her little dimple appear. She probably didn't know he used that as her happiness meter, a signal to show how content she was, and he silently promised to always make it appear.

He rolled them over until he was covering her and nudged her legs apart.

"*Mon amour*," he swept a hand up her chest to cup her breast, pushing it up to flutter his tongue against her pouting nipple. "I will show you."

CHAPTER THIRTY-ONE

Arno watched from the steps of the château the goings-on in the marquee with a satisfied smile. The thousands of fairy lights had just been turned on, chasing away the dark shadows, and the entire front garden was flickering, and making baby Mylo, who was sitting on his knee, kick out his legs in wide-eyed excitement.

Chillitara was busy taking photographs with the Super Supremes–the Diana Ross tribute band he'd brought in as a surprise for her birthday–and instructing her friend Vinny as they all posed this way and that, at the same time.

With Meredith's help, he'd secretly invited and flown down her friends from England and Noah and Kerry came over from the States.

What Chillitara thought was a garden party with the neighbours was, in fact, a birthday celebration with the people she loved the most.

She had been so surprised she'd cried, Arno remembered with satisfaction.

He'd finally met Horatio and his wife, too.

After the cake cutting, Horatio had cornered him and warned, with a smile on his face, that Chilli and Mylo will always be welcome in his village. Arno heard the warning and confidently stated it would never happen. They'd clapped backs and ate cake as though they hadn't just squared off.

Arno focused on Chilli as she looked for him and smiled brightly and wave when she finally spotted him in the shadows. His breath caught watching her walk towards him. She looked stunning in a yellow halter neck jumpsuit thing that stopped mid-thigh, showcasing her perfect legs, and she wore a wavy lace front wig in reds and golds, which hung down to the curve of her back. She called it Hot Spice, and she'd shyly told him it was from her line of wigs.

He'd watched and listened with fascination to the system she used to apply it, even the way she gently teased and smoothed what she called her baby hairs at her hairline.

Her face had been a picture when he'd asked if she would do a halo eyeshadow. He chuckled, remembering her swinging around to him wide-eyed, a palette of shadows in one hand, and a makeup brush in the other. That's when he admitted to watching every single one of her videos. Chilli had walked over, sat on his knee, touched his face, and let her eyes speak for her.

Arno was happy, although disappointed she hadn't yet opened up to him. He'd told her everything about himself that night at the cottage, and even on their slow walk home with Sebastian trotting obediently behind them, he'd told her things he'd never shared with anyone else. Arno trusted her explicitly, yet still, she kept secrets. When she thought he wasn't looking, he saw them in the shadows of her gaze. But he could wait.

"Hey you," Chilli said, once she reached them.

Because of Mylo's vulnerabilities to infections, they'd kept his interaction with their guests to a minimum. Therefore, pre-planned, Chilli, with Garen's help, had made a slide show of him for their friends. "And hey to you too, my most handsome baby boy in the entire world." She cooed, tugging gently on Mylo's legs, and nuzzling his neck, loving his squawk of excitement when he recognised her.

"Hey," Arno replied, liking the way she sat beside him, wrapping her arms around his, and leaning into him. He shifted slightly, so that Mylo was facing her. "Enjoying yourself?"

"I'm having the time of my life," she confirmed, tipping her head towards the tent. "It's all so beautiful." She sighed contently, and they both watched their remaining guests pull chairs around a single table to chat.

The DJ had left, but music still played from numerous outdoor speakers. For saying Arno didn't like the internet, he had a lot of manly toys, which Chilli teased him about.

Large flat-screen TVs throughout his suite, including his bathroom, surround sound speakers everywhere, the golf cart, a Segway, a quad bike, two electric scooters, and several motorbikes in various sizes. Boys and their toys. She'd rolled her eyes at him, and screamed when he caught her around her waist, plastered her against the wall, and made love to her mouth for apparently offending him. *That* had been her punishment.

"So," Arno began casually, "what's the plan?"

"Plan?"

"Yeah, the whole, you and me and baby makes three, thing."

Chilli gasped, knowing instinctively what he was alluding to. He'd said the phrase the night she'd gone into labour. He wanted them to be a family, a proper, official family.

There had been an uncomfortable moment today when one neighbour asked if they had set a wedding date. Arno's face had turned to stone, but his eyes had swirled hot verdant when he looked imploringly at her. It was Vinny who filled the awkward silence with an outlandish joke.

Chilli bit her lip, feeling the silence, hot and heavy, that suddenly engulfed only them like a private hurricane. She knew what he was saying, what he was asking. But they couldn't be what he wanted them to be. She turned to him carefully, slowly, knowing that no matter what, her next words were going to hurt him.

"Can't we just be as we are?" Chilli placed her hand on his forearm, sweeping her thumb over his warm skin. "Like this?" She encouraged.

"I want you as my wife Chillitara," Arno turned to her fully, giving her no option but to look at him directly. These past few weeks, hell, the moment she'd purposely fallen onto him on the train had changed him, giving him a purpose. He was a father. They were a family. "I love you and want us to be official."

Chilli searched for a light tinkle of laughter, desperate to lighten the moment. But even to her, it sounded forced. She knew she was hurting him, rejecting him like this, but it had to be done, even though it went against everything in her heart, a heart strangled by lack of choice. She had to lie, for both their sakes.

"You can be such an old fuddy-duddy," she teased. "I'm not going anywhere, Arno." She told him. "I'm happy just being with you, living here in France with you, Timon, and Grand-Mère. It's perfect. Why spoil it with that aged-old institution? That's for old people. It's just a piece of paper, after all." She added, flipping a hand in the air.

Arno felt a slash of fire shoot through him, and he fought to breathe through it. He'd promised himself he wouldn't put any pressure on her, and look at him, being a selfish idiot caught up in the moment like a loved-up fool.

She was right. Couples lived together all the time without that piece of paper. It *was* an aged-old institution, and she was a young, holistic, modern woman. She didn't need the security of a piece of paper to define their relationship. Why did he feel he needed it?

Arno raised her hand and smoothed his lips over her knuckles before standing and pulling her with him. "You're right," he kissed her, "we don't need a piece of paper," he agreed. "Come on. Let's put the world's most handsome baby boy to bed."

"Oh no, I'm not going upstairs with you," Chilli started laughing, and wagging her finger in his face, even though her lower body was curved suggestively into his. "At his last nap, you tossed up my skirt, had your wicked way, and my clothes were so wrinkled I had to change." She reminded him. "Everyone knew what we did!"

Arno laughed down at her. "So? I can't keep my hands off you."

"Are you saying it's my fault?"

"*Oui*, it is your fault," he tucked her under his arm, and with a silent nod at the small gathering under the tent, steered her into the house to put their son to bed, and maybe see how wrinkled he could get her clothes.

***

Chilli tipped her head back, giving Arno access to her neck, while she tried to pull his shirt out of his trousers to touch his skin at the same time.

They'd put Mylo to bed, and on another floor, in the shadows of Arno's closet, he was making love to her amongst his shirts, kissing her up against the wall.

"Take it off Chilli," Arno ordered with a mumble against her lips, skimming his hands all over her body, trying to get her out of the jumpsuit. Why did she always wear complicated clothes? He thought to himself in frustration, remembering her blue dress from the night they'd met. He was going to make her wear skirts from now on. Preferably without underwear, too. Giving up on looking for a zip, he scooped her breasts out of her top, pulled one nipple, and then the other, deep into his mouth.

Chilli gasped, liking the urgent roughness of it, but a thudding sound infiltrated her erotic fog.

"Arno?" she grasped his hair, trying to stop him.

"Hmm?"

"Do you hear that?"

"No." He moved to her mouth again, dancing his tongue over her lips before moving inside to tickle the roof of her mouth.

Chilli canted her head to the side, unable to concentrate on his magic. "No seriously, Arno, what's that sound?"

Breathing deeply, Arno stopped and listened. "Sounds like a helicopter or something," he acknowledged with a shrug, sliding his body down against hers and rubbing one palm against her sex.

"It's getting awfully close," Chilli stated, resurfacing from another one of his mind-blowing kisses a moment later.

Arno frowned, finally hearing what she was saying. The helicopter flew overhead, and it sounded like it was about to land on the roof.

"What the hell!" he exclaimed. "Stay here." He ordered, already leaving the room, planning on crucifying whomever it was who dared fly near his grapes. There wasn't anywhere safe to land one of those things. Who the hell would come here in a helicopter, anyway?

The noise was deafening and stalking through the house Arno peered through the windows along the way. It alarmed him to see a blue helicopter hover and carefully lower itself to the ground in the patch of flat land just beyond the stable block.

"Where's the baby!" Garen shouted, running through the house, almost knocking him down.

"What?"

"The baby! Where's the baby?"

"In the nursery, why? What's going on?" Arno asked, seeing Garen as he had never seen him before. Focused.

"I'll keep him safe with my life," Garen promised, running past him. "Protect the Princess!"

"What?"

"Go, Arno, go!"

Then he was gone.

Arno was about to turn back and ask what the hell Garen was talking about until he saw his grandfather and Meredith walk outside, their hands clasped, and with Rainor and Benny flanked protectively on either side of them. Was that the shadow of a gun in Benny's trousers?

Frustrated and torn, but knowing Chilli was safe in his suite, Arno ran outside, just as two men and a woman disembarked from the helicopter.

Arno would have laughed if the situation wasn't so alarming. They looked like brightly coloured peacocks trying to hold down their hats in the wind.

"Who are you?" Arno commanded, reaching the fountain at the same time they did, "and where do you get off landing on my land without my permission!" Arno charged, he was going to say more, but the light of fear in Meredith's eyes when she touched his arm, stopped him. "What is it, Meredith? Who are these people?" Arno demanded.

Meredith looked like a shadow to her former self, with hunched shoulders and pale skin. Even the pink flowy dress she wore seemed to lie flat against her legs. Arno watched her take a deep breath and step forward.

"It's okay, Arno, I know him," Meredith said in English, stepping in front of him.

"Your Highness," she said in French, bowing her head at the short man. He had dark skin and wore trendy white trainers that were at odds with his decadent, heavily embroidered blue and gold clothing.

"You are still as beautiful as ever, Meredith," he answered.

Her smile was slight. "Thank you."

"Meredith?" Arno interrupted. "Who are these people?"

One man looked vaguely familiar.

Just then, Chillitara walked towards them. Benny and Rainor moved together, making a human shield, but she walked around them, giving them a small nod of acknowledgement before moving on. They fell into step beside her. Protecting her.

The tall man and woman bowed.

"Princess," they said in unison.

Princess! This was the second time Chillitara had been referred to as a princess in as many minutes, Arno realised. As a matter of fact, ever since he'd known her, someone had used that title, but he'd put it down to an affectionate pet name.

In shock, and unable to process what he was seeing and hearing, Arno watched Chillitara take her grandmother's hand before addressing the trio.

"I don't want you here," she said in English, lifting her chin, her dark eyes spitting fire. "*We* don't want you here."

The man smirked but didn't acknowledge her words, turning to her grandmother instead. "I'm too young to become a grandfather, Meredith," he said. "The scandal alone has sent me across the world."

"Baba, stop teasing," the attractive woman beside him spoke for the first time, clicking her tongue and moving towards them. She picked her way across the gravel in gold stilettos and skin-tight blue clothing made from the same fabric as the man she had just spoken to. "You are scaring them," she smiled, flicking her long braids over her shoulders before holding out her hand to Chillitara. "It is my pleasure to finally meet you, Princess Chillitara. I am your father's wife, Grace." She explained in clear English.

Chilli stepped in front of her grandmother, shielding her. "I won't let you take him," she repeated, ignoring Grace's hand.

"I am sorry we came as we did," Grace explained, not at all offended by Chilli's rudeness. "Already we were in Paris when we received word of your birthday party. Your father thought we should come and visit."

"Why?" Chilli sneered. "He's never concerned himself with me before." Chilli refused to look at the man she had only seen online.

"He is a stubborn man," Grace answered, rolling her eyes and clicking her tongue several times, "too proud for his own good." She turned to Timon with a smile. "You must be Timon Tournier, the great-grandfather?" she asked, lifting a single, beautifully arched, tattooed brow. "Thank you for the invitation."

Timon shook all hands, then turned to sweep his arm wide. "This is my grandson Arno," he introduced, nodding towards his Arno, who was scowling fiercely at everyone. "Come, come," he ushered. "Let's go inside." Timon invited, holding out his arm to Grace.

Arno was confused and angry. Chillitara was a real-life princess. He would even say warrior princess because she stood proudly, regally, with her chin raised and shoulders back. This was a woman ready to fight. She didn't trust them. And if she didn't trust them, why should he?

"Grandfather?" Arno interrupted, unwilling to let these people into the château.

"It will be fine, Arno, trust me," Timon assured him, before turning towards the house. "Would you like some birthday cake? We are celebrating the Princesses' birthday..."

CHAPTER THIRTY-TWO

Arno held Chillitara's elbow, holding her back as the others walked ahead.

"Your father is a king or something?" he charged immediately, glaring down at her, "and you're royalty and didn't tell me?"

Chilli dipped her head before looking up at him. For months, she had wanted to share her secret. But couldn't.

"Grand-Mère had been warned no scandals and to keep me a secret. I had to stay away from the family or she would suffer the consequences," she admitted, feeling that furious streak of resentment at the rejection of an entire country. "I've never been to West Africa," she shrugged. "Besides, this is the first time I've ever met him."

"The first time?" Arno echoed, unable to comprehend such a thing. Who would not want to meet his lovely Chillitara? "Why is he here? Why now?" he asked, trying to understand what the King's sudden appearance meant to them all. "What does he want?"

"You heard what your grandfather said. He was invited," she reminded him, pressing her lips together. "What does he want?" she lifted and dropped a shoulder in a quick shrug, "My guess is our baby."

"Mylo?" Arno said in confusion, "I don't understand?"

"It's a long story, Arno. I'm sorry for not saying anything to you," she apologised, looking over her shoulder towards the Château. They'd all gone inside. "It's because we couldn't."

"We?" Arno asked, and then answered for himself, "You and Meredith?"

Chilli nodded.

"I still don't–"

"Arno, please," she touched his arm, her dark eyes wide when she looked up at him. "Please, we'll talk about this later." She turned to go, pulling him with her, but he didn't move.

"Is Mylo safe?"

Chilli turned back to him. "Garen has taken him to the cottage."

"Are you safe?"

Chilli tipped her chin up high. "I'm not afraid anymore."

"Are you safe?" Arno repeated, sensing the aura of fear she had just denied bounce around her like a thousand rubber balls. He was going to sort this out tonight. She would not fear another day. Arno was older, here to protect his family. He would kick her father off his vineyard to ensure Chillitara felt safe in her own home.

Chilli looked at him from under her lashes and placed her hand on his arm, knowing he would not like her next words. "Your grandfather brought in Benny, Rainor, and Garen as security." She admitted in a low voice.

Arno pulled himself up to his full height, and Chilli saw the flash of hurt she'd wanted to save him from.

He slung her hand from his arm and stepped back. "You didn't think I was capable of looking after you? Of keeping my family safe?" Arno yelled, "Fuck that shit!"

"It was to keep you safe too," she pleaded, blinking back tears. "We don't know how this will end. I didn't know about the invitation, although I'm not surprised. Timon said there was a lot happening in the Independent State of Java and–"

Arno looked down at her, his frown in tight pleats. "Independent State of where?" he'd never heard of it.

"Java," Chilli repeated. "It's a tiny country squashed between Nigeria and Benin," she explained, happy to change the subject. "It's like what Monaco is in Europe."

"Super rich too, and claimed by Nigeria, yet has its own laws to keep the peace, and avoid war. Nigeria has access to its wealth." She advised, knowledgeable about the country she'd never visited. "Apparently, a lot has been going on, changes and unrest, and Timon didn't like the threat of retribution hanging over our heads."

"Retribution?" Arno hated each ugly syllable of the word. "For what?"

Chilli looked everywhere but at him, realising he was probably about to blow another gasket, and lose his temper.

Arno slid his fingers under her chin and tipped her head up to see her lovely eyes large and glassy. "For what?" he growled.

"For having a baby outside of marriage." She admitted in a small voice.

Arno dropped his hand, and rocked back on his heels, as the guilt of everything he'd caused raised to the surface again, cutting off his breath from the inside out. He saw every memorable moment, from her landing on his lap, the ride up the lift, their lovemaking over the weeks, her great reveal on the train, her losing consciousness, and the horror of the night she'd almost died. He saw everything in a kaleidoscope of bright primary colours colliding into blackness in his mind's eye. He had ruined her entire life with a single lie.

Alarmed at his sudden paleness, Chilli quickly snaked her arms around his waist, squeezing him tight. She would have preferred if he'd shouted.

"I love you," she admitted aloud for the first time. She felt his chest expand within her arms and heard his heart suddenly beat a heavy tattoo beneath her ear. "I would go to that room a million times over," she whispered into his chest, "if the outcome was this. You and me, and our precious little boy." She defended. "I love you, Arno," she stated again. "I've loved you from the moment we met, and I realised your eyes were the same beautiful green in my dream that morning."

She squeezed him when he didn't react, simply looking over her head into the distance, his mind elsewhere, and she reached up, placed one hand at his nape, and forced his head down to her. "I love you," she told him, capturing his face between her hands, forcing him to look into her eyes. "Do you hear me?"

She wrapped her arms around him again, squeezing him over

and over, until he moved, placing his hands on her shoulders now, and taking a small step backwards, although sliding his palms down her arms to weave their fingers together. When he looked at her, his eyes weren't as dark, and his colour was returning. She'd hated lying to him all these months.

His lips turned up on one side, not quite smiling but not smirking. "I hear you."

She looked behind her. "We need to talk," she whispered, swinging their hands between them. "But not now."

Arno followed her gaze, finally noticing Benny, who was standing by the door, where he was watching over them, and also able to see inside with just a turn of his head.

"You're right," Arno conceded. "Now is not the time." He nodded for her to proceed him into the house. They walked through the kitchen with Benny at their heels, down the hall now lit by the soft glow of up-lighters on the walls, then on to the formal living room with dainty gilded chairs, and velvet damask wallpaper in cream and brown, where he saw everyone seated, and being served tea and birthday cake, by Agnes.

Benny went to the east corner of the room, opposite Rainor. The tall man stood close to the King.

Arno closed the door behind Agnes. "To what do we owe the honour?" he drawled, knowing his smile was not welcoming. He didn't like that they had all lied to him. He was the only one who didn't know what was happening. Seeing them all in the harsh light, Arno finally recognised the taller man as the orderly in the hospital all those months ago. He captured Chillitara's hand and pulled her close.

Placing her cup onto the saucer, it was Grace who cleared her throat, and spoke, but not before deferring to her husband's quick nod and tender encouraging smile. "We need to start at the beginning," she placed her tea beside her slice of half-eaten birthday cake on the small side table beside her chair. "My Baba was a young student in Paris when he fell in love," she began, and went on, knowing the story well, "and married Lea, the Princess's mother."

Meredith gasped and tried to stand, but Timon, who was standing behind her armchair, placed his hand on her shoulder, stopping her. "That's not true!" she accused, moving to the edge of her seat. "You didn't think she was worthy enough to marry. You broke her heart–"

"We married, Meredith," Baba interrupted softly, naming the date and place, waiting a moment for it to sink in, knowing the older woman would remember the significance of it. His eighteenth birthday. They had all gone to dinner at The Paris Seasons Hotel to celebrate. "But everything started happening. Lea wasn't feeling well and trying to hide it, and they ordered me back that night," he said. "We didn't get the chance to tell you."

"But you just left her."

"I had no choice." He stood then, obviously agitated at her words, hearing the veiled accusation. "I was the future King of the Independent State of Java, and at seventeen, away from home, from Africa, for the first time. I fell in love with a young western woman who liked to walk barefoot in the rain and write songs. I loved her Meredith; you know I did."

"She would have travelled to the end of the world with you, Baba," Meredith whispered. Tears pooled, then trickled down her face.

"I know, and I loved her too much to let her sacrifice who she was in Java," he admitted. His face crumpled for a moment, raw emotion for everyone to see. "Lea was French through and through." his smile was small, his eyes softening at his memories. "It was where she was loved. She was an angel on earth who touched me, everyone, in ways I can never describe." He choked around the laden emotion in his throat.

The hands Meredith used to push her hair behind her ears were shaking. "She loved you so much."

"And I loved her Meredith, never doubt that," Baba walked across the room to her chair, bending at the waist to clasp her trembling hands within his. "My father was backward in his thinking. If he'd known about us, God only knows what he would have done. I was scared for you both," he pleaded. "When she fell pregnant, the only way I knew I could protect you all was by giving her the security of my name. My father was a proud, controlling man. He would have killed her spirit, crushed her if she'd lived in Java," he went down on his knees. "I'd seen him do it with my mother, and my sisters," he revealed, his mouth tightening at the memories of an angry, ignorant man who reigned terror over the family within the confines of the tall palace walls. He would not expose Lea to that.

If his father learned of the marriage, he would have ordered them to live in Java. Baba had known it was safer for her in France.

"She was my life." he kissed Meredith's hands. "And then she died."

Meredith sniffed, before repeating more to herself, "and then she died."

Baba breathed in a deep stuttered breath, before saying, "I will forever carry the burden of her death, and the guilt of pandering to a man I never respected, when Lea needed me," he apologised, blinking away the tears. "I'm sorry, Meredith."

"You were just as young, Baba," Meredith forgave through her tears, and gently cupped his cheek when he looked up, his own tears flowing unchecked down his cheeks.

The room was quiet. They knew they were witnessing a private moment between two people who had lost a special person.

Wrapping his arm around Chillitara's waist, Arno pulled her in front of him, wondering what she was feeling seeing her father and grandmother like this. Didn't anyone think how Chillitara could be hurting? Did they forget her mother *died* giving birth to her?

Suddenly remembering where he was, Baba looked up and stalked to the fireplace.

In the thick emotional silence that followed, Arno cleared his throat, bringing all eyes to him. "Why are you here?" he asked Baba.

Baba shrugged one shoulder. "My father is dead."

"Should I say condolences?" Arno snorted, not at all impressed with that simple statement.

"Arno!" Timon admonished.

Baba laughed. "No. We're all better for it." He pressed his lips together. "He would have lived another hundred years if he'd known about Mylo. We knew he was fading and waited him out before leaving Java."

Baba picked up a small green and gold art déco vase, turning it this way and that. "This is beautiful, *Sevres*?"

"Yes," Arno confirmed, naming the famous French artist, before prompting with a flick of his wrist. "You were saying?"

"You are a very forward young man," Baba stated with a raised brow, before turning to Chilli. "You chose well." Then, replacing the vase said, "My father suffered a stroke the day before Lea went into premature labour." He huffed to himself, a faraway look in his eyes. "I needed to be in France with my wife. I didn't want to go. I planned to return as soon as possible, but then–

He didn't finish. Everyone was aware of what he couldn't say. Chillitara's mother had died.

"I couldn't come back." his agitation was clear by the way he grasped the back of his neck. "He had stroke after stroke and the entire state of Java relied on me. Hundreds of thousands of people.

"My authority was challenged at every turn, because my father had made it known how disappointed he was in me, as the only son who'd lied and enrolled at *Sorbonne,* to be an artist," his hand which had been smoothing along the mantle curled into a tight fist and then he shook his shoulders. "My state is small, but the richest in West Africa. We have oil and, of course, my diamond kimberlite pipes," he said with pride to them all. "Did you know it is rare to find such pipes in West Africa?"

Arno swore. "So, you left your baby and forgot about her," Arno challenged, ignoring his grandfather's gasp, "to reign over oil and blood diamonds?"

"My heart has always been wherever my daughter is," Baba clarified, searing Arno with a fierce look. "But I also had an obligation to my people. Europe, France in particular, have started skirmishes within my villages, instigating unrest to get their hands on my oil. If they knew of my daughter, of her being French, they would have kidnapped her, used her as leverage, got the locals to practise evil juju on her, and I wouldn't risk it. Very few people know of her existence, and her anonymity kept her safe."

"You say that like you cared what happened to Grand-Mère and I," Chilli spoke for the first time, unprepared to forgive the man who had overshadowed her entire life. "You know nothing about me!" She suddenly exploded.

Baba straightened and pushed his shoulders back.

Arno saw the authority behind Baba's small stature.

"I know everything about you," Baba began. "Your favourite restaurants, your friends, what sports you played in school," he listed lightly. "Sammy," he indicated the silent man standing alert in the room. "And many others, even Nurse Aimee and Kylian, have shadowed your every move, keeping you protected and safe your entire life," he gritted. "When you became an influencer, it was easier for me to be close and involve myself. I follow you on every platform, calling myself *'Getting It Right'*

"I double tap or press the like button! I *watch* everything," he gritted with a slight bite of annoyance before continuing. "We have talked privately. I sacrificed my whole life to make sure you could live yours!" He finished with a roar, slapping the marble mantle with his open palm in frustration. Not at her, but the circumstances of their lives.

"Stop lying!"

"Chillitara!"

Chilli swung to her grandmother. "What? He comes here twenty-three years later sprouting rubbish of loving France, knowing me, and pressing the stupid *'like'* button when all he wants is to take Mylo back to Africa." It wasn't about her anymore. She would do whatever it takes to protect her son from the likes of him, no matter what he said.

Chilli walked towards him, stopping barely an inch away to

look down at him, every bit the princess with her heated glare. "You will not take my child."

The tension in the room ramped up several notches. The tall African man, Sammy, who had remained quiet, quickly and silently, crossed the floor, placing a hand on Chillitara's arm to push her back.

"Take your hands off her." Arno growled, prowling towards the man.

Baba spoke sharply in an unfamiliar language and the man fell back. His head bowed.

The room was tense. Then Baba flung back his head and laughed. "Where did you hear such a thing?"

"African rulers always want sons," Chilli snarled. "Women are barely educated!" She knew it wasn't true, but she wanted to insult him. Like he had done to her all her life.

"Not this king," he huffed. "We embrace certain changes, knowing it can be beneficial for our country and our people," Baba interjected, his posture now stiff with offence. "Did I not say, like you, my heart has always been in France?"

"I don't understand?"

He canted his head to one side. "Can you make jollof rice?"

"What?"

"Jollof rice?"

Chilli knew Jollof was the name of the spicy yellow rice she sometimes ordered from her favourite West African restaurant. "No."

"Neither can I. We will learn together," he declared, smiling brightly. "With my father's passing, I am now free. I have changed the law, and my sister, your Aunt Ada, will take my place. The very first queen in the Independent State of Java, West Africa's most powerful state. It is a great time for Africa. A new Africa!"

"Yes, Baba," Grace started clapping her hands enthusiastically, with Sammy joining in, "A new Africa!"

"I don't understand?" Chilli frowned.

"My daughter," Baba reached out, and placed his hand on her

shoulder, "you are no longer in danger. I have abdicated with blessings from our Chiefs," he beamed. "My grandson is no longer in danger, and I am free to live my life."

"In France?"

"Did I not say my heart, you, are here?" he enquired, shrugging one shoulder.

CHAPTER THIRTY-THREE

"Arno–"

"So, imagine," Arno cut in abruptly. "You are a," he swept his green gaze up and down her body, "or should I say, *were*," he snorted. "A princess?"

It was after four in the morning before they'd made it up to her suite, stopping for a moment to stare lovingly at their sleeping son before tiptoeing out of the nursery.

Earlier on, Benny gave the all-clear, and Garen returned from the cottage with Mylo. It had been emotional seeing her father holding the baby, kissing his forehead, and gazing down at him with tears in his eyes. His love was genuine for everyone to see.

And then, after family photos, and later joined by their friends Vinny, Dr Gabriel, Kerry and her fiancé Noah, the party continued in the opulent living room with Timon asking Arno to go to the private family vault, and bring up a special bottle of Cabernet, which had been produced by Timon's grandfather.

Everyone toasted, Baba's abdication, and relocation to France, Mylo's birth, Chilli's birthday, Kerry and Noah, finally setting a wedding date, and even the fact that Arno had declared the grapes ready for harvesting earlier that day.

It had been hilarious when Grace suddenly started screaming like a star-struck teenager when she recognised Noah, who'd shyly fetched his guitar, and sang some of his famous, and not-so-famous country music songs, after Grace had dropped to her knees, begging and pleading.

And now, closing the bedroom door with a measured click, Chilli turned to Arno knowing she had a lot of explaining to do, and that his question was more a statement of grim detached fact.

She bit the side of her lip, trying to gauge his mood. He'd

rolled up the sleeves to his trendy collarless moss-coloured shirt she'd bought him in Paris all those months ago, and his hair hung in messy waves that reminded her of the first time she'd met him on the train. But his face was stark, his eyes dark and unreadable.

He'd been cordial, but not overly talkative downstairs, and she'd known he was simply waiting to get her alone before he went off on one of his wayward thought processes to vent at her. Therefore, she attempted to get in first.

"I'm sorry I couldn't tell you," she apologised, stepping out of her shoes to walk towards him, her arms outstretched. "But–"

"But nothing," he interrupted again, raking his hair away from his face with both hands, and moving away, putting the length of the enormous Persian rug between them. "You've been lying to me for weeks."

"I've never acknowledged the whole royalty thing, Arno," she clarified, dismayed by his accusation. "It doesn't mean–"

"It's not about the title, Chillitara," he snapped, slashing the air with one hand, "you came to France, to my home–" Arno took a deep breath, trying but failing to calm down. He'd been simmering with emotions all evening. They'd all been chatting and laughing, and all he could think about, *feel,* was that wealth of excitement, when he'd ridden into the courtyard, his heart bursting with love that she had come to him on her own accord. Yet she had lied, played games, and taken him for a damn fool. The chateau was nothing more than a safe house to her.

It had all been a lie.

"You came down here on false pretences," he continued, enunciating every syllable through gritted teeth. "Not because you missed me," he listed. "Not because you wanted us to be together," his voice became thin like brittle glass, and just as cutting. "To be a family," he said, impaling her with his darkened eyes. "To *love* me," he added. "You came here to hide."

"That's not–"

"Don't lie to me!" he bellowed suddenly, unfolding his arms, but his stance remained rigid, his hands held in tight fists at his sides. "Yes or no?"

"Arno, please."

His grimness frightened her. She'd never seen him look like this, so totally ravaged with flags of red flaring against his cheekbones, and the green in his eyes entirely swallowed by the darkness of hurt.

"Yes or no?"

"Yes, but–"

Chilli watched him draw in a deep breath, his chest expanding under the depth of it, where he stood across the room staring at her for long drawn-out seconds. Suddenly he moved, skirting around the frilled edges of the rug to leave the room.

Chilli stared at the rug. Seeing yet unseeing the aged burgundy and cream swirls. He'd walked all the way around it to avoid her, she noticed absently, biting her bottom lip.

She'd known he was going to be mad, but that look before he'd turned away made her heart bleed for them both. He needed to cool down before she approached him again, she reasoned, telling herself she wasn't avoiding the confrontation, but merely requiring a moment to herself.

Chilli walked into her en-suite to have a hot shower, pulling off her clothes along the way, and leaving them on the floor, trying to blink away the tears.

She was overwhelmed. Exhausted by the secrets and lies that shadowed her life until today. A new day. It was over.

She reached for her old-fashioned shower cap before ignoring it. Pulling off her wig and throwing it on the floor instead. She looked at it, a blaze of long hot spice-coloured strands against the much softer honey tones of recently laid porcelain tiles.

The bathroom had been decorated. Soft and feminine with gold and crystal accessories. This was now her home. A beautiful château occupied by a proud, green-eyed Frenchman who loved her as much as she loved him. Yet home was wherever Arno Tournier was. He was her heart. She didn't care if he lived in a tent, well maybe not a tent, she chuckled to herself–finding some humour in a humourless situation–but home was wherever he was. This was where she belonged.

Shampooing away her wayward thoughts, she placed a dollop of conditioner into her palms, rubbed her hands together, and smoothed them over her hair.

Her father. She had met Baba, the former King of Java. He was nothing like how she'd thought him to be. He was not arrogant or authoritarian. He was playful and laughed a lot. He sang alongside Noah and obviously adored his wife Grace, whom he kept stealing loving glances to throughout the night.

Baba and her grandmother were great friends, and she wondered at his harsh warnings all those years ago, the fear he'd made them live by, and concluded that he had behaved that way to scare them into silence for their own safety.

Yet he hadn't left them alone. He'd always had someone shadowing them. Protecting them. Chilli had noticed them, thinking they were making sure she wasn't about to embarrass the family or reveal who she was. She had been tempted, especially as her grandmother got older. It wasn't fair living as they did.

They had been cautious and suspicious of everyone. Moving house multiple times. Looking over their shoulders. The stress had been suffocating. When Chilli had lived her life openly via social media, she had taken control. Telling her father she wouldn't be hidden.

Imagine, she laughed to herself. Imagine, she'd been having long conversations behind the scenes with *Getting it Right*, not knowing *she* was a *he*, and her father, to boot!

Chilli should have felt betrayed, and she did in a way, but not knowing someone's true identity was one of the risks of being a content creator. You didn't know who you were befriending online.

She rinsed her hair, stepped out of the shower, folded a towel around her curls to soak up the moisture, and dried her skin. Then she swept Hopetone and Pinks, lotus flower-scented body lotion over her body, before roughly towel drying her hair, stacking the damp mass on top of her head, and securing it all with a single length of ribbon.

The trio was leaving tomorrow for Baba's last royal engagement and returning to help with the grape harvesting later.

From the way Baba kept dropping hints, they would be living at the château before the year was out, Chilli thought with amusement, not really minding. Her father loved France.

Hearing the gentle trot of a horse in the courtyard below. Chilli quickly pulled on a short pale-yellow nightie and sauntered to the windows. Arno was leading Sebastian into the stables. Chilli waited, watching, until he eventually walked out, glancing at her windows before walking into the house with his head bent.

She knew he was hurting, that she'd lied, but hadn't her earlier declaration of love account for anything? Did he not see her running to him meant she trusted him? Arno had a terrible habit of overthinking things, missing details, and coming up with the wrong conclusion where she was concerned.

What had he said recently? Ah yes, she made him feel too much. Blooming hell. In the last few minutes, he'd probably regulated her to acquaintance again, putting a formal spin on their relationship because of who her father was. Stupid man!

With a determined glint, Chilli made her way to his room.

He was in the shower.

Looking about, she spied two chairs and a leather footstool. With quick decision, she arranged them to her satisfaction, before going to his chest of drawers, opening and closing them until she found his white athletic socks to put on.

Eventually, Arno walked into the room with a large dark towel folded around his waist, his beautiful body glistening with water and drying his hair with a small white towel.

Foreseeing a disaster, but too late to stop it, Chilli watched in horror when Arno walked straight into the row of chairs, upending one, painting the air blue, hopping about, and rubbing his shin at the same time.

"What the hell!" He yelled, staring down at the row of chairs in the middle of his bedroom in disbelief.

"Oops," Chilli said, trying not to laugh and moving away from the wall she'd been leaning against to walk towards him.

Dropping his foot, Arno's smouldering green gaze scorched down her body, looking at her white athletic socks with a tip of a puzzled eyebrow, before slowly sweeping back up again, lingering at her breasts, watching with a small one-sided tilt to his lips, when her nipples poked the soft fabric of her nightie.

Chilli preened under his heated stare. Confident she had him, when his tongue swept across his bottom lip. Unfortunately, a second later, she saw the moment he remembered he was mad at her. He blinked several times, snapping his lips tightly shut and narrowing his eyes at her.

Chilli let her breath out with a noisy whoosh, walked over, picked up and repositioned the chair in the row, before facing him with her hands on her hips.

"What are you doing here?" he asked, turning his back to rub his hair roughly. Arno knew he'd acted like a complete fool. He'd intended to apologise for his stupid behaviour after his shower, but she'd beat him to it, and he was egotistical enough to see how this was going to play out.

"I need you to do something."

He hadn't been expecting that and swung back to her.

"What?" he asked. "It is late, and I am tired."

"It will only take a second, Arno."

Chillitara walked over to him, took his free hand, pulled him towards the chairs, turned him about, and then pushed his chest. Realising what she wanted, Arno allowed her to push him into the middle seat.

With his gaze guarded, he crossed his arms. "What–" he began.

"Shh," she pressed a finger to his lips, "you're ruining it." Kissing him quickly because he looked so cute trying to look mad at her, Chilli sauntered away, walking across the room, very much aware his lovely eyes were probably glued to her bottom.

He always said he loved her curves.

Turning around, and holding his gaze, she stepped slowly towards him, before falling onto his lap. His large hands immediately went to her small waist to keep her from falling.

"What–"

"Oh! I am so sorry," she apologised with feigned innocence, wrapping one arm around his neck and pressing her chest into his. "My fault."

Arno grimaced, then sighed. "Chilli," he said wearily, finally understanding why there was a row of chairs in the middle of his room.

Chilli pushed the chairs away on either side of them and moved so that she was facing him. Her nightie rode up, allowing her sex to nestle intimately against his. The towel was no barrier, and she snuggled into his body to smooth her other hand up his chest to rest on his strong shoulder.

"Falling onto your lap that day was the best thing–after Mylo," she slotted in with a wink. "Was the best thing I've ever done."

He smirked, his lovely lips softening at her declaration, "oh yeah,"

"Yeah,"

"So, you admit to intentionally falling?"

He was fastidious about this one thing, she thought, mentally rolling her eyes. Yet loving him all the more. "I do." Chilli confessed.

"Do you make a habit of falling onto men on trains?"

"Oh no," she shook her head, "only this man." She declared, walking her fingers along his collarbone and up his neck. Droplets of water still clung to his skin, and she leaned forward and licked a few of them off.

"It was his hair I noticed first," she admitted. "I had this crazy urge to run my fingers through it." She did just that, massaging his scalp with her fingertips, disturbing the fragrant, citrusy scent of his shampoo.

"Oh yes?"

"Then it was his eyes," she told him, touching his face. "They were the green of my dreams that morning."

"So you said." He remembered she'd alluded to her dream when they were by the fountain several hours ago.

Tipping her head to the side, she said, "no more secrets," and went on quickly, feeling his body stiffen at her words. "You already know the biggest secret, Arno. This is nothing in comparison," she soothed. "I'm special," she revealed. "An anomaly."

"Oh yes?"

Chilli was aware he was letting her do all the talking with his lack of vocabulary, but didn't mind. She had his full attention.

"I dream in one colour," she gloated, nibbling his earlobe. "One of like zero point one per cent of people in the world. I'm so rare I was once asked to do a dream study."

Although his eyes were dancing, he was shaking his head when she leaned away to see his reaction.

"What?" she asked.

Arno's lips twitched at her cute petulance.

"I'm not special?"

"From what I remember of my dreams last night, Chillitara, everything was tinged with a glow," he revealed. "A single yellow glow," they both looked down at her nightie, "and you wore it all day today."

"And I dreamt in green." They looked at the pile of clothes on the floor. His green shirt was on top. The ribbon in her hair was the same hue she remembered, reaching up to touch the velvet strip.

"I love you, Arno Tournier," she sighed, feeling a connection which could only be theirs.

"Hmm-mmm."

"I simply wanted to be with you, ok?" Chilli stated matter-of-factly. "I missed you when you left England, so when Grand-Mère suggested we come here, I jumped at the chance," she confirmed, dipping her head. "Forgive me for not telling you?" she asked, knowing she needed to hear him say it.

"You completely emasculated me Chillitara," Arno admitted,

moving to readjust her to his liking on his lap. "Never doubt that I would protect you, my family, with my life."

"I know," she confirmed, kissing the underside of his jaw, liking the rough feel of his bristles against her lips. "I'm sorry. I'm used to keeping secrets to protect the people I love." She leaned even closer, plastering herself against him, loving the way his hardness jumped and pulsed beneath her bottom, reminiscent of that day on the train. Good. This had been her aim.

"So," she began, slowly circling her hips, "I was thinking about our plan." she wriggled her bottom, and touched his brow, smoothing a single finger along the length of one, and then the other.

"Plan?" Arno placed his hands on the luscious soft globes of her bottom and did what he'd wanted to do the day they'd met. He lifted her slightly, and smoothed his palm along her centre, only to smirk, and arch a single eyebrow, finding her already bare and wet for him.

"Y-yes," Chilli stuttered, rocking against his fingers, trying to concentrate on her next words at the same time. "The w-whole you, me and baby make three–" she breathed, opening her legs wider and giving him better access. "T-thing."

Arno quickly shifted the towel out of his way, grasped her hips, and brought her down onto him. "Ah, that thing," he leaned forward, capturing her sweet gasp in his kiss. "Tut-tut Chillitara, tomorrow we plan," he advised, rocking her hips forwards then backwards against him, his mind utterly blown as all his fantasies from all those months ago on the train were coming true. "Tonight, we play trains." he buried his face between her breasts, pulling the narrow straps off her shoulders to greedily capture one nipple deep into his mouth.

"Ahh," Chilli gasped, holding his head to her. "Is that what we're doing, playing trains?"

"*Oui.*"

EPILOGUE

Chilli jumped, startled, when the alarm on her phone sounded. She needed to get ready.

If Arno thought his annual ball was extravagant before, now, four years later and being organised by her stepmother Grace, it had expanded to include vintners and vignerons from around the world.

Grace had planned events for the entire week. From wine tasting tours of local vineyards, to cultural events in surrounding cities and villages. It all culminated in tonight's ball. Timon, her grandmother, Baba, and Grace were the primary hosts.

Massaging the back of her neck, Chilli kicked off her shoes, leaned into her chair to have a peaceful moment to herself. They may be entertaining, but she had spent a few hours in her office, which had been moved to a converted outbuilding behind the stables. From here, she could look out and if not physically see Arno within his beloved grapevines, she could at least picture him there.

She breathed in deep with contentment and smiled at the array of picture frames on her desk before she locked up and joined the family.

Mylo, a happy and healthy four-year-old who was now taller than his peers, was smiling back at her. He had a thick mop of dark curls that flopped adoringly into his eyes. He was a replica of his father, but had her temperament.

Mylo was popular with all the children in his nursery room, and everyone considered him their best friend and would fight for his attention. He had the room cheering when he said they were all best friends. She had cried when his room teacher had told her.

Chilli fiddled with the wonky ceramic paperweight her father had made. The chateau now housed more glazed pottery vases, plates, and jars than the apartment in Paris. Her father had made the picture frame that held a formal photograph of himself, Grace and Obi, their one-year-old son. They were all wearing matching traditional gowns in golds and browns on her desk.

Baba, her father, had thrown himself into his art, that they'd had to convert another outbuilding into a craft studio for him, to keep him organised. It even housed a Kiln.

A smaller picture frame featured Timon and her grandmother standing at the altar. Her grandmother, a woman who had sworn to never get married, had glowed in a simple lilac dress and crown of wild flowers.

Chilli leaned forward and picked up the next frame which Baba and Mylo had made as a present for her. It was of Arno. She had taken the photograph on her phone. He was wearing jeans, a white sweat-stained t-shirt, dusty boots and a black bandana held his long hair back. He was sitting casually astride Sebastian, holding the reins loosely in one hand, leaning forward and looking back at her with a look she had never seen before. The air had been sticky and heavy, the sky cloudless. It had seemed closer somehow, as though she could reach up and stroke its underbelly.

Chilli felt heat flood into her cheeks as she remembered what they had done after she had taken that photograph. The air had closed in. Her skin had felt tight, her body laden. Arno had been still, his verdant gaze smouldering. Feeling trapped, Chilli had turned and fled.

She had ducked under and in between the vines. Hearing Arno's growl of frustration, she stopped and watched as Sebastian reared, before man and horse, took off down and around the avenue of grapevines. Chilli had moved swiftly, going horizontally to him before making a run for the golf cart she had used to look for him.

It wasn't long before she had heard the powerful thunder of Sebastian's hoofs coming up behind and then racing past her.

Arno had jumped down, stalked towards her and pulled her roughly into his arms. She would have fainted if this was a 19th century romance. Instead, she'd felt every part of her being ignited with licks of fiery flames.

They'd made love on the ground, within the vines. It had been the most primal love making of her life. Rushed yet so deep, she felt as though they'd become one. Where he began, she ended, where she began, he ended. It was surreal. Out of body, and she'd screamed and cried from the pleasure of it.

Someone laughing outside, pulled her from her erotic thoughts and Chilli reached for the flask of water, poured herself a small glass before tidying her desk.

Chilli was living her best life. She still had her many channels, and would do the odd beauty vlog, but now she had another channel and a podcast where she talked business, motivation, and finance. She had lost some followers during her transition, which her team had expected, but her new channel was flourishing. Chilli was enjoying herself, happily balancing the family brands with her own.

As she was about to close her laptop, an email came through and, with her heart racing, she opened it.

***

Arno was getting used to it, but still felt self-conscious. Chilli said it was his sheepishness that endeared his followers to him.

Arno couldn't believe he had followers. He didn't post often, as he preferred his bi-weekly podcast on a Sunday evening. Talking wine, he could do, taking pictures of himself within his grapevines, not so much.

Arno wiped the sweat from his brow. He gazed upwards to see the sun lower than he wanted it to be. He had to get back to the chateau before Chillitara started ringing him.

Arno had let the foreman and his field labourers have the afternoon off, so he was in his vines alone. He could see the chateau and pick out his wife's building in the distance. She should be getting ready to leave now too, he thought and with a self-mocking smile, and wondered if they'd be able to get some loving in before hosting the ball.

His wife. Arno smiled into the distance. Chilli had asked him to marry her the morning of their first Christmas together. He couldn't believe she'd actually been nervous when asking. Of course, he made her suffer all of ten seconds before sweeping her off her feet and taking her back to bed.

Arno was so proud of her. Taking over the business side of things. Re-structuring, re-branding and making their brand so exclusive, their profit margins were thriving. They didn't need to compete with anyone. He'd been called out for being a wine snob and he accepted it. Tournier Wines had one thing others didn't. Baba.

Although abdicating, his father-in-law was still royalty, and he was shameless with promoting their wine within exclusive circles.

Arno walked towards the golfcart thankful tonight was the last of a week-long interruption to his sweetly calm life.

He was nearing the outskirts of the field when he heard the distinct sound of racing horse hoofs. Puzzled as no one should be out riding, Arno squinted into the distance.

He wondered if something had happened. He felt sick and even more so when Chilli came bounding over the ridge on Sebastian as though the hounds of hell were behind them.

Arno stepped into the open and waved to be noticed. She was wearing her office clothes; he saw with alarm. A black pair of trousers, a pink t-shirt–the colour of his dream this morning–long curly hair he knew was a V-clip wig from her wig line, flew behind her and it looked like her feet were bare. Why was she out riding, dressed as she was? What was wrong? What had happened?

Arno waited. Apprehension keeping him frozen. He could feel his blood flowing throughout his body. It was going to be bad. Why else would his wife come bounding through the fields on his horse when she had her own gentle mare to ride? Sebastian was a powerful horse. Chillitara was *not* supposed to ride him unless he was with her.

Sebastian came to a stuttering holt in front of him. The horse's nostrils were flaring as he trotted over to Arno, his golden eyes looking guilty for letting Chillitara ride him.

Chilli jumped down, her eyes intent on Arno.

"What is it?" Arno rushed, seeing the tears streaming down her cheeks unchecked when she closed the gap between them.

Chilli tried to speak through the swell of emotion clogging her throat. She reached for his hands, knowing she was making a mess of things. His complexion had turned grey. Arno was a fatalist. His immediate thoughts were always that something bad had happened.

She placed her palms against his chest. "The email," she blurted, looking up at him.

Arno's body was stiff and unmoving and Chilli wrapped her arms around his waist. Squeezing him tight. She could hear his heart racing where it pounded beneath her ear. "It came," she sniffed unladylike, burrowing her head into his chest.

Realising she was being unfair to him, she took a deep shuddering breath to collect herself and moved back so she could see his face. "We did it," she breathed with a wobbly smile. "We've been accepted."

Accepted? Arno frowned down at her. For what?

Sebastian moved, feeling the confused vibes of emotion around his master, and trotted closer, nudging them both.

Seeing the happiness radiating in Chillitara's eyes, Arno guessed, "The adoption?"

Chilli tipped her head back, sniffing, smiling and nodding at the same time.

"For both of them?" Arno asked, not daring to hope they could adopt the seven- and eight-year-old brother and sister.

"Both of them." Chilli confirmed.

Arno pulled her into his chest, wrapping his arms around her to rock her back and forth within his tight embrace.

After a deep sigh, Arno moved to cup her face. "The best thing you ever did to me was fall onto my lap that day on the train." He whispered, his eyes reflecting the love blazing from hers.

THE END

Join Caroline's influencer list for more fun reads & freebies!

ABOUT THE AUTHOR

Caroline Bell Foster

Caroline was born in Derby, England, and went on a six-week holiday to Jamaica with her family. She stayed for years!

Ever the adventurer, Caroline bought her first pair of high heels in Toronto, Canada and traded her pink sunglasses for a bus ride in the Rift Valley, Kenya by the age of 18.

A self-proclaimed cat person, Caroline is looking forward to one day being called 'The Mad Cat Lady. She enjoys writing sweet or spicy romances.

The multi-award-winning author is also the author of the Amazon Bestselling Call Centre Series, Call Me Royal and Call Me Lucky, where she pays tribute to all those who work the night shift in call centres as she has done.

With themes of substance, Caroline's latest novels defy convention and celebrate modern-day Britain with several titles set primarily in The East Midlands.

Caroline has been listed as one of the most influential creatives in her region.

Caroline has come full circle and lives in Nottingham, England, just twelve miles from where she was born. She married her college sweetheart David (Mr Sunshine) and they have two children.

If you would like to keep up to date with Caroline's new releases, please sign up to her twice-yearly newsletter via her website.

www.carolinebellfoster.com

BOOKS BY THIS AUTHOR

Sweey & Spicy Books For Every Mood

Distracting Ace – (International Heroes Book 1) It took thirty-six hours for Ace to fall in love. But longer to find it again and keep it.

Convincing Kyle – (International Heroes Book 2)
First, love and family interference spelt disaster for Kyle and Camille. Years later, they tried again, but even more, interference threatens their love.

Avoiding Matthew – (International Heroes Book 3)
Special Government Operatives Matthew and Lacy hooked up every chance they got. But wanting to make the world a better place, Lacy has to avoid Matthew at all costs. But it's so hard!

The Pussycat Trap - 3 stories in one - Who knew the pitter-patter of tiny paws could melt the hearts of these powerful men. (Sweet Romance)

The Cat Café - London banker Blake enters the cat café by mistake. Not only is he shocked to see so many cats in one place, but to also fall in love with the mad cat lady Trinity Peters.

Amazon bestselling Call Centre Series:

Call Me Lucky - Teddy could not believe the foul-mouthed girl he once knew had changed so little. He needed to show Felicity the world could be better and brighter with him.

Call Me Royal - Della now lived her life by one word, safe. Could long lost love Spencer remind her how it used to be?

Spicy Tropical Romances:

Saffron's Choice - . Engaged to a man she hadn't seen in 5 years. Saffron gives in and falls in love with the man that had always been in front of her.

Caribbean Whispers - Could Merrissa escape her past and take a chance on Alex, or does her past continue to haunt her?

Ladies Jamaican. - Three friends, three kinds of love. Could they make it?

CPSIA information can be obtained
at www.ICGtesting.com
Printed in the USA
LVHW021210240523
746432LV00023B/366